"*Major Wyclyff's Campaign* is a splendid, witty romp."
—Romantic Times

LADY SOPHIA'S CHOICE

"No!" She had not intended to say it so forcefully, but the word seemed to explode out of her nonetheless, leaving everyone slightly dazed. Suddenly she was on her feet, pacing the room in a hurried rustle of skirts. "Major, I am free for the first time in my life. There are no rules to govern my behavior, no gossip following me, nothing ahead but a free life as a spinster. I even gave my dowry so that no one would be tempted to offer for me—"

"You underestimate your charms."

"Nonsense!" She spun back to face him directly. "My point is, I am finally free. Why would I throw that away for a life spent at a husband's beck and call?"

Other *Leisure* books by Katherine Greyle:
RULES FOR A LADY

KATHERINE GREYLE

LEISURE BOOKS  NEW YORK CITY

A LEISURE BOOK®

October 2001

Published by

Dorchester Publishing Co., Inc.
276 Fifth Avenue
New York, NY 10001

ISBN 0-8439-4920-1

Printed in the United States of America.

Visit us on the web at www.dorchesterpub.com.

Loose.
Relaxed.
Easy.

Thanks, Bob,
for everything.

And special thanks
to Chris, a great editor.

MAJOR WYCLYFF'S CAMPAIGN

Prologue

"I danced with young Blakesly yesterday. I am quite sure he purposely stumbled so that he could catch himself on a most inappropriate place on my person. It was most mortifying, but . . ."

Lady Sophia continued to prattle on, trying to sound bright and cheerful, but her thoughts weren't on her words. Instead, she was looking down at the gaunt man in the hospital bed. He had been handsome once, she was sure of it. But now his angular face looked thin and bony, and his rich brown curls lay flat against his slick brow. He was a man who should have been surrounded by military honors, but now his companions were pain and dreariness.

"I am quite certain," she continued, "that Lord Blakesly would not dream of being so impertinent if you had been there. You must rouse yourself, Major Wyclyff. I do believe I need your escort."

He would never accompany her, she knew. Even were

he the picture of health, the major and she did not travel in the same circles. However, it had become a game between them in her last month of hospital visits. While he lay on his sickbed, they would speak of what they would do together when he was better. She spoke of picnics and strolls, of Vauxhall and the museums. And when he tired of that, they would argue politics or religion, spring as opposed to fall, or any other nonsense in between. He liked to argue and, while she did not, she would do anything to help him pass the time while he lay abed, his mangled leg stretched out before him.

For a while, she had believed their daydreampt plans would happen.

But then, a week ago, the major had taken a turn for the worse. His wound turned an angry red. All too soon, his smile faded into a grimace of pain and his skin grew flushed with fever. Yesterday, he had been delirious. Today, naught but a low moan escaped his parched lips.

He was dying.

Sophia stroked his broad hand, tracing the length of his fingers, her heart feeling frozen within her body. In five years of hospital visits, she had seen many men die. She knew the signs, and knew that her major would not last much longer.

A tear slipped down her face to land on the back of his hand. Blinking, she wiped away the moisture, startled by her reaction. "You see what you have done, Major? I am crying because of you." There was a touch of amazement in her voice, surprise that his imminent death would move her so deeply. After all, she had never cried before. Not for any of the other soldiers. Not for anyone, including her own father.

"I hold you directly responsible," she said with mock severity. "You must wake immediately or I shall be forced to take drastic measures. Crushed strawberries on the eyes to take away the redness. Cucumbers to suppress the tendency toward puffiness. My word, think of the expense and time such a toilette requires, Major. Truly, you must wake immediately. I command it."

She had not expected her words to have any effect. She spoke them to distract herself from what she knew was coming, so it was with considerable shock that she looked up to see his eyes had opened.

They were a mysterious brown, fever-bright, and so intense, she wondered if he had not been possessed by some spirit. No man on the verge of death could look right through one, as though to one's very soul. She should have been frightened, but for some reason she was not. It was her major lying there, looking at her not only with lucidity, but as though his very life depended upon it.

"Oh, Major," she whispered. "You have come back to me."

"Sophia," he croaked.

She nodded, and then with swift movements she poured him some water, lifting his shoulders and helping him drink. He watched her the entire time, his gaze hotter than his skin, burning her as she eased him back down.

"You must fight your illness, Major," she said softly. "Fight it as hard as any invading army. His Majesty expects nothing less from one of his finest officers—"

"Marry me." Even deathly ill, his voice had the ring of command.

Sophia's hand did not slow as she tugged the wrinkles out of his blanket. "Of course, Major. But you must be able to walk down the aisle, you know."

He grabbed her hand, pulling it and her gaze up toward his face. "Marry me," he ordered again.

In five years, she had received dozens of marriage proposals. It seemed to be a favorite pastime among wounded men. At first she had been flustered, but before long, she had developed an answer. To those who would mend, she simply smiled mysteriously. To those who would die, she would swear anything upon their recovery.

"I will wear a long white gown, and you will be in your regimentals," she said softly. "Everyone will stare because we are so happy together." She reached forward with a cool cloth, mopping his brow. "But first you must get well." She smiled down at him, focusing not on his wasted body but on the strength that literally shone in his eyes. "It will take a long time for me to prepare for our wedding, you know. In the meantime, you must swear to get better."

His eyes slipped shut. They did not close willingly, but slowly, as if he fought with everything in him. Then all was still except for the harsh rasp of his breathing.

Sophia sat back down beside him, her hand still clutched in his. She sighed softly, believing she had heard the last words he would ever utter. But moments later, when she thought him long since asleep, he whispered two words.

"I swear."

Chapter One

"Lady Sophia, what can your humblest servant say?" Lord Blakesly droned. "Your smile glows like polished pearls. Your hair falls in neater folds than the greatest cravat. And as for your laugh . . ."

"It tinkles like the bell on a dainty swine," quipped Lydia from her left.

Sophia slowly turned, her gaze landing on her dearest friend, who had apparently just joined her circle of admirers. Seeing Lydia's bright eyes and animated expression, Sophia knew the young woman wanted to speak with her. Unfortunately, the gentlemen would not let her through. Instead, Lydia had contented herself with tossing witticisms into the group, hoping that at least some of them would get the hint.

Normally such a situation would have earned at least a smile. Especially since Blakesly seemed more boorish than usual tonight. But Sophia had no heart for even the slightest twist of her lips. Indeed, she seemed to have little strength for anything lately.

"Ah, listen, Lady Sophia," inserted Blakesly, as he pointed limp-wristedly in the direction of the orchestra. "A waltz. I believe—"

"I am in desperate need of some lemonade, my lord. Could you not please . . ." She didn't need to say more. Though disappointment pulled his sallow face downward, Blakesly managed to straighten with almost military speed, his eyes darting about the ballroom for the nearest servant.

"Any feat, my lady. Any desire. Any—"

"Lemonade, Blakesly. Please."

With a swift nod, the young boor waded off into the crowd. Unfortunately, plenty more fops surrounded her, each one eager to take Blakesly's place. All the while, Lydia hovered on the periphery, her impatience obvious.

"Perhaps," she offered, "you could accompany me to the withdrawing room." Lydia glanced regretfully at the men circling Sophia. "Please forgive me, gentlemen, but I fear I must take my friend away from you."

Good-natured groans rang out, some more heartfelt than others, but Sophia could do no more than nod. Indeed, that alone took Herculean effort. She was forced to smile insincerely, pushing her way through the crowded ballroom. By the time she and Lydia reached the stiflingly hot withdrawing room, exhaustion had almost consumed her.

"Thank Heaven it is empty," said Lydia, scanning the small room. Not even a servant waited in the tiny space.

Sophia shrugged, her thoughts disjointed. "They don't even seem like people to me anymore," she murmured softly.

"Who?"

Sophia waved vaguely back toward the ballroom to indicate the overdressed souls that were England's *ton*. "Just birds. Bright, dull, fat, or thin, it doesn't matter. They are all the same: here one moment, gone the next. Birds."

Lydia frowned, her elfin face pinching with annoyance. "You went back to the hospital today."

Sophia lifted her gaze, startled out of her numb emptiness. "No. I have not been there in a month. Not since . . ." Her voice faded away.

"Since your major died. Sophia, this is outside of enough. I swear you have become downright cold since that poor man's death."

"Cold," murmured Sophia. "Yes, that is the word for it. I feel cold." And alone.

"Sophia!" Lydia exclaimed, clearly exasperated with her friend's inattention. "I have news!"

Sophia did not even raise her eyes. "Percy has offered for you."

Lydia's mouth dropped open in stunned surprise. "Yes," she gasped. "How did you know?"

Sophia nearly groaned aloud. How could she *not* have known? Indeed, in five Seasons of parties, five long years of dancing and dressing and displaying herself, there was little that Sophia could not guess. Though the faces and the names changed, the gossip remained the same. Those who married and those who did not seemed exactly the same. The boys who bored her seemed obsessed with exactly the same things. Indeed, the bitter game of who was more important, more beautiful, more perfect than anyone else seemed exactly the same, and exactly as insubstantial, as the year before.

"It just doesn't seem real," she whispered.

"That is exactly how I feel!" her friend exclaimed, clearly misunderstanding. "When Papa told me, I nearly fainted with excitement. Oh, Sophia, I am to be wed!"

"You shall be a beautiful bride," she replied automatically. But as Sophia stared at her friend, seeing Lydia's face flushed with joy, she couldn't help but wonder.

When had she herself last felt so happy? So filled with life? In her heart, she was pleased for her friend. Truly, she felt glad for Lydia's happiness.

And so, why did it seem so meaningless to her—as if she had spent five years of her life, five Seasons among the *ton*, in a child's game? Instead of play tokens, she'd traded gossip. Instead of moving wood figures around a board, she had herself traveled from party to party, carefully acting according to Society's rules.

And now, she was oh so weary of it all.

"Oh, Sophia," cried Lydia, her expression filled with sympathy. "You should not despair. You shall get married, too. I know it. Perhaps Lord Kyle will finally come up to scratch."

"Reginald?" Her thoughts twisted, trying to understand her friend's thoughts. "Why would I wish to marry him?"

Lydia did not hear her; she was too caught up in her own fantasy. "Why, it shall be wonderful! You and I could have a double wedding. We shall be like sisters. And our children will grow up together. And come out in the same Season. Or perhaps I shall have a son, and your daughter could marry him. Oh, that would be wonderful! Can you not envision it?"

Indeed, Sophia could, and the thought filled her with horror. An entire second generation trapped in the same meaningless circle of noise and prattle. "Oh, heavens, Lydia, do not even think it!"

Lydia stopped, her mouth hanging open at her friend's harsh tone.

Sophia tried to calm her thoughts, but her words tumbled out nonetheless. "I assure you," she said coolly, "I have no interest in marrying Reg."

"But I thought you grew up together." Lydia's eyes fluttered in confusion. "Just like Percy and I did."

"Of course, Reg and I are friends. Or we were. But then there was that scandal with that girl and the Scotsman and he . . ." She raised her hand in a helpless gesture. "He left." She leaned forward, touching her friend's hand as her thoughts returned to the bright collage of people just outside the door. "Eventually, they all fly away. We women are always abandoned."

Lydia's face contorted in horror, her lower lip quivering with tears. "Oh, Sophia, how can you say such a thing? Percy would never . . . He would . . ."

Sophia felt shame flood her soul, and she immediately moved forward, gripping her friend's hands. "Oh, Lydia, of course not! Percy is as constant as the sun. He would never leave you alone." She pulled her friend into a fierce hug. "He adores you. Oh, please do not let my horrid mood affect your happiness."

But Lydia would not have any of it. She shoved Sophia away with surprising fierceness. "I blame it completely on those visits to that dreadful hospital. You have become so strange since then."

Sophia allowed her hands to fall away from her friend, her body and her thoughts crawling to a stop. It was as if she became encased in ice, chilling even her words as she spoke in a low whisper. "I am so sorry, Lydia. I never meant to hurt you."

"I am not hurt. I am angry! You have become so maudlin. I don't know who you are anymore. But whoever it is, I don't like you." And with that Lydia stomped away, abandoning Sophia in the suddenly chill room.

As arguments went, this was a minor one. Sophia knew she could mend the breach with a simple shopping trip. But she had no heart for it. Indeed, she could barely contemplate the expedition, much less embark upon it. So rather than follow her friend back into the glittering ballroom, she remained where she was, sitting in the corner, her thoughts silent as death.

Unfortunately, even that respite was denied her. Within moments, her mother came to search her out, admonishing her for abandoning her admirers, and chatting as brightly as any magpie. Too quickly, she shooed Sophia back into the ballroom. It took a scant two minutes more before the same circle of men surrounded her, their droll banter sounding like so much chirping—all notes with no meaning. And then Lord Kyle appeared at her side, her childhood companion as foppish and nonsensical as the rest. More so, in fact, because they had once been friends.

While he prattled on about the fold of some man's cravat, Sophia thought of the major. It was unfair, she knew, to compare Reg—a rich, pampered rake—to an injured soldier lying in his deathbed, but she could not stop herself. Even feverish, the major's words had always touched her. His most trivial banter seemed more real to her than the most serious discourse with Reg.

Yet, the major was dead. And Sophia had been left behind to listen to a comparison of black cravats and dark blue ones.

Reg had just loudly taken up the part of pure black when Sophia stood up. She did not know what prompted it, but abruptly her body filled with anger. Her cheeks burned and her vision snapped into focus. "I am leaving," she said.

Reg stared at her, his mouth half open. If she gave him time, she knew he would offer his escort. As it was, no less than three gentlemen presented themselves, offering to find her mother. She simply shook her head.

"I am leaving for Staffordshire in the morning," she declared to each and every one of them. "And I will never return." If life was a game, she decided, it was high time she played it according to her own rules.

Major Anthony Wyclyff stood on the London townhouse stoop and stared at the bare doorway in shock. There was no knocker on the door. That meant the family was not at home. But Sophia could not be gone, his mind repeated numbly. She could not have left London. "But where is she?" he asked aloud.

There was no answer. Indeed, he had not expected one. Still, he turned to glare at his batman Kirby. "Where could she be?" he repeated.

The man remained silent, having no answer. Instead, a voice spoke from the street.

"Lady Sophia has left London."

Anthony spun around on his bad leg, his eyes fixing on a tall, foppish man, about whom there was something familiar. He searched his memory. Reginald Peters, Lord Kyle. That was the man's name. They had known each other as children, attended Eton at the same time. It had been years since he'd last seen the man. Kyle was the heir to a rich title, handsome, elegant, and adequately educated, while Anthony himself had been thick, heavy, and something of a lackwit in school, especially in the classic languages of Latin and Greek. But, more importantly, Anthony was merely the second son of an earl. After his education, his father had bought his colors, and that was the last he had known of any of his childhood companions.

Yet here was Kyle, greeting him warmly, as if they were still at Eton. "Anthony, old boy, is that you? And in your colors, no less. My, what a figure you turned out to be."

Anthony nodded stiffly at the compliment, knowing it was a significant one from the dandy before him. But his thoughts remained on his future wife. "Where is Lady Sophia? The Season is barely over. She could not have left so soon."

Lord Kyle shrugged, leaning negligently against the fence as he spoke. "She has gone to Staffordshire to live with her aunt."

Anthony stared at the man, seeing the truth in the fop's eyes, and ground his teeth at the delay. Now he would have to ride halfway across England when he had matters to attend to in London.

"Very well," he snapped and began to descend the steps. He still had to move carefully. His leg had a constant ache that occasionally turned into sharp pain. Unfortunately, he had no time to coddle the injury, especially now that he needed to travel to Staffordshire. At the base of the steps, he nodded politely to his childhood acquaintance. "Thank you for the information," he said. He knew he was being unnecessarily rude, but he could not help himself. It rankled him that a mere difference in birth allowed Kyle into Sophia's inner circle, privy to her movements, whereas he, her future husband, was left standing stupidly on her doorstep.

Unfortunately, Lord Kyle was not dismissed so easily. As Anthony began striding toward his temporary quarters, the man fell into step beside him. Typically, a major in His Majesty's army would be able to easily outdistance any unwanted company, but Lord Kyle possessed a long stride and Anthony's injury prevented such escape. Instead, he was forced to continue conversation when all he wanted was to find his bride and get on with his life.

"May I inquire as to your business with Lady Sophia?" Kyle asked. When Anthony slanted him an irritated look, the fop was quick to explain. "I only ask because she and I have been friends for ages. Perhaps I could be of some assistance."

Anthony frowned. Had Sophia ever mentioned Lord Kyle? They had talked about so much during his stay in the hospital, but the majority of it was muddled. He had been in considerable pain, and yet . . . "I do not remember her mentioning you."

"Ah, well, our friendship tends to wane during the Season. There is so much to do that even should we cross paths, our conversation is brief by necessity." Then he smiled, a fond, nostalgic expression that grated upon Anthony's nerves. "But our estates align the one against the other. Our families often spend the Christmas holidays together."

"Well, I would not count on her presence at table this winter," he ground out, again irritated that Kyle could so easily expect Sophia's presence. "Come August, she will set sail for India with me."

His pronouncement had the desired effect. Lord Kyle stopped dead in his tracks, his bored expression wiped clean. He gaped at the major. "Truly! Whatever for?"

Normally, Anthony would not have said it. He certainly would not have done so with a smirk that fairly begged the man to doubt him. But he was frustrated and in pain, and he so much wanted to put this particular irritation in its place. "You may wish us happy, Kyle. Sophia and I are to be married. I have the special license in my pocket. And then we are away to India in service to His Majesty."

This time Lord Kyle did not gape at him. There was a moment's hesitation, time enough for Anthony to believe he had at last silenced the man, but then Lord Kyle burst into laughter. He actually guffawed. Right there in the middle of the street. The peal was loud, musical, and filled with a good humor that seemed to burn painfully into Anthony's soul.

"Ah," sighed a merry Lord Kyle when he could at last draw breath. "Truly, I have always loved your sense of humor, old chap. You did not use it much at Eton, but when you did, I swear you kept us amused for days."

Anthony did not respond. He merely remained still, his cold stare the very one he used to discipline unruly recruits. Bit by slow bit, it had its effect. Lord Kyle's laughter faded until it was slowly replaced by a dawning horror.

"Good God, you cannot be serious," the man finally gasped.

Anthony let his heavy glare speak for itself.

"But I was with her the day before her departure. I assure you, Lady Sophia does not consider herself engaged." When Anthony did not comment, the fop actually took a step forward. "She has foresworn all men, declared herself on the shelf, and is happily content in the solitary state."

"She has sworn to marry me."

Kyle shook his head in dismay. "My God, man, you make it sound like a military tribunal. Are you feeling quite the thing?"

"I am quite well, thank you," Anthony snapped. Then he spun on his heel and began walking away as quickly as his injury would permit. He did not allow his expression or demeanor to alter. No one, and certainly not the silly Lord Kyle, would ever suspect what terror now chilled his heart.

Could Sophia have forgotten? Could she have allowed their engagement to slip from her mind? Impossible. A woman did not forget a proposal of marriage.

But she had never returned to the hospital. She had visited daily, and then not a word. He assumed she had begun preparations for their wedding. Indeed, she had said as much. But to leave for Staffordshire? Without word?

"She spoke quite clearly," he said aloud to himself. "We are to be married."

"Then perhaps you ought to inform Lady Sophia of the matter," Kyle drawled from slightly behind him.

Anthony turned on the man, his anger a palpable force between them. "I intend to do just that," he practically bellowed, planting his fists on his hips.

Kyle's grin widened. "Oh, yes, I can see you have not changed since Eton. Your smooth manner is sure to win so great a prize as Lady Sophia."

Anthony felt his hands clench into fists. "We will be married!"

"Of course you will," returned Kyle smoothly. Then he leaned forward. "I wager she shall have you booted out on your ear in a trice."

Anthony clenched his teeth, trying to control his fury. Mentally, he listed all the things he needed to do before heading for Staffordshire. The catalogue was much too long. He needed to complete this business with Sophia immediately. But then Lord Kyle's arrogant voice slipped into his thoughts.

"I wager a monkey you find yourself disengaged within a fortnight."

It was not so much the bet itself, but the insinuation behind it. The suggestion that he, Anthony Wyclyff, a decorated major in His Majesty's army, was not good enough for Lady Sophia. And more than that, that this popinjay, this fribble in elegant clothing, had the right to her presence at Christmas merely because he had the fortune to be born first.

"Wager a hundred guineas or a thousand, whatever you like," he practically growled. "Sophia and I shall be wed before I set sail for India."

Lord Kyle quickly extended his hand. "Done! A thousand guineas that she tosses you out on your ear."

Anthony glared at the man's long, elegant hand, seeing that it was neat and free of calluses. Kyle had never done a day's hard labor in his entire life, and yet he thought he could wager on Anthony's future. It was ridiculous.

"Come, come, Major. Surely your virility is worth a thousand guineas?"

As insults went, it was a minor one. Anthony had no need to prove himself to anyone, much less this jack-a-dandy. But his long illness had weakened him, and anger made him reckless. He grabbed the man's hand with the same motion he used to draw a blade.

"Done," he said, his voice holding the ring of steel. "A thousand guineas that Lady Sophia is mine by August!"

* * *

"Die, you wretched tormentor of women!" Sophia cried, and her voice echoed in the small clearing of the dark, Staffordshire wood. With great glee, she lofted her most hated corset high into the air, then gleefully tossed it up into the night sky.

She watched it fly, hurled heavenward where it hung, suspended just for a moment, as if being perused by God, then tumbled downward into the pit. In her mind's eye, Sophia imagined the corset as rejected, judged evil by the Almighty, and then spat downward into Hell.

"Amen!" she cried. Then Sophia reached down to the bag at her feet, quickly grabbing another hated corset. She felt its familiar weight, saw the dangling, pale ivory strings, even paused a moment to stroke the hateful whalebone ridges. With gleeful delight, she again threw it to the heavens and watched it land with a dull thud in the black pit at her feet.

"Another punisher meets his doom!" Sophia uttered.

Another, then a fourth of the horrible contraptions was swallowed by the hole. Finally she added the rest of the contents of her sack, tossing in anything she owned that had stays, itched, or had to be laced in any way.

"Never again shall you touch my skin!" she cried.

She watched as the night seemed to absorb the offensive items, obliterating them from existence. In her imagination, all the rules of a restrictive and vindictive London society went the way of her corsets and stays. Every cruel matron, every gossip-ridden soul was rejected by God and tossed into the hole at her feet.

Grabbing her shovel, she lifted up a spadeful of dirt. "Gone and done!" she crowed. Then she tossed dirt in, imagining every one of her hateful memories suffocated beneath the earth. She giggled with true joy as she listened to the steady thud of the soil as she began to bury them all.

But it was not enough.

Sophia wanted more. So, with a sigh, she pulled off her too-tight walking boots and kicked them straight into the black hole. They disappeared before she drew another breath.

"I must get rid of it all," she said softly. All the sniping, lecherous leers, the inane round of parties and social calls, and, most importantly, all the ridiculous rules that hemmed in a young lady on every side. Those restrictive and judgmental codes of conduct designed for a lady who wished to be wed; they no longer applied to her, just as corsets and laces would no longer cut off her breath. She was on the shelf, too old to marry, and that suited her just fine.

Still, she did not want her delightful ritual to end. Unfortunately, there was very little else to bury except for the clothing on her body. And she did not wish to get rid of her dress. She had made it herself—a simple muslin drape. It was a most comfortable attire, especially suited for ritual sacrifices of unpleasant underclothing.

There had to be something else. But what?

Suddenly, she knew. It would be difficult. Furniture was not an easy thing to drag out of one's house, but she would manage. Then it would all be well and truly gone. . . .

Major Wyclyff shifted uneasily on his horse. The saddle cut painfully into his injured leg, and he knew he would be stiff and sore in the morning. But, for now, he wished only to think of his destination and his bride-to-be.

Sophia. Even her name was refined. She was cool, composed, and everything that would be perfect to his diplomatic post.

He had it all planned. He had entered Staffordshire a little less than an hour earlier and had quickly settled his gear and batman into the nearest inn. Then he had mounted his horse and come here, to Sophia's current residence, scouting out the lay of the land. He wished to be completely prepared when he visited her tomorrow.

He would arrive at tea, the most civilized time for social calls. Then he would speak with Sophia, telling her that he was now well enough to marry. The wedding, thanks to his special license, could be dispatched with immediately. At last, they would remove together to India.

Perfect. And precisely planned.

Anthony smiled, seeing a neat lifetime ahead of himself and his wife. The thought even managed to take his mind off his pain.

He saw the torches stuck into the ground long before he reached the clearing near the Rathburn home. Their illumination glowed brightly in the clear night. Frowning, he narrowed his eyes, trying to make sense of the shadows in the flickering light. Had some gypsy or poacher fashioned a campfire to roast his dinner? Surely not so close to a residence.

Then, to his shock, he saw a large shape pass out through the door of the Rathburn manor.

Anger burned swift and sure through his body. This was no gypsy cooking his dinner. This was a thief, stealing items directly out of the house!

Anthony spurred his horse on. Fear for Sophia clutched at his throat. He could only pray she was safely away from home. But what if she were here? What if the thief had harmed her? The thought was insupportable.

As he drew closer to the clearing, Anthony could hear the grating of something heavy pulled over stones. What was it? He could not see what was being dragged, or who was dragging it, but they had come from the house. Of that he was sure.

Could it be a body? Fear overcame his military sense.

Rather than taking a moment to the assess the situation, he drew his sword and kicked his heels hard into his stallion's sides. Demon obediently broke into a gallop, bursting like an avenging angel into the clearing.

It took less than a second to size up the situation. He saw one person, a woman cursing as she pulled at something immense. It was not a body as he had feared. Instead, it looked something like a desk flipped on its side, its drawers and lid flopping about like a broken toy.

Narrowing his gaze, he focused more on the woman. As she was between him and a rather large torch, her contorted body was a dark shadow outlined by a brilliant orange glow. Still, he caught the shape of crudely shorn locks and a pert little nose.

He reined in his horse mere inches from her, glaring down at the woman as he bellowed, "What are you doing? By God, if you have harmed Sophia, I will split you from end to end!"

He waited, expecting the woman to drop the furniture and immediately flee. Most sane people did when he used that tone of voice. But she merely lifted her head and frowned at him.

"I am burying corsets," she said calmly. "And you are in the way."

"I beg your pardon?" he said stiffly. Then he squinted, trying to shield his eyes from the glare of the torch while still seeing her clearly. He only partly succeeded. He saw a white, breathless smile and long, dirty legs exposed by a rip in a shapeless smock.

"My corsets. I never liked them, you know. Awful contraptions." Then she straightened. "And you are ruining it. Go away."

Anthony frowned. Something about her voice teased at him, reminding him of . . . But he shook his head. The woman could not be Sophia. His future wife would never be out of doors at such an hour, acting like a Bedlamite. Right now, she was no doubt drinking tea, her maiden aunt probably nearby, reading aloud books of poetry.

In the meantime, this thief seemed intent on making off with her furnishings.

"Put everything back!" he ordered, brandishing his sword.

"I will not!" she snapped.

Furious, Anthony jumped from his saddle, intent on forcing the woman to comply. He hit the ground hard, the impact jarring his already strained leg, but he ignored it as he took a threatening step forward.

Except the ground was uneven, the earth soft and muddy from the recent rains. It eroded beneath his feet. "Wha—!" was all he managed as he stumbled and slipped into a deep pit. His sword went flying, as well as his grip on anything solid. He was rolling end over end, but then he abruptly stopped, landing on his shoulder at the very bottom.

"Oh, bother!" he heard her exclaim from above him. "Really, you must get out so I can throw in the escritoire."

He ignored her words, having already concluded that the woman was mad. Still, even madwomen could be dangerous, and he was bound to protect Sophia, even from the likes of this deranged creature. He pulled himself painfully to his feet, frowning as he felt strange items beneath him. He felt fabric and ribbons, but then his hand ran across an item sticking straight out. It was long and hard and had the unmistakable feel of bone.

Bone? The very thought was chilling.

"What is in here?"

It was at that moment that he chanced to look up. "Good God!" he exclaimed. "What are you doing?" It was a stupid question. He could see quite clearly what she was doing. She was still dragging what he now saw was a large and rather heavy desk—right toward the lip of the pit.

"Stop that!" he roared.

"But if I get this on the very edge, you can climb up. Do not worry about scratching it. I intend to bury it in any event. It is a silly thing with all sorts of nonsense cubbies perfect for the inane correspondence that I wrote day after miserable day. Truly, what can be more symbolic than getting rid of it?"

Then she grunted, clearly straining as she pushed the heavy wooden piece to the edge of the hole. Anthony watched in horror as the item teetered. Good lord, if it tumbled down on him, it would kill him immediately. And she likely couldn't see where he was.

"Have a care not to come too close until I have it settled!" she called needlessly, but Anthony wasn't listening. He was well beyond the point of being careful. He was already scrambling out of the muddy pit as fast as his injury would allow.

"No! Wait—" she cried as she saw him.

But it was too late. In her efforts to help him, she lost control of the desk. With a ponderous groan, it shifted and began slipping, heading directly toward him.

Fortunately, he was prepared. Jumping rapidly out of the way, he narrowly missed being clubbed in the head by one of the desk's legs as it crashed past. Unfortunately, the madwoman was also reaching for him, effectively blocking his best escape route up to solid ground. He scrambled, and she reached. He grasped her helping hand and pulled hard, using all his strength to escape the now tumbling desk.

It was too much. She was stronger than she looked. With her pull and his push, he practically shot out of the pit. Then, before either could adjust, they were flying together, tumbling through the mud, rolling one on top of the other as they fell away from the hole.

It was a few seconds before he could stop their movements, and by that time, they were both covered in filth and gasping for air. He'd landed on top, her long, pliant body warm beneath him, her eyes wide with surprise.

"Well, this certainly was not part of the ritual," she said with a low chuckle. The sound was rich, and despite the circumstances, he could not stop his reaction. His body heated as her movements played against it.

He meant to speak, but all he could manage was a strangled groan as he slowly tried to shift off of her. The strain of their acrobatics had set his leg to burning with the intensity of a brand, and despite the enticements of his current resting place, his awkward position only intensified the pain. He had to get off of her, but the slightest movement sent bolts of agony through him.

Nevertheless, he persevered, gritting his teeth as he struggled to respectfully disentangle himself from her. It was agony on many different levels, and he was soon sweating with the strain.

She remained silent throughout the entire wriggling and shifting experience, no doubt as aware as he was of her every curve and hollow. But before he could disengage from her completely, he felt the soft tremors invade her body, the slight gasps and jerks as she began to cry.

"Damn," he said softly, feeling extremely awkward as he finally rolled onto the soft grass nearby. "Where did I hurt you?"

His question produced a fresh surge of muffled sounds, and there passed some few moments before he realized she was laughing, not crying. By that time, her hilarity was quite audible as she guffawed like a soldier in his first drunk.

"Madame," he began.

"My, but I have done it correctly now!" she said between laughs. "I have actually cavorted upon the ground with a man!" She curled on her sides, holding them tight as the laughter poured out of her.

"Madame!" he said stiffly. "I rescued you from tumbling into the pit. I certainly did not *cavort*—"

"Yes," she interrupted. "Yes, you did! And I heartily thank you for the experience. It was the perfect ending for my ritual." She pushed halfway up from the ground, her weight resting on her elbow, as she continued to giggle. "Aunt Agatha will be so proud of me! Do say you will come for tea."

Anthony blinked as he stared at the long column of her neck. Clearly, she had lost her mind. He sat up slowly, keeping his injured leg straight before him. Then he patted her hand, trying to make the touch reassuring. "Give me a moment to rest, then I shall help you bury . . . whatever it is you lost."

She lifted her head as she focused on him. "Lost? Whatever do you mean? Did you lose something?" Then she looked about her, scanning the woods as if to find some item hidden beyond the trees.

"Of course, *I* have not lost anything!" he said, exasperation making his voice short. "You have!"

She turned and stared at him.

"The bones," he clarified. "In the pit."

"Bones?" she asked, clearly confused. Then, suddenly, her expression brightened. "Oh, those. What about them?"

He was perilously close to shouting. "Whose bones are you trying to bury?"

She merely blinked at him. "I have no idea whose bones those are. Some poor whale, I believe, sacrificed for the sole purpose of torturing me."

Her words made no sense, but he sifted through the nonsense to light upon one word. "Whale?"

"Yes. Those are whalebones. From my corsets."

"Your corsets?"

"Exactly!" She clapped her hands, as if he were some slow student only now catching on to his sums.

It was too much for him. He exploded, leaning forward despite new bolts of pain in his leg. "Do you mean to tell me you nearly killed me so that you could bury your corsets?"

"And my boots. And my escritoire," she responded calmly. "We must not forget the escritoire. It was extremely heavy."

Then, in the single most irritating moment of an entirely unbelievable conversation, the most terrible thing happened.

He recognized her.

Chapter Two

Anthony frowned at Sophia.

She had changed drastically. Her stunningly beautiful blond locks had been haphazardly cut away. Her long, regal body lay sprawled across the muddy ground. Her elegant clothing was now a smudged and torn smock. And her cool, sweet face looked at him as if *he* were the one who had lost his mind. But he recognized her, nonetheless.

"Good God, Lady Sophia, what has happened to you?"

She blinked, slowly sitting up straight as she focused on his face. The torches shed enough light for her to peer closely at him. He no doubt looked different than the ravaged face and wasted body she remembered. He was no longer in a hospital, his body thin and wracked with fever.

"Major? You are alive!" Her whisper confirmed his darkest thoughts. This tormented soul before him was indeed his angel of mercy, his Sophia, his intended bride.

He saw her gaze travel the length of his body, skipping to his injured leg.

"It hurts," he said before she could ask, "but it is whole. I hope to regain full use in time. Indeed, I can ride again." He glanced back to where Demon waited patiently at the edge of the clearing.

"Thank God," she said. "Oh, thank God," she repeated, her voice shaking with the force of her emotion. Then she reached out a slender hand only to leave it hovering over his injury without touching him.

He smiled as he reached out and pressed her hand down to land softly upon his leg. How many nights had he dreamed of just this? Of her touch, warm and soothing on his pain. "It is quite whole," he said. "Though I am supposed to rest it, not scramble out of pits."

She did not seem to catch his mild admonishment. Indeed, she was still staring at him, her eyes wide with stunned amazement. "They told me you died. They were most specific."

"They were wrong. I am well."

She shook her head. "They were very clear."

"They were wrong," he repeated. Then he smiled. "I recovered. Thanks to your promise."

It took a few more moments of her staring at him, looking at his face, then his leg, then his entire body, but eventually she seemed to accept that he was real. That he was alive. She burst into tears.

Tender feelings flooded his soul. Reaching out, he gently pulled her into his arms, gathering her close as he stroked her trembling shoulders. "Shhh, my lady," he whispered. "The nightmare is over. I am whole."

She wrapped her arms around him, tightening their embrace, as if still reassuring herself of his strength. He held her quietly, caressing her arm in long strokes, allowing himself to relish every second of their reunion.

"I could not have done it," he murmured against her

hair. "Your promise kept me alive. You gave me hope when nothing else mattered." Her sobs were subsiding now, her body stilling as she began to compose herself. "Oh, Sophia," he whispered as he dropped a gentle kiss on her brow. "I have waited for you forever."

She raised her head, tilting her face toward him. He helped her move, shifting her to a better position, one that allowed their mouths to touch. To kiss. But before he could claim her lips, she spoke.

"Promise? What promise?"

He felt his breath freeze in his body. There it was: the hard reality that Sophia did not remember their engagement. It cut at him more than the sword that had crippled his leg. More than the fever that had ravaged his body. And more than the knowledge that his entire future was now in question.

But how could he be surprised? Looking at the dirty creature in his arms, he knew she was unbalanced. Her mind was unhinged, perhaps by the very event that had separated her from him in the first place.

Naturally, he could understand. Upon hearing the false news that her fiancé had perished, Sophia's delicate constitution became overbalanced. She was distraught. So much so that she quit the fashionable whirl for a lifetime of mourning in Staffordshire. Now the shock of his recovery was too much for her delicate sensibilities.

All he needed to do was gently remind her of what had occurred. Of her promise to wed him. Then, her mind would naturally return to the calm demeanor which was its natural state.

Smiling, he stroked her cheek. "You promised to marry me."

She pulled free, out of his arms. "I most certainly did not!"

His empty hands clenched, and his patience began to

fray. "In the hospital. When I was ill. You promised to marry me."

"But you were *dying*." Again she stared at him, her gaze roving over his body. He waited, allowing her the time to look her fill and assure herself that he was whole.

"As you can see, I am recovered."

"Well, I cannot help that," she shot back. Then, suddenly, she pushed up on her feet, straightening enough to tower over him. "In any event, what are you doing here? And how dare you interrupt my ritual!"

He paused at the abrupt change in her tone, but he reined in his temper. Shock often sent delicate constitutions into strange mood shifts. He gestured to the yawning hole at their feet. "What is this ritual?"

She turned to look into the pit, and he caught a flash of reflected torchlight in her eyes. "I was sacrificing . . . well, you among other things."

"Me?"

"Yes! For arranging and planning my life like every other person has tried to do since I came of age! My word, even when you were delirious, you were ordering me to marry you. I had to agree just to silence you." Suddenly, she planted her hands on her hips. "Indeed, I should throw you back in the pit along with the rest of the constrictions and burdens. How dare you ruin my moment of symbolic relief from all of London?"

"Relief from London? What nonsense is this?" He straightened, ignoring the bolt of agony in his knee, pulling himself tall enough to stare her in the eye. "Besides, you said I created the perfect ending for your ritual."

"That was before I knew you were *you!*" she snapped. "Now I shall have to do an entirely new ritual with new corsets. And whalebone is terribly expensive, you know."

He stared at her, and suddenly his temper broke. "This is insane!" he bellowed.

"It is not!" she yelled back. "It is symbolic, and I believe you should have to buy the corsets."

He reared back. "What?"

"You are the one who ruined this experience. It is either a whole new ritual or you shall have to throw yourself back into the hole. Your choice." She folded her arms across her chest as if daring him to deny her.

"I will not throw myself into your pit—"

"Your effigy, then."

"Absolutely not! And I will not buy you corsets. Not yet, at least. What I will do is marry you, *then* buy you new corsets; then I shall take you to London before we leave for India!" The words were out before he could stop them, but once said, he did not regret them. Perhaps this was no way to tell a lady they would marry, but then again, a lady did not bury innocent furniture in the middle of the night!

Unfortunately, as the silence stretched between them, he realized that perhaps this was not the most ideal circumstance to reunite with Sophia. Especially as he was beginning to glimpse her stubborn streak. It was possible that she would be stubborn enough to cry off their engagement just to spite him.

In fact, the more she stared at him, her mouth sagging open in shock, the more he believed he might have erred. At last she drew back, smoothing her muddy dress as if it were the most costly of court gowns.

The motions reassured him. For the first time since this whole bizarre episode began, he recognized the Sophia he knew—despite her attire. She was cool, composed, and almost regal as she looked down at him and smiled.

"I do not wish for any new corsets."

And with that, she strode away, head held high, stomping most effectively on her small, bare feet.

He watched her go, doing nothing to stop her. He was in too ill a temper to continue their conversation. And she was obviously not in an appropriate frame of mind.

He instead busied himself with filling in her pit. It didn't take long. He moved quickly, doing the minimum necessary to ensure any wandering strangers were safe from her handiwork. Then he mounted Demon and rode toward the Rathburn home.

It was not far to her house, and he saw her immediately, but he did not detain her. He merely wished to make sure she returned home safely. And as he watched the moonlight wash her silhouette with silver, he could not restrain a smile.

She was magnificent. Her body was tall and slim, her carriage graceful. She was a true aristocrat, her blood nearly as blue as that of the Regent himself. Even when tiptoeing back to her manor door on bare feet, he could see the pride in her movements, the generations of breeding.

Tonight's episode he excused as merely a temporary female aberration. After all, she had just completed her fifth London Season. She had thought her fiancé dead and was now facing a lifetime spent on the shelf as too old to be marriageable. A woman on the verge of spinsterhood would certainly undergo enormous emotional distress. Her actions tonight were merely a symptom of her fears.

She was perhaps only now realizing that her worries were at an end. He still intended to marry her, despite tonight's show of temper. Then he planned to spend the rest of his life caring for her.

The thought gave him so much pleasure that he whistled all the way back to his room at the inn.

The following morning, Sophia stared at her drawer of unmentionables and frowned. They were all gone. All her stiff corsets, itchy underclothes, and even her walking boots. All buried.

Which was exactly as she had intended. Until the major had shown up, of course, and ruined the entire thing. Now she wanted to repeat last night's ritual, except that she had nothing worthy of burying. She actually liked everything that remained.

She closed the wardrobe with a sigh and sat back down on her bed. It did not matter, she told herself. Her arms ached from last night's digging, and she did not wish to repeat the process.

So what was she to do today?

She turned her head to stare at the steady hands of the gilt clock on her dresser. It was not even teatime yet. My goodness, the days went ponderously slow in Staffordshire.

In London, she would have already attended one or perhaps two functions, frittering away her time with idle chatter and insipid gossip. Thank goodness that part of her life was over.

Of course, now that she was in Staffordshire, she was merely frittering away her time doing absolutely nothing except feeling bored. She tapped her fingers together. What exactly did a free, unfettered spinster do with her time?

The morning's correspondence had brought some relief to the tedium. She fingered the missive from her sometimes friend, Reginald, Lord Kyle, and re-read his message. It began with the usual *on-dits* from London, nothing that she cared to know or follow, though she did manage to read every word at least twice. It was only at the end that his correspondence shifted to the odd.

Staffordshire must be overrun with madmen. I fear I sent one to your doorstep in the form of a major recently released from hospital. The other is a man I call Uncle Latimer. You would know him as Lord Blakesly the elder (the younger one being both presumptuous with the title and an idiot to boot). Have you heard anything of him?

It ended with the usual farewells, mixed with dry comments about his difficult tailor. Sophia knew nothing of Lord Blakesly the elder, though she absolutely agreed with Kyle's assessment of the younger. As for the realization that Reginald was responsible for directing the major to her here, she had every intention of chiding him for it when next they spoke. She would have written him a letter stating her opinion, but her escritoire was currently buried in the side yard.

What struck her as particularly odd was that Reginald considered the major insane. True, Lord Kyle dubbed all military men as madmen. Swordplay and bullets tended to disrupt one's attire, and that, to Reginald's thinking, was proof of a weak mind. But perhaps he had a point. The major had just recovered from a severe illness. Perhaps it had weakened his normal reason.

But he had not seemed mad last night, she thought with a sigh. Indeed, he had looked magnificent riding in on his huge stallion. At first, she had thought him a conjured spirit, tall and dark, like King Arthur riding to battle. The torchlight had turned his brown locks to a reddish gold like a magical helmet. And when he had bellowed at her, all she could think of was keeping the spell alive so that he would remain by her side.

There was no spell, of course. Only the major, still as handsome and commanding as ever, even after his illness. Even now, she could hardly believe it was him. Alive and seemingly unhurt. *I am well*; that's what he had said.

He was well, but she remembered all too clearly the hours spent by his bedside. The pain that had wracked his body. The agony of watching his strength slip away. And then that horrible moment when they told her he'd died. She could not stop her tears even now, despite the sure knowledge that he was alive.

But the Major was not some mythical creature, she reminded herself. He was a man. A man who had been desperately hurt. Who even now could catch another fever. What if last night's events had reopened his wound? What if he had returned only to die again? Only to abandon her once more? She did not want to need someone, to want someone, who might slip away so easily. She did not want to hurt like that again. Her body clenched at the horrors she envisioned. And yet, at the same time, she kept remembering how glorious he had seemed last night. How strong.

Yet how forceful and opinionated! He was as bad as the worst of the condescending fops who graced the London ballrooms. No, he did not live for his tailor or the latest *on-dit*, as Reginald did, but he, like the others, expected to be obeyed unquestionably. He practically ordered everything and everyone about him. Why, his interruption of her ritual was typical of him, and all because he thought she was doing something silly.

Oh Lord, she groaned into her pillow. Her mind was spinning in circles. She kept remembering him looking so virile. Not sick at all. Thinking back to her removal from London, she knew she should have spoken directly with the doctor. But the nurse had been adamant that the major had died, and Sophia had been heartbroken. After all, they had all seen the signs. The major had been going to die. Had died. Or rather, she thought he had. And the pain had been too much to bear.

Still lost in her confusing thoughts, Sophia was startled by a discreet knock at the door. "Beggin' yer pardon, miss," said Mary—her maid at her aunt's estate—as the girl pushed into the room. "But yer aunt wondered if you planned to attend tea."

Sophia blinked, her gaze skipping straight to the clock.

"Oh, my, yes. I had clean forgot." She hopped up from the bed, using the motion to force thoughts of the major from her mind. "Tell Aunt Agatha I shall be there directly."

She did not waste time on her appearance. It was just she and her favorite aunt. What she did do was grab the book of scandalous poetry that she had purchased secretly in London. The two of them absolutely delighted in reading it over crumpets.

It was, in fact, one of her favorite times of the day.

With a small skip, she tripped down the stairs of the small house. From there it was a single hop before she burst through the door. "Aunt, I have just been reading this poem about a whore in Peru—"

"Sophia! Your guest has arrived."

Sophia froze with one foot over the threshold. There before her, painfully gaining his feet, was the very person who had been drifting in and out of her thoughts all day. And all night.

Major Wyclyff.

And if she thought he was handsome last night, today he was truly magnificent. He was in his dress uniform with gold braid and medals. He stood rigid and tall, the pride of all of England clear in his broad shoulders. He looked magnificent, not sickly at all.

"Oh!" was all she could say.

"Oh, dear," gasped Aunt Agatha, her hands fluttering before her. "Have you forgotten the major's appointment? Truly, my dear—"

"Appointment?" gasped Sophia, her gaze still riveted on her guest's rugged face. She noted lines of strain about his eyes and a lingering leanness to his features. "What appointment?"

"For tea," he answered as he executed a bow worthy of the king's court.

"Tea?" she gasped as she finally found her breath. "Not

my tea with Aunt Agatha. Goodness, Major, first my ritual and now teatime. Why must you be always popping up at the most inconvenient places?"

"But, but," stammered her aunt, her lavender ribbons fluttering about her gown, "he said you invited him."

"I most certainly—"

"Did," countered the major before she could finish. "I believe you said I was the crowning touch to your ritual, and would I please come to tea."

Sophia thought back, belatedly realizing that she had said something to such effect. "But that was before I knew it was you."

"Nonsense," he countered. "I know a lady as refined as yourself would never invite strange gentlemen to her aunt's house." Next, to her total mortification, the major's gaze traveled leisurely down her body, no doubt taking in her flyaway hair, her rumpled gown—without stays—and, of course, the scandalous book in her hand.

She whipped it behind her back.

"You are mistaken," she said tartly, the words out before she could think to stop them.

"About your refinement or the strange gentlemen?" He smiled as he spoke, and she could tell he was trying to tease her, but she could not respond. Not when he stood there in his dress uniform, looking magnificent in every way, and she . . .

Good lord, even her hem was smudged!

But there was nothing to be done. She could not stand there fighting with the man. Not when he was still recovering from his death. With as much grace as possible, Sophia settled down on the settee. On top of her scandalous book.

Her aunt handed her a cup of tea, and Sophia smiled politely. With a little luck, she would pass through this most horrid incident with a modicum of self-respect.

"Do tell me about the whore from Peru," said the major, his expression forbidding.

Sophia felt her face heat. He would remember her unguarded comment upon entering the chamber. It was on the tip of her tongue to deny the whole incident when she noticed something. Whereas the major's face appeared somewhat censurious, his eyes were alight with humor. He was practically daring her to deny she'd said it.

Very well, she thought smugly. She would take a great deal of enjoyment from giving him more than he bargained for.

"Oh, yes," she said, awkwardly removing the book from beneath her. Nearby, Aunt Agatha dropped her teacup into the saucer with a clatter, but the major merely raised his eyebrows in curiosity. "It appears," continued Sophia as she turned to the correct page of poetry, "that she had four breasts rather than two." Sophia looked straight at the major. "Remarkable, is it not?"

He nodded sagely. "Absolutely. Did they cause her any problems?"

She heard her aunt choke, but Sophia continued gamely on, determined to see the thing through. "No," she said, keeping her gaze on the major's face. "It appeared to increase her popularity with an entire ship's crew."

He did not even blink, and she saw the mirth dance in his eyes. Suddenly, he was laughing loud and hearty while both Sophia and her aunt stared at him as if he were having a fit. The officer usually was too formal to laugh with such vigor.

"Major?" asked Aunt Agatha, her voice shaky with concern.

"You are an absolute hand, Sophia," he said between chuckles. "You shall make an excellent diplomat's wife." Slowly, he sobered; then he leaned forward, placing his arms on his knees as he looked intently at her. "I am so pleased that I discovered you while you were yet unattached. I cannot express how fortunate I feel."

Sophia merely gaped at him. Far from being offended by the scandalous topic, he seemed truly entertained. And as for the rest of what he said . . . She took a deep breath. It made no sense whatsoever. He could not possibly mean what he seemed to suggest.

"Well, Sophia?" he asked as he awkwardly shifted out of his chair. It was a few moments before she realized what he intended, but then it happened. He settled down onto bended knee.

"Major!" she squeaked. "Your leg!"

He continued as if she had not spoken. "When will you do me the honor of becoming my wife?"

She heard her aunt clap her hands in delight, but all Sophia could do was gape as her world spun out of control. "I spoke of a Peruvian whore and you still persist with this nonsense of our marriage?"

"I prefer the traditional womanly form for my wife," he returned with a twinkle of mirth. Then his aspect sobered as he regarded her. "Surely this comes as no surprise. I did mention it last night."

"Last night I wanted to bury you!"

"Last night you were burying corsets and furniture. Of course, some would say my face bears some resemblance—"

"Do not be absurd!" snapped Sophia. "You know you are devilishly handsome. In fact, I believe you told me that yourself once."

"I was sick with fever."

"Are you sure you are not still suffering from one?" She raised her hands, then let them flop back down in her lap. "Oh, do get off your leg. Please." Her anxiety was clear in her voice.

"Not until you pick the date of our nuptials."

"You will do yourself further injury."

"I have a special license—"

"And then the fever will come."

"We could be wed immediately—"

"No!" She had not intended to say it so forcefully, but the word seemed to explode out of her nonetheless, leaving everyone slightly dazed. Suddenly she was on her feet, pacing the room in a hurried rustle of skirts. "Major, I am free for the first time in my life. There are no rules to govern my behavior, no gossip following me, nothing ahead but a free life as a spinster. I even gave my dowry to my brother so that no one would be tempted to offer for me—"

"You underestimate your charms."

"Nonsense!" She spun back to face him directly. "My point is, I am finally free. Why would I throw that away for a life spent at a husband's beck and call? Please do get up off your leg!"

He did not move. In fact, if anything, he seemed to settle more firmly onto the floor. "Lady Sophia, I wish to marry you, not strip you naked and chain you to my bedpost. I am offering you my name."

She sighed and dropped back down on the settee, rushing her formal words in the hope it would speed his return to his seat. "I am cognizant of the honor which you bestow upon me, but I cannot accept. I have grown much too fond of my freedom to toss it away."

He folded his arms, frustration clear upon his face. "Freedom? You call burying corsets freedom?"

"I call it my choice," she said with a touch of asperity. "Just as you are choosing to harm yourself by crouching upon my floor!"

"With me, you shall see the world," he coaxed. "We shall serve England together. You shall grace our corner of the world with culture and dignity while I remind them of Britain's stronger side."

She pursed her lips. "Are you suggesting I marry you out of duty to the Crown?" It was as if he were calling her to enlist in the military.

The major grimaced. "Do not deliberately misconstrue my words, Lady Sophia."

"You are hard to misconstrue, Major," she snapped as she once again rose from her seat. "As I said last night, I have no wish for new corsets. Good day, Major."

Then she turned and quit the room.

"You turned him down? Sophia, I had not thought you lacking in wits, but I cannot credit that you could be so reckless! Whatever possessed you to—"

"He did not want a wife." Sophia's dry comment effectively silenced her aunt, who suddenly stood stock still in her niece's bedroom. Then the woman frowned, and Sophia knew her reprieve was over.

"But I was sure he said marriage, Sophia. I distinctly heard the word."

Sophia groaned as she rolled onto her stomach and dropped her head forward onto her pillow. If she closed her eyes very tight, she could pretend the world did not exist.

"Did you see the major's face when he left?" began her aunt. "He looked heartbroken."

Sophia lifted her head, fear clutching her heart. "Was he flushed? Pale? Did he seem ill?"

Aunt Agatha shook her head, clearly baffled by her niece's question. "I said heartbroken, Sophia. His batman did not say a word. The man just knew from the look in the major's eyes."

Sophia rolled onto her back and stared at the lace canopy overhead. "More likely he overheard what happened. Kirby is always popping up everywhere—or at least he did at the hospital, always showing up where I was. I am convinced he listens at keyholes."

Her aunt sighed, then settled down next to Sophia on the bed, her ribbons and bows fluttering with her every movement. "The major said he was staying at the Stag's Heart Inn. You could send around a note—"

"Aunt!" interrupted Sophia. "I thought you of all people would understand my decision."

"Me?" the older woman squeaked. "Whyever would I understand? I think it is the most mutton-headed thing you have ever done."

Sophia pushed back on her elbows, levering herself upright on the bed. "You have everything I want, Aunt Agatha. You are free to do what you want, when you want. You are alone, with no one constantly harping at you to do this or act as such. . . ."

"You mean I have no husband to love, no children to hold," countered the older woman.

"You have only yourself to please. You are free."

"Which is a nice way of saying I have no one to please me when the days grow short and cold." Her aunt slanted her a look. "And believe me, Sophia, they do grow short and cold in Staffordshire."

Sophia sighed and pulled her knees up to her chin. "You are deliberately misunderstanding me."

"Sophia, darling, I understand you quite well." Her aunt leaned forward and gathered up her niece's fingers, her cherubic face drawn and sad. "You are young still. You cannot imagine life will ever grow tedious or empty."

Sophia lifted her gaze to her aunt's face, trying to sound serene but only succeeding in seeming cold. "On the contrary, I know quite well about tedium and emptiness. It is called London and five years of endless routs, card parties, and wide smiles that cover souls filled with malice." Sophia clutched her aunt's plump hand. "Surely you know what I mean. You must see why I cannot settle for the polite slavery the major offers."

"Slavery!" her aunt exclaimed. "Whoever put such notions into your head?"

Sophia lifted a single eyebrow in a skeptical expression she had perfected over the last five years. "You did, Aunt. Years ago when I asked you why you never married."

Agatha's gaze widened, then slid away, dropping to her fingers, which toyed with the tail of a purple ribbon. She did not speak for a long time, her thoughts obviously turned inward, or perhaps into the long-ago past.

"Yes, Sophia," she finally whispered. "I suppose I did think that years ago—about a young doctor who ended up marrying a minister's daughter instead of me. But now I am older. I know there is something worse than London." Her eyes focused, bringing with it that rare twinkle Sophia so loved. "It is called Staffordshire."

"Aunt Agatha—"

"Whatever has happened to you, Sophia?" her aunt cried. "You were lively and free and unrestrained once, following your heart wherever it willed."

Sophia leaned forward eagerly. "But that is exactly how I am now," she pressed. "Now that I am free. There is no one to order me about!"

Her aunt shook her head, the sadness clear on her worn face. "No. Now you are cautious, nervous about everything and everyone. I suppose I can understand your reticence in London. There is so much to fear with the *ton*. But even here, you do not trust yourself. You have put your faith in silly rituals and childish nonsense about freedom."

"That is not true!" Sophia's response was loud and vehement, but inside she cringed, not wanting to think too deeply about her aunt's words. Instead, she shook her head, taking refuge in the phrase that was now her watchword. "I am free now. I will never listen to anyone but myself ever again."

Her aunt frowned. "You are hiding. I think you have

been doing so for a very long time. Probably all the time you were in London." She reached forward in a quick motion, taking Sophia's hand in an earnest grasp. "Is there someone else, Sophia? Someone who has stolen your heart?"

"Of course not," she responded, her voice strong and firm. Who else would there be? She could never trust a member of the *ton* to prefer her to the enticements of town. With her decision to remain here in Staffordshire, she would be abandoned within hours of her own wedding.

"You had so many suitors, your mother and I were sure you would be wed in a fortnight. But not a one claimed you."

Sophia grimaced, remembering each and every one of her so-called suitors. "Not a one truly wanted me. I was simply a passing fancy for flighty boys."

"Perhaps," commented Agatha, her thoughtful gaze heavy on her niece. "But I think you are afraid."

"I fear nothing!" Sophia exclaimed. "Except men who would bind me to their name, then run off to do whatever they wish, leaving me to fret and worry alone."

"Your Major Wyclyff does not seem so inconstant. Indeed, you once told me that was why you so liked military men. They dedicate their lives to a sense of duty and responsibility."

Sophia glanced away, her eyes tearing despite her determination not to cry. "Military men die, Aunt Agatha," she whispered. "And the end is just the same."

"But Major Wyclyff has left the army. He is to be a diplomat."

Sophia fell silent. She had no answer for that, only a numbing coldness and the memory of a nurse telling her that Major Wyclyff was dead.

She felt her aunt's hand on her chin, gently drawing her back to the dear lady's earnest expression. "There is still time to change your mind about the major. You need not write to him, you know. I am positive he shall be back. He does not seem a man who gives up easily."

Sophia bit her lip and considered her aunt's comment. It was true. Even feverish, with the doctors and nurses all waiting for him to die, the major had a power in him. It was the most overwhelming reason she had said "yes" in the hospital. His strength had enveloped her even when he was wracked with fever. Though he was thin, wasted even, moaning in pain, she still could not deny him his last wish—their engagement.

She never thought he would survive. But in the end, he'd defied them all—doctors, nurses, even Death. He'd risen from his hospital bed and, assuming he did not re-injure himself, was now beginning a respectable diplomatic career. No, the major was not a man who gave up easily.

"You think he will come back for me?" Sophia asked softly.

Aunt Agatha shifted uneasily on the bed. "He will act according to his nature."

Sophia looked up at her aunt, unable to fathom what she was suggesting. "What?"

Her aunt gave a fond smile, pushing up as she prepared to leave her niece's bedroom. "He is a military man. Think, Sophia; what does a good officer do when faced with clear defeat?"

"Retreat."

The older woman nodded. "And then what?"

Sophia shrugged. She had not the slightest clue.

"He tries an oblique assault, my dear. If I were you," the woman added with a slight wink, "I would prepare for a flanking maneuver."

"But whatever is that—" she began.

Agatha waved her to silence. "And when he does," she continued, "perhaps we could arrange a simple test, a way for him to prove his commitment to you. You find him arrogant and demanding? Perhaps we could force him to serve—with constancy and humility." Then before Sophia could demand an explanation, Agatha rose and wandered from the room, a pensive smile on her face.

Sophia frowned at her aunt's departing form, wondering what test the dear lady could devise. It did not matter, she decided. She had her own plans for thwarting the major.

Chapter Three

Anthony's leg was stiff as he dismounted in front of the Rathburn house, but it was not the pain that made his movements so awkward. It had been years since he had brought a gift to a lady. In fact, the last time had been when he was no more than fourteen, carrying a bunch of wildflowers to his mother for her birthday.

This time, he was bringing a whalebone corset to the woman who had summarily dismissed him only three days before. Still, he reminded himself, he had no cause to be awkward. She was a reasonable woman who no doubt had come to see the error of her earlier decision.

He did not come to this conclusion lightly, but had spent a great deal of thought on the probability of it. If he guessed correctly, Sophia had spent the first day after his appearance in righteous indignation. His continued existence had obviously come as a shock, and her reaction had been one of confusion and distress at so unexpected an event. In his experience, it generally took women approximately a day to calm their emotions.

The next twenty-four hours had likely passed in silent thought as Sophia's temper cooled and reason once again asserted itself. It would have taken a little less than another day for her to step logically to the realization that she had made a mistake in trying to cry off their engagement.

So it was this midafternoon, three days after Sophia's refusal, that Anthony arrived with corset in hand, intending to once again ask Lady Sophia to set the date of their wedding.

"She will not receive you."

Anthony paused in the act of handing his horse to a servant, turning slightly as he searched for the source of the muffled voice. "I beg your pardon?"

"I said, 'She will not receive you.' "

The sound came from behind him, and Anthony once again twisted awkwardly, scanning the near gardens for the source of the female voice. The woman emerged slowly, backing out from beneath a large hedge, her round posterior quivering as she wiggled and twisted.

Lady Agatha, Sophia's aunt.

"These vines are terribly difficult," she muttered as she tugged on a rather long and twisted vine of unknown progeny. "They were a special gift from a dear but dotty old friend, imported from the Continent. The plant, not the friend. I thought to simply kill the thing, but everywhere I turn, there it is again, growing in the most difficult places. Here," she continued, pushing the greenery in question into his hand. "Have a tug."

Anthony had no choice. Good manners insisted that he comply with the lady's request. Wrapping the vine around his glove, he pulled . . . to no avail.

"Come now, Major," Lady Agatha chided as she finally

stepped out of the shrubbery, her ribbons trailing behind her. "Put your back into it."

"Perhaps your gardener . . ."

"Nonsense. This will take but a moment."

Anthony sighed, impatient to see Sophia, but the girl's aunt appeared blithely ignorant of his desires. Finally giving in to the inevitable, he put aside his wrapped package and added his other hand to the first and began to tug.

Nothing.

Frowning, he set his feet wider and pulled again. This time, he was rewarded with a slight hitch as at least one root gave way.

"Oh, bravo, Major. Please, keep pulling."

"Madame—"

"Pull!" The lady added force to her command by laying her hands on top of his and adding her own bulk to his weight. Together they hauled on the vine while her ribbons brushed his nose and fluttered in his eyes.

"Madame," Anthony sputtered. "Your bows . . . madame!"

But it was too late. Though he tried to fight the urge, the sneeze was as undeniable as the persistent tickle of her ribbons. It exploded through him with the force of a gale, ripping the roots from the soil and throwing both him and Lady Agatha backward.

He landed flat on his gift of fashionable unmentionables and skidded directly into a patch of mud.

"Bravo, Major!" Lady Agatha cried as she tumbled off of him, further mangling what was left of his package. "I feel certain we have finished this usurper once and for all!" She waved the uprooted vine, then gained her feet, calmly shifting the vine to inspect its dirty base. "Oh, bother! I thought you would be strong enough to get more of the root system." She sighed heavily. "But I supposed there is a limit to what even a major of His Majesty's army can achieve."

Anthony did not dare comment; he was busy surveying the damage done to the poor corset, not to mention his now soiled attire. Surveying his damaged gift, he realized the shopkeeper had been less than expert in his wrapping. The box had split open and a whalebone corner had cleaved a deep rut through the mud.

Really, he thought as he lifted the item from the muck, why did women subject themselves to such torment? The corset looked most uncomfortable to him.

"A corset, Major? That is a tad unusual."

He glanced up, feeling his face heat to the roots of his hair. "Lady Sophia suggested, um, that I purchase her new ones as I, uh, ruined her—"

"Ah, yes, that silly ritual." Lady Agatha shook her head and turned away. "I thought it would be good for her at the time, but I can see it has just confused her mind even more."

Anthony frowned as the lady began walking away. Confused her mind? Perhaps this sweet lady possessed the answer to Sophia's strange behavior. "Lady Agatha," he called as he hurried to catch up with her. "What do you mean, confused her mind?"

"Hmmm? Oh, she wished to be rid of everything related to London, and burying corsets has always sounded like a perfectly delightful thing to me, so I suggested she do it. Now it appears she was more interested in burying you." She bent down to lift up a basket of cuttings, pausing to take a frowning look at his muddy clothing. "I suppose I cannot blame her for refusing you, if that is your choice of attire when calling."

He looked up at the lady, frustration washing over him as he catalogued the things he now must do before finishing his business with Sophia. Not only would he have to go back to his room to bathe and change, but he would have to purchase a new corset, a most humiliating affair, to be sure. By the time that was accomplished, Sophia would no doubt be bedded down for the night.

"Well, you need not glare like that at me," exclaimed the lady as she calmly folded the vine into her basket. "I am not the one who has barred the door to you."

It was not until Anthony had given up trying to clean off his pantaloons that her words sank in. But by that time, the woman had already begun wandering to the near gardens, and he was forced to catch up to her there. "Sophia has barred the door to me?"

Lady Agatha grasped one of her fluttering ribbons and tugged on it far enough to pull back the wide brim of her bonnet. "Did I not just say so?"

"Well, of course," muttered Anthony as he measured his pace to hers. "But that must have been two days ago. By now your niece has reevaluated the situation enough to—"

"To be seeking your visit?"

Anthony smiled. "Yes."

"No."

"But . . ."

Lady Agatha took a sharp turn to the right, and Anthony had to struggle over a rather strange purple hedge to remain by her side.

"She will not see you, Major. She will not even go out of the house in case she might chance to meet you. In fact, she has vowed to remain inside until her mother writes that you are safely ensconced in London, wooing some other girl."

It was fortunate that Lady Agatha chose that moment to suddenly stoop down over a broad-leafed weed, for Anthony stopped dead in his tracks to consider her words.

"Sophia is not nearly that stubborn," he said, as much to himself as to the girl's aunt.

"Oh, I assure you, Sophia is that stubborn and more. You shall have quite a time if you intend to continue wooing her."

Anthony did not answer. He was too busy considering his options. There were not many. "She has truly barred the door?"

"Most explicitly."

"Does she take walks?"

"Not anymore."

"She must ride."

"She sold her horse in London."

"Damnation! Then how am I to see her, short of dancing on the rooftops and dropping whole into her bedroom?"

"Oh, pray do not do that!" cried Lady Agatha. "You would undoubtably crush the rare plants I have cultured by her window."

Anthony stared at the plump woman digging gingerly at some weed as if she was born to the task. Then, suddenly, she turned her head and he gazed into her pale green eyes. He had not realized they were so keen, but here with the sunlight falling full on her face, he felt the weight of a stare his commanding officer had never managed.

Instinctively, he stiffened his spine. "Madame?"

She stood slowly, bringing the muddy weed with her. "So you intend to continue wooing my niece."

It was not a question, but he answered it nonetheless. "Yes, my lady."

"Why?" she asked. "Certainly there are other girls available to you."

"Lady Sophia has already consented."

The woman snorted as she tossed the weed away. "Sophia is locked in her room for fear that she might see you. Is that how you wish to spend your married life? With a wife who bars the door to you?"

"Of course not! Sophia is not truly so intemperate."

"You know full well she is," the lady snapped. "I repeat my question: Why Sophia?"

He answered without thought, as if commanded by a superior officer. "Because she is perfect in every way."

Clearly that was not the correct answer; Lady Agatha shook her head, and her eyes narrowed as she inspected him from head to toe. "Sophia finds you domineering and inflexible. I cannot say that I disagree."

Shock jolted him out of his rigid posture. "But that cannot be true," he said, as much to her as to himself. "Our conversations in the hospital were spirited and entertaining." His tone softened in memory. "She even said I had a stimulating perspective on the world."

"Are you certain she said that?"

His posture stiffened, and he found himself somewhat offended. "Those very words."

The lady sighed, then ambled forward through her garden while Anthony hurried to fall in line with her. But even as they moved, his gaze shifted upward, to Sophia's bedroom window. He had to speak with her. Surely, face to face he could find a way to convince her.

Then her aunt was speaking, jolting him out of his thoughts. "You must prove to her that you can be flexible. That you can serve."

Anthony frowned. "I was a soldier in His Majesty's army. I served every day of my career."

Her chuckle set her ribbons to dancing about her hair. "A wife is a much more difficult taskmaster than His Majesty."

Anthony stopped walking, his impatience getting the better of him. "My lady, I beg of you, call your niece outside. Allow me to speak with—"

"Major, I have decided it is time for Bowen to visit his mother. He is our butler, you understand, but he neglects his poor parent so, I really feel I must insist he visit her more often."

Anthony frowned, wondering at this apparent non sequitur. What could the butler have to do with anything?

"My lady, if I could just speak with Sophia—"

"I shall have to find a replacement, you understand," she continued without pause. "Starting tomorrow." Her keen gaze once again fell full on his face.

Suddenly, he understood. He felt his eyes widen, and his shoulders pulled back with astonishment. "You cannot possibly think I would make a good butler!"

"Well, of course not!" returned the lady. "You will, no doubt, make a perfectly wretched butler, but for Sophia's sake, I feel I can make the sacrifice."

"Madame, I am the son of an earl!"

"Well, what is that to the point? I am the daughter of an earl, and yet I tend my own garden. If rank made a difference with Sophia, she would no doubt already be married to that stiff-rumped duke with the watery eyes and wandering hands."

Anthony clenched his teeth in anger. Sophia had not told him about any duke with wayward hands. But he was not given time to dwell on such things as Lady Agatha continued, her voice as sharp as his old nurse's.

"The only way to see Sophia is to come into the house. And the only way into the house is as a servant."

"Could you not just invite me in?" he asked, his voice heavy with sarcasm.

"Well, of course I could, but she will not come down. And she asks now if we have visitors to dine before coming to table. I told you, Major, she is as stubborn as that vine, but together we can move her."

Anthony flinched, not appreciating her analogy, but he was nevertheless forced to admit certain similarities. "Why are you helping me?"

"Because I must see you two together." She turned to him, and her face softened into a mischievous smile. "And because you make her mad as I have never seen her before."

"But—"

"Never underestimate passion, Major. It stirs the blood to all sorts of things. Anger. Recklessness. Sometimes even love." Then Agatha wandered off, her basket once again on her arm. Her last words floated over her shoulder. "Do try not to get mud in the house, Major. As our butler, you must be more careful with your appearance."

Then she was gone.

Sophia's defense against the Major's "flanking maneuver" had been well planned. She left word with Bowen to refuse posies, sweets, or even impassioned letters; she refused to take trips into the village for fear of "accidentally" meeting him; and she even stopped her daily walks in the dale near her aunt's house.

Nothing happened. In the three days since the major's proposal, no letters were refused at the door. No trinkets were pushed through her window. Indeed, no impassioned cries came from the front walk. Anthony had disappeared from her life, no doubt riding back to London on his magnificent steed, leaving Sophia once again alone.

Perversely, the situation left her mood decidedly flat.

Obviously, her aunt had been exaggerating the major's intentions. As a practical and logical man, Anthony clearly understood her refusal and had left for London. She was now free to resume the normal course of life in Staffordshire.

Naturally, she was pleased that the situation had been resolved so easily, she told herself. It was merely the cloudy day that effected her mood.

So, on the fourth morning after the Major's teatime appearance, she dressed in one of her prettiest gowns to cheer herself up and went down to breakfast. She spotted her aunt immediately. Indeed, who could miss a plump woman adorned with more than a dozen pink bows, when suddenly a deep, rich, very male voice interrupted her thoughts.

"Good morning, Lady Sophia," the major called as he backed awkwardly into the breakfast room toting a tray of breakfast. "You look quite lovely this morning."

Sophia did not know how to respond. She simply stared at him.

"Would you care for some poached eggs? Toast?" he continued almost gleefully. "Cook's kippers are delicious this morning."

Sophia continued to stare. It could not possibly be true. But it was. It was the major, dressed in a butler's knee breeches and stockings, his limp masked by his careful pace. And he was serving her kippers.

"Close your mouth, Sophia," commented her aunt in a merry undertone. "You are catching flies."

Sophia snapped her jaw shut.

"Would you care for some eggs, my lady?" repeated the major.

Sophia lifted her gaze to look directly at him. His eyes were twinkling. Sparkling, actually, which was an odd thing for meltingly dark brown eyes to be doing. Still, somehow he had accomplished it. Just as somehow he had managed to appear in her breakfast room, serving her eggs and morning chocolate.

She swallowed convulsively. "Are you quite well?" she asked before she thought to stop her words. "Does your leg pain you?"

He grinned as he poured her chocolate. "Of course I am well. Thank you for asking. Eggs?"

She watched him a moment longer, searching his face for telltale signs of a fever. There didn't seem to be any.

"Kippers?" he inquired.

Slowly, she dropped her eyes to the cart. "No, thank you," was all she managed.

"You may go now, Major," called her aunt sweetly.

The man nodded and quit the room, his manners impeccable. Sophia watched, her mind still reeling from the sight. The moment the door swung shut behind him, she rounded on her aunt.

"What is *he* doing here?" she hissed.

"I told you last night that Bowen had left to visit his ailing mother."

Sophia clenched her fingers in her bright canary skirt. "Yes, you did. But I fail to see what that has to do with the major serving kippers to us."

Her aunt raised one finely drawn eyebrow. "Is there something wrong with the kippers?"

"I have no idea; I have not tasted any," she snapped.

"Oh, then did the major spill as he served your chocolate?"

Sophia gritted her teeth but was unable to keep the frustration from her voice. "You know quite well that he did not, although it was a near thing there for a moment." The major obviously was not used to handling fine china while wearing white gloves. Which was all the more reason to suspect her aunt of hidden motives.

"I fail to see the problem," claimed the older woman serenely.

"Well, I do. The major cannot act as our butler!"

When she so chose, Aunt Agatha could look like a cherub being cruelly and unjustly tortured. Now was one of those times. She placed one hand on her chest and opened her eyes wide with shocked horror. "Goodness, Sophia," she gasped. "You must know I had to hire another butler until Bowen returned."

"Of course, but—"

"And the major came to me looking for employment."

Sophia gave her a skeptical look. "Really? The stiff major, an earl's son, came to you looking for employment?"

Her aunt colored. "Well," she answered slowly, "he is only a younger son." Her voice trailed away.

"Out with it, Aunt Agatha. What have you done?"

The dear lady stiffened, her face flushed with embarrassment. "I could not allow one of our dear casualties of war to starve. Especially when I had a job available."

"He is not on the point of starvation!" Sophia snapped.

"Well, I fail to see how you could know that. After all—"

"*Aunt!* Why is he here?"

Aunt Agatha looked down at the lacy tablecloth, her expression too innocent. "We, um, had a long conversation yesterday."

"Regarding?"

The older woman lifted her gaze until her light green eyes were flashing irritation at her niece. "Regarding your ridiculous refusal to see him. Goodness, Sophia, you have practically gaoled yourself in this house."

"I have not!"

"Excuse me, Lady Agatha," interrupted the major's deep voice. It was so unexpected that Sophia nearly jumped out of her chair. "The gardener wishes to speak with you," he continued. "Shall I bid him wait?"

Sophia frowned at their erstwhile new butler, showing every ounce of displeasure available to her. "It is customary to wait until we bid you to speak, Major. My aunt and I were in the middle of a discussion." Her tone was haughty, almost rude, and she had the satisfaction of seeing the major's face flush with the effort to hold back his response to her words.

Taking advantage of the man's temporary silence, Sophia turned back to her aunt. "Surely you can see he is not fit to be a butler. A general, certainly, but not our butler."

Her aunt did not respond. She simply gave her niece a serene smile as she turned to the major. "I will see the gardener directly. Thank you." Then, with a slight nod to her niece, she stood and withdrew from the room, the delicate wave of her pink ribbons her only good-bye.

Which left Sophia alone with her increasingly cold breakfast and her suitor.

Sophia was not by nature a confrontational person. She preferred polite inanities to open arguments. In fact, it was one of the things she most disliked about the major—that whenever she was with him, even in the hospital, they seemed to descend into heated debates about one thing or another.

Here again, she thought with a deep sense of injury, he was forcing her into a clearly adversarial relationship. Well, she would not stoop to that. She would speak to him reasonably, calmly, like a rational adult. He would just be made to see he could not get around her by becoming a servant in her aunt's household.

She lifted her chin and pinned him with her steady regard. "What are you doing here, Major?" she asked, her voice cool yet civil.

He looked up, his expression completely bland, his tone clearly deferential. "I am clearing your aunt's dishes. Shall I return at a later time for them?"

Sophia kept firm control of her temper and focused on speaking calmly, rationally. "No, you should not return," she said. "You should not be here at all."

He raised his eyebrows. They were thick, arching over his dark eyes. She found the sight oddly mesmerizing. "Is there something wrong with my service?" he asked, his manner excruciatingly polite. "Perhaps I should lay the dishes out on the sideboard in the mornings. Would that be satisfactory?"

Sophia shook her head. She knew he was being deliberately obtuse. She had to focus on the meaning beneath his actions. "I suppose this is what is meant by a flanking maneuver," she grumbled.

"I beg your pardon, my lady?"

She sighed, feeling the strain on her control. It was clearly time to be blunt. "Why are you here, Major?"

He frowned and gestured to the dishes.

"That doesn't fadge, and you know it. I cannot credit that a man of your standing, an earl's son, no less, would stoop to become our temporary butler."

She did not see how it happened. One moment the major was across the room, bowing his head and looking very servile. The next moment he was towering over her, using his full height to impressive advantage as he glared at her with outraged dignity.

"Do you imply that the position of butler is a dishonorable occupation?"

Sophia blinked, tilting her head back to look him in the eye. "Of course not," she stammered.

"Or that I, the son of an earl, should disdain such lawful employment?"

She shook her head. "Naturally you should work at whatever occupation you choose—"

"Then you have some objection to my person? Perhaps I have an offensive odor."

"Not that I can detect," she said, feeling her temper slip past its restraints.

"Am I perhaps too ugly?"

"Do not be ridiculous," she snapped, frustration making her curt. "You are quite handsome, as you well know."

He grinned, clearly pleased with her unintended compliment. "Then I fail to see why you object to my employment."

"Because you are doing this simply to get me to marry you!" She blurted the words out, heedless of her intention to remain cool and detached. But even so, she did not regret them. She spoke the truth, and they both knew it.

Except he apparently did not. If ever there was an expression of outraged shock, he was wearing it. If one discounted that ever-present twinkle in his eyes.

"I beg your pardon, miss, but I fear you have gravely mistaken the situation." He paused, as if suddenly struck by a confusing thought. "Do you often consider new employees are angling for a proposal?"

She glared at him. "You are not an employee."

"You are sacking me?"

"Do not be ridiculous!"

"Ah," he said with an understanding smile. "Then you are proposing to me. I must say this is an odd turn of affairs. Was it my overwhelming beauty that first attracted you, or my lack of a distinct odor?"

"You are insane!"

He frowned. "Not last time I checked, but if you would like, I shall obtain a doctor's certificate affirming my sanity. I perfectly understand how you would not wish to marry a madman."

Sophia pushed to her feet, feeling the need to level the field somewhat. But despite her great height, she was still only eye-to-chin with the wretched man. "You are deliberately provoking me, and I will not tolerate it."

He bowed slightly, backing away from her in a falsely submissive gesture. "My deepest apologies, my lady. I had no wish to offend."

Sophia ground her teeth together, wondering how she had lost such control not only of the situation but of her own temper. She glared at him. "Why are you doing this?"

He was silent a moment. Then, without moving a muscle, he suddenly changed. Gone was the provocative butler pretending a subservience that never seemed real. In his place stood the major she remembered—tall, commanding, a leader of men despite his servant's clothing.

"I wished to see you," was all he said.

She sighed. Finally, they were getting to the heart of the matter. "This is not the way."

He raised an eyebrow. "You refused my visits."

"You never came."

"You left orders you were not at home to me or any of

my gifts. And you have hidden in the house so that my only choice was to join you here."

"That is not true!" Nevertheless, Sophia felt her face turn scarlet.

"Of course, my lady." Though his tone was deferential, there was no mistaking the doubt in his voice.

Sophia dropped down into her chair, quietly yielding him this battle, but not the whole war. Never that. "Very well," she finally conceded. "Perhaps I was a trifle too, um, firm in my actions. But I only wished to make my position clear." She looked up at him, meeting his eyes with her own steady gaze. "Now that you are seeing me, can you also see that I will not change my mind?"

He folded his arms across his chest and looked down at her—not condescendingly, but as a man studying a particularly difficult puzzle. "You said you will not marry because you cannot support becoming a slave."

"Correct."

"I wished to show you that I can be flexible. I can serve. I have, in fact, served every day of my life. I serve England and the Crown."

Sophia released an inelegant snort. "You cannot maintain this farce, Major. Look at you." She waved at his imperious stance. "Even as a butler, you cannot resist trying to control the situation. Our marriage would be less than an hour old before you issued your first command. Then I would be forever carrying out your orders, falling to whatever line you drew."

"I would not make you into a slave!" he countered hotly.

"Then your subordinate. Perhaps a leftenant . . . or a private!"

"You would be my wife!" But even as he spoke, he dropped his hands onto his waist and took an angry step forward. She had no doubt this was exactly how he looked when disciplining an unfortunate underling. And from the sudden flushed cast to his face, he knew exactly what he had done.

Dropping his arms to his sides, he shifted his demeanor back to one of a butler. Of course, having seen him as a commanding officer moments before, she knew his subservience was merely an act, a guise put on in this ridiculous campaign to win her hand.

"You cannot maintain this posture," she commented quietly. "It will drive you mad in less than a day."

He simply lifted an eyebrow, his expression one of quiet challenge. "You do not know me as well as you believe, Lady Sophia."

She met his challenge with one of her own. "I know I will not change my mind, no matter how many tea cakes you serve me."

His smile was slow in coming, secret in its arrival, and sweetly exciting when it appeared. It was a man's smile, filled with masculine pride and quiet daring. It thrilled her down to her toes. It also made her extremely suspicious.

"What are you thinking?" she asked.

He raised his eyebrows in an expression of complete innocence. "Only that I shall have to serve you something other than tea and cakes."

Chapter Four

Four hours later, Major Wyclyff did not think he was up to serving anything. His leg ached, his back was stiff, and his head throbbed from a brigade-sized headache. But most of all, his hands and wrists ached from polishing silver so tarnished it reflected only gray. Why, his thumbs even felt flat.

"Well, 'ere's a sight," interrupted the gravelly voice of his batman. "A decorated major o' the Hussars, bent over like a hobbled horse polishing an old tabby's silver. Why, it be enough to stir a man to suicide."

Anthony groaned and turned around on the high stool in his cramped little butler's closet. "Stubble it, Kirby. We have been in worse situations than this."

"Aye," the short man agreed with a solemn nod. "But never one wot smelled so bad."

Anthony could not help but agree. The polishing solution the maid recommended reeked to high heaven, especially in this cramped room. "Did you come here for a reason?" he asked, thankfully setting aside a badly tarnished teaspoon.

"Aye. Came t' see if ye regained yer senses. We can be back in London by tomorrow noon."

Anthony thought lovingly of his small, sweet-smelling rooms in London and sighed. "I cannot go back until I am married."

"But the appointment—"

"Is for a married man."

Kirby's thick face compressed into a tight line of disapproval. Anthony had seen it too many times before to miss it now. It said in silent anger that his superior officer and current employer was ten times a fool. And for once, Anthony wondered if the sullen batman was right. "Say your piece, man."

Kirby did not disappoint him. He squared his shoulders and started in. "Begging yer pardon, sir, but there's many a woman to bed without dressing in knee breeches and polishing silver."

"I do not want a woman to bed, Kirby. I will have Sophia to wife and none other."

Kirby frowned, his whole face quivering with frustration. "But why, sir? Wager or no wager, I can't see 'at she's worth all this." He gestured disdainfully at the tiny butler's closet.

Anthony felt his body clench as anger burned in his gut. It was not a reasonable reaction. His batman was only repeating what he had told himself for the last few days. But the irrational anger still poured like hot lead through his blood.

"A thousand guineas, man," he said curtly. "You know I have not that much, not to mention what winning the wager will do for me."

Kirby shook his head, clearly dismissing the thought. "Your father can pay the debt."

"I will not run to my father!" He said the words, but

inside he cringed. He had considered doing just that at least a dozen times. He still did not understand why he had made so impulsive and clearly reckless a bet. But wager he had, and now he was forced to honor it. The thought of trying to explain the entire wretched situation to his father made him wish he had died in that hospital bed.

"She ain't worth it," Kirby pressed. "I know that yer thinking she's an angel. She pulled you back from the dead, and there ain't a day that I don't thank God in Heaven she brought ye back from the Grim Reaper's fist when I couldna done it." Kirby paused, squaring his shoulders in what for him was an unusual display of awkwardness. "She's a right fine woman, sir, when she ain't burying furniture in the dales. But she weren't there just fer you. She went ta all the men, Major. The dying and the poor. She visited ever' one of them like clockwork. Ye can't be basin' a marriage on a visit t' the sick."

Anthony did not answer. He knew all of this. Even sick with fever, he knew Sophia had visited all the patients in that hospital. But despite the doubts that plagued him each night, he believed her visits with him had been different. They had spoken of so much together. She had told him her dreams, and he had seen the longing in her eyes when she looked at him. Only when she looked at him.

With a clenched jaw, he glared at his batman. "You have said your piece. Now get out."

He did not wait to see Kirby leave, but turned his back. Swinging stiffly around on his leg, he specifically ignored the man who had seen him through swamps and battlefields, who had shaved him, nursed him, and even bathed him. He turned his back and waited in anxious tension for the sound of Kirby's heavy footfalls as the man stomped away.

Instead, he heard *her* voice. "If you will not explain it

to him, Major, perhaps you will explain to me."

He spun around, shock coursing through his body at the sight of Sophia standing directly beside his orderly. Never had he thought to be startled by her soft voice. The sound of her footsteps was imprinted in his consciousness. He listened for them in his dreams and waited for them by day. And yet she surprised him, coming upon him when he was least prepared to speak with anyone, much less her.

"Sophia," he whispered, his throat closing up at the sight of her serene face surrounded by soft waves of golden hair, short though her curls now were. Beside her, Kirby bowed formally to him and took his leave, but Anthony barely noticed. His angel was before him, demanding answers he was not prepared to give.

"Was your man correct? Did you propose to me because I visited you in the hospital?"

He shifted awkwardly, thankful that she had not heard him discuss the unfortunate wager. "I offer you the protection of my name and my person," he said stiffly. "The reasons are unimportant."

She was implacable. "I have already refused your most generous offer, Major—"

"You accepted in the hospital."

"I have already cried off your most generous offer," she corrected. "If you wish me to change my mind, you will need to offer your thoughts. Why is it so important that I marry you?"

He flexed his shoulders backward and lifted his chin. He might have been facing a firing squad for all the tension that surged through his body. Why was this so confounded hard?

"I owe you my life, Lady Sophia. You were the sole reason I recovered from my fever. The doctors said it was a miracle. I know it was you."

"Your remarkable constitution and bullheaded stubbornness are the reason you recovered. I merely gave you a little incentive."

He nodded, his muscles straining with the movement. "You were an angel of mercy—"

"And a paragon of virtue," she added dryly. "So build me a shrine and throw flowers on it. There is no need to twist yourself into a knot cleaning my aunt's silver."

He did not move; his body gave no reaction. Yet deep inside, he felt a quickening, a stirring of emotion that only she seemed to inspire. No one else could lighten his soul as she did. Laughter rarely seemed to touch him, but around her—playing with her, arguing—he felt it inside, and that made him all the more determined to have its source in his life.

"Come out of the butler's room, Major," she coaxed. "Perhaps we could sit in the parlor." He felt her hand, warm and life-giving on his arm, tugging at him. More than anything, he wanted to follow her. But he knew it was her first step in removing him from her life. She would take him from the closet to the parlor, and before he knew it, she would have him out the door riding back to London. Alone.

He stood firm. "I am your butler," he said stiffly. "It is not my place to sit with you."

"Oh, stow it, Major," she snapped. "You cannot seriously believe I developed a *tendre* for you in the hospital. You were one of hundreds with whom I spoke. What you are feeling is simple gratitude," she said firmly. "I accept your thanks. I tell you I enjoyed our conversations immensely, but that is hardly a reason to marry."

He felt her every word like a knife wound cutting at him. It tore at his confidence and weighed him down. But he was a major of the Hussars, and so he lifted his gaze to hers, studying her expression more intimately than any battle plan. He knew every nuance of her face, every shift of her eyes and what each would mean.

If she lied, he would know.

"I was merely another patient to you?" he challenged, forcing her to say it to his face. "Another wounded soldier?"

Her eyes flickered but did not slide away. "Yes."

"You never gave me another moment's thought after you left my bedside?"

Her jaw firmed, but, most telling of all, her breath nearly stopped. "Yes," she agreed.

She was definitely lying. He sighed in relief, his expression finally relaxing into a near smile.

She stood there dumbfounded. "Major?"

"I waited for your visits," he said calmly. "Every day, I counted the seconds until you returned. And while I waited, I remembered. I recalled your every word, your every motion."

She shook her head, clearly disturbed by the casualness with which he spoke of his obsession.

"You were the one thing that kept me sane when there was nought else for me."

"But—"

"And do you know what all that taught me about you?" He tilted his head back, admiring the way the sunlight tinted her curls with flashes of red. His angel had fire in her, he thought, and he smiled in appreciation even as she stared at him as if he were mad.

"You are a woman in motion. When you laugh or speak or smile, your body moves about. Your hands, your hair, even your eyes sparkle. It as if you are dancing wherever you are."

Her eyes grew wider with shock, flashing her irritation and dismay. "On the contrary, Major," she finally sputtered, "I am the Ice Queen, or so I was dubbed. I am the cold woman who froze her way through five Seasons in London."

"Aye." He nodded. She had spoken of that many times.

Even now, he could see pain in her expression whenever she mentioned that cruel label.

"But—"

"There is only one time when you freeze, Sophia. One thing that makes you inflexible, cold, and lifeless." He leaned forward as though confiding a secret. "Do you want to know what that is?"

She stared at him, mesmerized, her breathing short and quick as he moved close enough to whisper into her curls.

"When you are lying."

She stiffened in outrage. "I never lie!"

He grinned, suddenly pleased with himself and with her. Finally, an honest argument with the woman. He was determined not to let the opportunity pass.

"On the contrary, Lady Sophia, your entire five Seasons in London were a lie. The only time you were truthful was with me. I saw you come alive, Sophia. With me." He reached out, daring to touch her flushed cheek. He stroked it as he had longed to for months, while his other hand gently drew her forward into his cramped alcove.

"You have never been more honest than when you spoke of your love of literature, your desire to see the world, even your need to please your family." He drew her closer still. Soon, her soft belly pressed against his knees. She watched him warily, her movements reluctant, but he saw the hunger in her eyes and felt an answering cry in his own blood. That knowledge emboldened him to pull her even tighter against him.

"Sophia—"

She stiffened. "It is every daughter's desire to please her family. It is her duty—"

"Liar." Her body was taut, but he continued to brush his fingertips along her face, feeling Sophia's tender flesh softening beneath the warmth of his touch. "You never looked more lifeless than when you told me how you longed to marry that duke or that you had danced with some viscount. You lied when you said you enjoyed those parties and routs."

"No—"

"A dying man sees everything, Sophia."

"You were obviously not that close to dying," she countered.

"I was."

"*No.*" The word was a bare whisper, her body as still as a statue.

He leaned forward. He felt the hard ridges of her hips pressed against his thighs. She was nestled between his legs, and he was on fire for her. His voice became husky as he finally set his lips against the soft down of her cheek. "You could be alive again," he whispered. "Marry me, Sophia, and be happy again."

He did not know what he said wrong. She was sweetly willing, her breath soft pants of a desire that went beyond the simply carnal. Then, suddenly, she went rigid in his arms, her fists pushing him away with a strength he had not expected from a woman.

"You presume too much!" she said, her voice as cold as it had ever been.

"Sophia?"

"Do not ever touch me again," she cried, then spun away from him, storming down the hall like an ancient fury. He watched her go, his body throbbing painfully, his frustration a bitter taste in his mouth.

What had he done wrong?

Sophia ran long and hard, her breath coming in painful gasps against the needle of strain in her side. She ran through the small grove behind her aunt's house, tore through the dale, running until she dropped to her knees beside a crystal-clear stream. She did not know where she was, nor did she care.

All she knew was that she had almost given in. Again.

She had almost allowed a man to convince her to do something he wanted because it would be "for her own good."

Hypocritical bastards.

Sophia let herself roll onto her side, closing her senses to everything but the sweet babble of the brook and the rich smell of wet summer grass.

How could she have allowed it? One moment, she'd been lying through her teeth, telling the major he never meant more to her than any other injured soldier. The next, she'd been standing between his knees, her body aching for his kiss. She had been ready to do anything, to say anything, even marriage vows, if only he would let his mouth follow the excruciatingly sensitive path of his fingertips to her lips.

Her face burned in mortification. She had been wanton, lewd, and so . . . needful.

Sophia groaned and buried her face in her hands. Thank God she had come to her senses. Thank God he had revealed himself at the last moment. "*Marry me, Sophia,*" he had said, "*and be happy again.*" Arrogant ass. As if she could not be happy on her own! As if her only choice for joy was his arms!

She was not stupid, so why did men always assume she was?

Sophia flopped onto her back with her arm over her eyes. Her skirt was twisted beneath her, pulling it up almost to her knees. It was a totally undignified position, but she did not really care. She was free. She would not marry the arrogant major. She would do whatever she wished, because she was free.

Free.

She frowned. Why did the word suddenly seem so empty?

It was at that moment she felt the hot sun blocked from her body. A shadow had fallen across her arm and face. Sophia tensed. She was abruptly conscious of how isolated this land was. After five years in London, she was used to having people everywhere she turned, always someone within earshot of a healthy scream.

But not out here. Not in Staffordshire, where one could walk for miles without seeing a soul.

Sophia shifted, lowering her arm from her face. There was a man standing over her, his body short and stocky, his red hair curling in an unkempt riot about his craggy face.

It was Kirby, the major's batman.

Sophia relaxed, then sat up, shifting her skirt to a more decorous position. He watched her movements, his green eyes oddly intense, but he did not say a word.

Obviously it was up to her to fill the silence. "Is there something you need?" she asked formally, her imperious tone as cold and proper as she could manage.

He shook his head. "The major sent me down to keep an eye on ye." As if to mock his orders, he let his gaze travel the length of the lonely dale. "Not fitting for a woman to wander off alone."

"Not in London," she countered. "But here—"

" 'Ere there's bandits to watch fer."

She nodded, knowing that tone of voice. It was the tone of a man who hated what he was doing, hated why he was doing it, but nevertheless did it because he was somehow forced. Sophia had heard that tone every time some gentleman was obliged by his mother to dance with her, every time her father gave her some gift . . . and every time she came in contact with the major's surly batman.

He did not like her, yet he was being forced by his loyalty to the major to tolerate her.

She smiled lazily. Perhaps she could use that to her advantage. She leaned forward, resting her elbows on her knees. "It occurs to me, Kirby, that you and I are on the same side here."

He raised a skeptical eyebrow but, in true military fashion, refused to comment.

"You do not wish the major to marry me, and I do not wish to marry him. The question now is how to convince the major that I am not the woman for him."

"The major makes up his own mind." Kirby's words were curt, but she saw the gleam of interest in his eyes.

"Yes, he does. Why is it, do you suppose, that he is so set on marrying me? I cannot believe he would put so much stock in my visits to the hospital. There must be something else."

The batman shifted awkwardly, turning his gaze to the distant hills as he clearly hesitated. He wanted to say something but did not dare.

"I need to know, Kirby. What is it?"

The man was practically squirming.

"Why is he so intent on marrying me?"

Finally, he spoke, his words quick in the afternoon heat. " 'E wants a diplomatic post."

Sophia frowned. "He told me his appointment is to India."

"Only if 'e's married."

Sophia straightened slightly, absently smoothing out the wrinkles in her skirt as she considered this newest information. It was certainly a piece of the puzzle, but it did not give her all the answers she needed. "There are plenty of women still in London," she said slowly. "Why would he come all the way out to Staffordshire for me?"

Again the dour man was silent. As she raised her eyes to study his profile, she was struck by the batman's solid appearance. Like the major, he was almost elemental in nature; strong and stubborn, as immovable as a mountain.

She folded her hands and released a sigh of disgust. Men. When would they learn they could bend and not break?

" 'E thinks ye could be a proper diplomatic wife."

Kirby's words were harsh, as if forced out of him against his will. Or as if he were betraying the one man to whom he most owed his loyalty.

Sophia studied the man's impassive face. "Are you saying that he wants me because . . . because I am cold?"

"Regal," he countered stiffly.

"The Ice Queen." She looked away, fighting the tears that clouded her vision. The title had dogged her every footstep in London, and now it followed her here to Staffordshire. Of course the major knew about the hateful appellation; they had spoken of it in the hospital before fever claimed his reason. More than that, he knew how much the term hurt her.

Could the major want her for the same thing she most hated in herself? Could he possibly be attracted to that very coldness, that deadness she had felt all those years in London? What he had cited when she had talked of her experiences with the *ton*? The betrayal felt like a knife in her soul. But such an aloof nature was indeed perfect for a diplomat's wife.

"If I was wishin' to discourage the major," Kirby said, his voice pushing into her thoughts, "I would show 'im that I was not the stiff-rumped woman 'e thought."

Sophia frowned, suddenly wanting to be done with this whole business. Whatever it took, she would rid herself of her suitor. "You mean," she said slowly, "I should show him I would be a terrible diplomat's wife."

Kirby nodded but did not offer any suggestions. Which left Sophia to ponder the possibilities.

"I could not do anything truly scandalous. It would hurt Aunt Agatha too much." Sophia idly pulled at a scarlet wildflower, carefully stripping away its petals as she focused on her newest plan. "But it would not have to be public. He is our butler, after all. He can see me as I am privately." She flushed at her misspoken word. "I mean, as I am at home." She frowned, the beginnings of an idea occurring to her. Suddenly she twisted, pinning the batman with a hopeful stare. "Kirby, what does the major abhor most of all? What absolutely disgusts him?"

It was the oddest thing, seeing the dour batman slowly blush to a fiery red. Apparently the man had thoughts that embarrassed even him. She pulled at another wildflower, her speculations running riot.

"Strong drink, my lady," Kirby finally choked out. "He abhors a man in his cups."

Was that all? she thought with a slight shrug. And here she had been imagining all sorts of strange things. Still, strong drink had its possibilities. Sophia allowed herself a triumphant smile. "Very well, Kirby. Tonight, I shall get myself thoroughly castaway."

Kirby cleared his throat, obviously uncomfortable with the thought. "Um, ma'am, 'ave you ever imbibed in excess?"

"Of course not!" She pushed to her feet. "But that shall make me all the more susceptible."

He shifted again, a frown puckering his face. "Ma'am, it ain't so easy—"

"Nonsense. It is the perfect suggestion. Except . . ." She paused, trying to remember the contents of her aunt's liquor cabinet. "I am not sure if my aunt has enough of any one drink." She shrugged. "Never mind. I shall just drink it all."

"But—"

"Tut tut, Kirby," she said airily as she began walking briskly back to the house. "It was an excellent notion. Pray do not try to take it back now." She steeled her spine with determination. "With luck, you shall be on your way back to London on the morrow."

"Aye," he commented grimly. "Or I'll 'ave me 'ead busted in for starting this in the first place."

Chapter Five

"My," exclaimed Sophia with a large and rather false yawn. "It is getting late." She glanced at her aunt. "Are you not the least bit tired?"

Aunt Agatha raised her gaze from her embroidery and stared so hard at her niece that Sophia began to fidget. "No, Sophia," she said slowly. "I am not fatigued. In fact, I feel I am becoming more alert by the second."

Sophia felt herself flush from her aunt's suspicious gaze. She knew she was bungling this whole affair, but she found the thought of becoming thoroughly cup-shot in her aunt's presence a bit more than she could bear. Still, there was no help for it. She had to start imbibing soon. Before long, the major would finish his tasks and retire for the night. Cook and Mary had already sought their own beds.

With a final glance at the clock, Sophia sighed and gave in to circumstance. She would simply have to explain herself to her aunt later. Right now, her task was to get thoroughly and disgracefully foxed.

She wandered over to the array of bottles on the sideboard. She had no experience with anything other than wine and champagne, and very little with even those. But her father's drink of choice had been brandy, so she supposed that would do.

She selected the largest glass she could find and poured.

"Sophia!" exclaimed her aunt. "I had no idea you enjoyed brandy."

"Oh, I—"

"So that is why you have been trying to shoo me off to bed. But, my dear, there is nothing to be ashamed of. I often enjoy a glass. To be honest, I was refraining so as not to offend your delicate sensibilities." She winked at her niece. "But now that I know you enjoy the odd glass . . . well, pour me some, too."

Sophia gaped at her relative. "But—"

"Come, come," interrupted her aunt. "Enough of this false modesty. We shall toast to a wonderful summer together."

"Er, very well." Sophia had no choice but to do as she was bid. She poured a modest portion into a glass and carried it to Agatha, marveling all the way. In her experience, ladies did not drink brandy.

"I can see you are still somewhat young," said her aunt with a rueful glance at her half-filled glass. "No matter. Just bring the bottle over here, and we shall have a comfortable coze."

Sophia did not dare gape any more, especially since she herself was the one who had opened the bottle to begin with. So, she brought the brandy to the table between them and watched in amazement as her aunt poured another large dollop into her glass.

"Come, Sophia," Aunt Agatha said after taking a healthy swallow. "Tell me something about London."

"Er, yes." But Sophia could not think of anything to say. She could only stare at the unusual sight of her aunt quite easily draining her glass.

Then her aunt glanced at her, her cheeks already turning a blushing rose. "Is there something wrong with the taste?"

Sophia glanced down at her still-full glass. "Oh!" Suddenly recalled to her purpose, she lifted her glass and drained it. Or rather, she tried to. She managed only two gulps before she nearly choked to death.

It was like swallowing fire, and it burned her all the way down past her stomach to her toes. She was coughing and wheezing like a dying old man while her aunt pounded her on the back and chortled heartily.

"My goodness, Sophia. From the way you were acting, I thought you had been sneaking your Papa's brandy since you were five. And now I have corrupted you."

"Nonsense, Aunt," gasped Sophia loudly, mindful that her voice had to carry enough for the major to overhear. "I enjoy brandy whenever the occasion arises."

"Of course you do," laughed the older woman cheerfully. "So drink up. Unless, of course, you would rather retire." She cast a significant glance out the window at the fading sunset. "It is rather late."

Sophia bit her lip in consternation, then finally relaxed into a smile. "You are gammoning me, Aunt. You are getting even because I tried to send you to bed."

Agatha leaned forward. "You were a bit obvious, my dear." With a deft twist of her wrist, the dear lady topped off her niece's glass. "Now, drink up, then tell me what is bothering you."

Sophia shifted uneasily. "But, nothing is bothering me."

"Um-hmm," responded her aunt with a solemn nod. "Finish that glass; then we can discuss why you left London before the last Season was out. And perhaps we might mention the major a time or two?" She gave her niece a look that suggests a wealth of understanding without explaining a thing.

"But—"

"Tut tut." Her aunt pressed the glass back into Sophia's hand. "Finish your drink first. Then we shall talk."

Anthony was checking the front door before retiring when he heard uproarious female laughter emanating from the upstairs parlor. Gone were Sophia's familiar mellow tones. What he heard instead was loud giggling—high-pitched and delightfully mischievous. It was as if his intended truly laughed with unrestrained glee for the first time in her life.

That thought drew him upstairs, his steps silent and slow, though he was certain neither woman would hear an entire regiment if it were banging on their front door.

"Do allow me the honor of tramping on your toes and breathing foul liquor into your face." Sophia's words were low and thick, and the major did not need to hear her aunt's high-pitched squeal to know she was imitating some crusty beau. "What!" she continued. "Why do you not swoon at the honor I bestow upon you? I am a peer o' the realm, don't you know!"

Anthony reached the parlor and carefully eased the door open. Sophia stood with her back to him, but he could tell from the haughty angle of her head that she was peering down her nose at an empty bottle of brandy. The poor container was apparently supposed to be her dance partner.

Her skin was flushed and glowing from drink, but that did not hinder her from mimicking some stuffed London popinjay. She continued to pretend to dance, moving stiffly, posturing with every step. Her hair, which had grown a bit, was working its way out of several pins she had inserted to keep it neat, and as he watched the golden curls tumbled loose.

She was beautiful. How could anyone have called her an "Ice Queen"? She seemed now like a flame, literally burning with energy and life as she strutted about the room with her bottle-*cum*-partner in hand.

"Oh, you have Harrington to a *T!*" exclaimed her aunt, holding her sides to contain her laughter. "Goodness, he was an old goat when I made my curtsy." The older woman drank heartily from her glass before peering owlishly at her niece. "But what of the major? How does he dance?"

"I have never danced with the major," came Sophia's response. Then she stepped forward, lowering her voice to a drunken whisper that nevertheless could have been heard in the next county. "But I know exactly how it would be."

"You do?" Her aunt was on the edge of her seat with curiosity, and Anthony could not help but lean closer to the door to hear Sophia's response.

"Goodness, Aunt, have you ever seen the major do anything but at attention? I expect he even stands so during his baths."

"Sophia!" her aunt exclaimed, but her shock was belied by a delighted giggle.

"It is true," Sophia continued. "Can you imagine the man on the dance floor?"

Lady Agatha pursed her lips and stared pensively at her drink. "I suppose with his bad leg—"

"His leg has nothing to do with it. Even were it whole, he would dance like a poker, marching one foot in front of the other." Then Sophia began to demonstrate, stomping her feet as she held the brandy bottle at rigid arm's-length before her. "And far be it for anyone to miss a step," Sophia continued. "Why, that would be grounds for a firing squad!"

"Oh, unfair!" cried her aunt. Insulted by Sophia's caricature, Anthony was pleased to hear someone defend him. Then he heard, "He would simply give her a dishonorable discharge!"

Sophia roared in appreciation even as Anthony stifled a curse.

"And can you not guess what sweet nothings he would pour into a poor girl's head?"

Lady Agatha leaned forward, her eyes glittering with amusement. "Military drills?"

"Naturally!" Sophia clapped her hands as she continued to strut about the room. "And he would tell her that she was doing her duty to England by partnering him."

Anthony felt his teeth grind together as the slow burn of embarrassment heated his face. He had said that to Sophia his first night in Staffordshire, and again when he asked her to marry him the next day. To have his own words tossed back at him like this . . . He shook his head. He could not really have sounded that stiff, that arrogant—could he?

Perhaps he had, he admitted ruefully. Clearly, Sophia thought him high in the instep. So high, in fact, she took great delight in her parody of him, marching like a bad puppet about the room.

Well, he thought with a tiny thrill of anticipation, it was time he disabused her of the notion. He was as passionate as any man. More so, in fact, when it came to her. Perhaps she needed to learn exactly what that meant.

With a firm shove, he pushed into the room.

Lady Agatha saw him first, her laughter fading into a mortified gasp. But Sophia was too busy strutting about the floor to immediately notice. It gave him the opportunity to slip in behind her, easily catching her and drawing her close. She was in his arms before she could do more than gasp in alarm.

He smiled down at her, allowing himself to revel in

the sight of her full red lips parted in a perfect O of surprise. He was going to claim those lips, he decided. Tonight. Before Sophia mustered the wits to fight him. His smile spread into a grin. His body was already tightening in anticipation.

"I believe this is my dance," he said softly, pulling her tighter into his embrace.

"But—"

He gave her no time for anything else. Ignoring the twinge in his leg, he swung her about, using all the grace and style within him to sweep her off her feet in a waltz that he hoped would leave her breathless.

There was no music, but he did not need any. She was warm and fluid in his arms, and if he started out as a man on a mission, all too soon her heat softened his determination. Within moments, they were flowing about the room in a dance that had more to do with a man holding a beautiful woman than the scandalous German waltz he had thought to show her.

"You are stunning," he whispered, wishing he knew what sort of words she wanted to hear from him.

"I am drunk."

He smiled. "Yes, you are that too."

"You are suppo—" She gasped as he spun her around, and he grinned at her closed eyes. The poor woman was clearly torn between throwing her head back in abandon and keeping everything excruciatingly steady to avoid upsetting her brandy-soaked belly. Out of pity, he slowed the pace and let her compose herself.

"You . . ." she began again. "You are supposed to be disgusted."

"Disgusted?" he cried. "By what? You are beautiful, even when you drink. Your face glows, your eyes grow wide, and your lips are full and red and aching to be kissed." He let his gaze wander to her mouth, wondering how long he could resist the lure. Not long now, he knew.

He was already leaning forward, dipping his head forward as her breath skated across his cheek.

Then she pulled back, obviously swallowing before opening her mouth wide. She looked like a beached fish, and he straightened as he wondered at her strange actions. Then, to his shock, she repeated the process.

"What are you doing?"

She frowned and did it again. Then he felt her entire body slump as she released a heavy sigh. "I cannot do it!" she moaned.

"What?"

"Burp. My brother Geoffrey used to do it all the time. But, I cannot seem to manage it." She swallowed again, then opened her mouth. When no sound emerged, she released a load groan. "I found it most crude, and I am sure you would too. If only . . ." She tried again to no avail.

He could not resist. He began to smile. Laughter bubbled up within him, popping like champagne bubbles in his blood until he was grinning from ear to ear. "My dear, you are a delight."

"I am trying to be repulsive."

"You are adorable." Then, just to tease her some more, he spun her around again, ignoring the ache in his leg, aware only of the weight of her body pressed so intimately against him. He twirled them faster and faster, forcing her to join him in his happiness until she released the laughter that he rarely allowed in himself.

And together, they danced.

Somewhere in the shadows, Lady Agatha began to snore.

He had no right to kiss Sophia. It was a liberty no honorable man would take until they were wed. Yet he had no will to resist. He stole a kiss, taking it from her lips as he had so often dreamed of doing. He tucked her against him so tightly, she had nowhere to run and no choice but to let him taste the glory of her mouth.

She did not object. She melted against him, letting her hands trail through his hair, drawing him down to her though he meant to resist.

They kissed again.

It was like tasting innocence. Her mouth was pure, simple, and untrained. But she learned quickly, and soon they were dancing in a whole new way. There was no space between them. Every part of her was pressed intimately against him. Her heat invaded his blood, making him mad with hunger. Better yet, he felt an answering desire from her. Her hands were no longer exploring but pulling, demanding, pressing him closer and harder against her.

"Sophia," he rasped, twisting his mouth away as he tried to regain some sense of reason. "I cannot resist you much longer. Say you will marry me."

She paused. He felt her body tense ever so slightly. Then the word escaped her lips: "No."

She gave her denial, but she did not release him. Instead, she began kissing his face, his eyes, his brow. His head dipped down against her neck, and he nuzzled the pulse point at the base of her throat.

"Sophia. Marry me." He was begging her.

"No."

She was driving him insane. He could not believe that after everything he had done, after the way she felt in his arms, she could still deny him. Suddenly a fierce anger mixed with the heat in his blood. In one swift move, he leaned down and lifted her into his arms. She did not cry out, but clutched him even tighter, her body pliant and willing.

He did not pause to consider his actions. He strode away, carrying her out of the parlor and straight to her bedroom door. She did not seem to notice. She had wrapped her arms around him, her desire apparent in her short, sweet panting which stroked his neck as she kissed his face, his neck, all of him that her greedy lips could reach.

He paused, claiming her lips with all the force of his desire, feasting on her mouth, demanding she respond to him as feverishly as he wanted her. She did. Taking his mouth as never before, she dueled with him. Their tongues meshed and fought as furiously as any battle he'd ever known.

In a haze of desire, he kicked open her bedroom door, the solid wood slamming backward against the frame, but she did not flinch. She did not seem to care if he woke all the servants with his lovemaking.

He cared, though.

He dropped her unceremoniously onto her bed. The movement was abrupt, and she was unable to keep hold of him. Still, he felt tied to her, mesmerized by the dark mystery of her eyes. Her lips were swollen from his kisses, her dress in disarray. How could he resist?

"Marry me, Sophia," he said again, his words soft and gentle. Even as he spoke, he leaned over her, feathering kisses across her skin, already anticipating her sweet surrender.

"No." Then she drew his lips to hers for another kiss. He took it, claiming her mouth again as he braced his arms on either side of her head.

"I want you, Sophia," he whispered into her lips, even as he lowered his body on top of hers, pressing intimately against her. She arched against him, her soft moan of hunger driving him wild. "Marry me."

He did not think she could understand him, as he was nearly gone himself. His hand had found the sweet contours of her breast, kneading it as she writhed beneath him. But somehow, somewhere, she found the breath to refuse him.

"No," she said one last time. He stilled.

Frowning down at her, he pulled his hand away. She was not denying him access to her. Already, she was reaching up for another kiss, her breast arched into his hand, her body pressed against his length.

He did not move. "Sophia, you must marry me."

"No."

Anger grew like sour fruit within him. Why would she do this? Why would she offer herself for a night, but not for a marriage? He did not understand. But he would not take her like this. He would not take just this.

Though it took every bit of willpower he possessed, he forced himself to move away. He pulled backward, off the bed, while his hands clenched into fists before he drew them down to his sides.

"I will bed you as my wife and not before," he ground out between clenched teeth.

She stared at him, her eyes going wide, her gaze darting over her room, skittering over her bed and her disheveled clothes. It was as if she had just noticed where they were and what they had been about.

"Oh!" It was a tiny gasp of shock and surprise, but Anthony still saw the desire swirling in her blue eyes. He could still have her if he wanted. But he did not need a wanton for one night. He wanted a wife.

"If your aim was to give me a disgust of you, you have succeeded," he snarled. He watched her beautiful blue eyes widen in horror and guilt. She had not truly thought she was in danger, had not understood what he'd intended. What any man would intend . . .

The knowledge sickened him. She was an innocent. And yet, seeing her now, lush and seductive, he had to fight the blood that pounded in his ears.

His mind reeled. This was not his Sophia, he told himself. The woman had always been composed, sophisticated in every way. She would never lie drunk and disheveled on a bed. He would not want her if she did.

That was not what he needed as a wife for a diplomatic career. What he wanted.

But he did want her. Now and in every way.

He took a step forward, toward her and the sweet heaven her body promised. Then he stopped himself, groaning out loud in his confusion. This was not Sophia, he repeated to himself. And yet it was.

He could not make sense of it. And his confusion infuriated him.

Spinning on his heel, he stormed out. His feet pounded down the hallway, delivering agony to his leg with every step. He welcomed the pain. It cleared his mind.

And then he saw Kirby waiting at the foot of the stairs, hat in hand, face pale, and his demeanor anxious.

Anthony slowed his steps, his eyes narrowing at his batman as the knowledge hit him. "You put her up to this." It was not a question. He'd known the truth from the moment he'd seen the orderly standing there.

Kirby shifted awkwardly. "I—"

He did not have the chance to finish as Anthony shoved the man out of his way. Then, without a backward glance, Major Wyclyff quit the Rathburn home.

"D'ye want anything else?" the barmaid asked, her dark eyes pulled wide in false innocence as she thrust her ample figure forward.

Anthony frowned up at the woman. In his experience, most barmaids were grateful for quiet customers, ones who paid their bills and made few demands. But not this woman. This one, apparently, was offering more than a serving of ale.

Anthony leaned back and perused the woman's delights. Short, bouncy, and with more than a handful of charms, she would make a soft pillow indeed for the night. Especially after Sophia had raised his hunger to a fever pitch.

But the mere thought of Sophia's cool blue eyes and her regal body had him shaking his head at the barmaid. He didn't want obvious charms. He wanted a statuesque refinement, able to both grace the king's court by day and heat a man's bed at night.

The barmaid flounced away, turning her attention to the more customary clientele of this quiet Staffordshire inn. After storming out of the Rathburn house, Anthony had headed straight for the nearest drink. His horse had brought him here, but three ales and hours sitting among Staffordshire's locals had not brought him relief. Indeed, his mind and body were as tormented as ever.

Sophia had surprised him tonight. Up until this evening, she had reigned supreme in his thoughts simply as a perfect complement for a man intent on political advancement. Like his mother, Sophia seemed a composed hostess, expertly designed to navigate social waters with the surety of Nelson. His mother had changed his father from a crass, nobody earl to a powerful political figure, well respected by all.

Sophia, he knew, could do such things for him as well.

In fact, at first he'd had no hopes that he could ever win her. A sick man on a hospital pallet could never dare to expect such a woman's hand. But then they had conversed, discussed, even confided in one another. Sophia had whispered about her dreams, and Anthony knew at last God had answered his prayers. God had handed him the perfect companion to his ambitions.

Sophia wished to see foreign parts. Anthony's ambassadorial career would certainly provide that. Sophia wished to be released from all the restrictions of a young debutante in England. A marriage to him would free her to act as a matron. In addition, Anthony was a relaxed commander. He would overlook many small infractions, counting on Sophia's excellent social skills to see her through.

But more than that, he recognized the underlying boredom in Sophia. She longed for a challenge. Something to interest her beyond who was whispering what nonsense to whom, the silly gossip of the *ton*. He knew that Sophia would launch herself into whatever he did, providing him with keen insights and invaluable assistance along England's diplomatic path to civilized world leadership.

In short, he could give Sophia everything she longed for, and she in turn could provide him with the exact support he required. When she had accepted his proposal in London, he had believed she understood all that.

Instead, she had been told he was dead; then, sick with grief, she had run to Staffordshire. Or perhaps, he thought morosely as he stared into his ale, she had simply given empty words to ease a dying man into Heaven.

His mind rebelled at such a thought. It wasn't possible, he told himself. Except, more and more, it appeared to be true. Her promise to him had meant nothing. Her future had been planned without him.

Still, he would not allow himself to be discouraged. After all, the reasons for them to wed were ample, and they remained as true now as they had two months ago. More so, since his mind and body were at last whole.

Yet everything had changed.

He had spent many long hours in the hospital dreaming of what it would be like to kiss Sophia. He had imagined warming her with slow strokes, teaching her carefully about passion. Never had he expected the fiery response he'd gotten tonight. Not even in fantasy had he thought Sophia capable of such untutored hunger, such open responsiveness. It was as though a single kiss had sparked a hot, wet, carnal enthusiasm that would rob any man of his reason.

Sweet heaven, his body was still pulsing with lust. He still could not credit that the two women—the cool, refined Sophia he knew and tonight's passionate wanton—

were one and the same. But they were. And oddly, that only made him more determined to marry her.

Earlier today, he might have released Sophia from her promise. There were many logical reasons he would have accepted for her refusal to wed: That she did not wish to leave her family for years on end. That she had a hobby completely unacceptable to the Crown—a desire for sculpting the naked male form, for example, or worse yet, a reforming zeal unchecked by common sense. But she claimed none of those things.

Instead, she had kissed him, and he had realized that God had provided him with not only a mate for his ambition, but a match for his passion. No power on Earth would keep him from her now. She was too perfect a woman to be released. He had never expected ardor in his marriage bed, merely an acceptable camaraderie. To know now that she had such fire within her was to know she was a pearl beyond compare.

Unfortunately, Sophia remained stubbornly immovable on this issue. It made no sense. There had to be a reason beyond what she said. Yet, after hours of thinking, he was still no closer to an explanation for her illogical behavior. He finished off his drink and waved for another, wondering at the puzzle.

After another hour of drinking, he had an answer. It was simple, really. Her illogic was simply part of the package; Sophia made no sense. Yet that did not deter him. He had fought in wars that made less. What he needed now was a plan. A campaign, as it were, that would bring sweet, illogical Sophia to his side.

He allowed a slow smile to creep over his face. Things were different. He now knew the battle they were waging. Whereas before, his only weapon had been logic, now he had a much more potent club to hand. What had Lady Agatha said? Passion. At the time, he had not believed it. Now he knew the older woman was exceptionally clear-sighted.

Sophia had passion in spades. She was obviously untutored, inexperienced in matters of the flesh. He must use her feelings against her, turn her newfound hunger toward him. That was the only way to succeed. Simple pleas had not worked. He would have to bring out the big guns.

It would be a difficult thing, though, he knew. He had to seduce her without bedding her; it was dishonorable to do otherwise. And he would not dishonor her. No matter what, he would not satisfy their mutual hunger until she said, "I do."

He had little doubt that he could accomplish the task. He was a man of great discipline who had never broken before. Not when the outcome was so important. All that remained was to draw up a battle plan. He needed to find a way to push Sophia out of her customary calm. The more disquiet she felt, the more she was likely to yield to her natural inclinations. The more she ached for satisfaction, the more she would turn to him. From there, it was one small step to the altar. Then India. Then a lifetime of glory by day and passion by night.

He grinned as he set aside his ale. Calling for paper and ink, he set himself to the task of writing out a plan.

Chapter Six

Sophia awoke to the horrid screeching of some demented bird only to be stabbed in both eyes by a white-hot poker of light. She moaned and buried herself in her pillow, deciding to wait until it got dark before she rose for the day.

Unfortunately, there was some other horrible creature nearby, humming. Loudly. Fit to wake the dead.

"Stop that infernal noise!" she snapped, then immediately regretted it as her head began to pound. It felt like it would explode.

"Oh, I be right sorry, miss," her maid said. "The major told me ye liked humming. Said it was the right proper way to wake up in London, he did. An' him being in all those foreign parts, I thought he knew. But—"

"Be quiet," Sophia begged in a whisper, clutching her head as tightly as she could.

"Oh, miss, but the major said—"

"Shhhh!"

"Oh!"

Sophia gritted her teeth, taking deep breaths as she tried to still the pounding in her head. It did not help. Nothing helped. Certainly not the baleful sight of her maid with a face so woeful it would shame a kicked puppy.

"Oh, go away," she moaned softly. "I am not fit company for anyone today."

"Yes, miss." Tears shimmered in her maid's eyes.

Sophia felt her conscience kicking her and sighed. "You sing beautifully, Mary."

The girl brightened considerably, and she bobbed up and down in a curtsy. "Thank you, miss. But I certainly will not sing in the mornings anymore. I swear. No singing—"

"Mary!" Sophia snapped, feeling the tight leash on her temper strain to near breaking.

"Yes, miss?"

"Do not ever listen to the major again."

"But—"

"Out!"

She was in no mood to listen to reason or explain herself to that chattering magpie for one more second. All she wanted was to lie down and sleep for a thousand years. Or until her death, which she prayed would come soon.

As she lay back down, a strange thought kept coming back to her, climbing over the blacksmith and his hammer in her head, stepping up before her sluggish mind and demanding to be heard. It said one thing:

Why is the major still here?

It was a bizarre thought, to say the least. The major was their butler, after all. He was supposed to be here. But the thought persisted, despite all her attempts to shoo it away.

Why is the major still here? He should be halfway to London by now.

Sophia did not know what to make of it. She did not feel capable of sitting up in bed, much less confronting her thoroughly aggravating suitor, but here she was, pulling on a wrap, apparently intent on determining for herself if the major was indeed still their servant.

Clearly, she had gone mad.

Still, that thought was secondary to the primary one. The one that wondered if the major truly could have stayed here, even after claiming such a thorough disgust of her last night. That thought pushed her down the stairs toward the breakfast room. On the way, she had to turn her extremely unwieldy head from the light blazing through the windows. At least it served to push her toward the breakfast room, if only to get away from its uncompromising glare.

The major was there.

Indeed, he was dressed impeccably in his dark knee breeches and starched white cravat. He was banging and clanking dishes like Cook on one of her tirades, but when he looked up at her, his expression was almost amused.

If it were not for the dark circles under his eyes, she would have thrown her slipper at him.

"Good morning—"

"What are you doing here?" She had not meant to sound so abrupt. In fact, she had meant to approach him with elegance and poise. But her throat was dry and her head throbbed, so she opted for expediency.

He merely smiled, an infuriatingly slow, masculine smile filled with smug satisfaction. "I am your butler. Where else should I be?"

She peered at him, trying to both see him and filter out the relentless sunshine. "But I disgust you. You said so yourself!" At least she thought she remembered something like that. She frowned, trying to sort through her jumbled thoughts.

"What an impertinent thing for me to have said!" he exclaimed, his voice carrying just the right tone of offended dignity and apology. "I gave my word to remain as your butler until Bowen could return."

"Your word?" She took a half step forward. "Do you mean you will not leave until Bowen comes back?"

"That is what I promised," he responded, his back stiff, his face set. "Honor requires nothing less."

"Honor? But I behaved . . ." She reached for a chair to steady herself and came up short against the wall. Still, it kept her upright as she tried to think. "But I was appalling last evening."

For a moment, she thought he grinned. But when she looked again, he was as stiff and rigid as ever. "I am your butler, my lady. It would be a gross impertinence for me to comment on your actions, one way or another."

She blinked. She frowned. Her head was still thick and slow, but his words seemed clear enough. He would not leave for London no matter how much she annoyed him. No matter what she did.

He could not possibly be serious. Could he?

"But—" she began.

"Would you care for some breakfast, my lady?" he interrupted. "Perhaps some kippers? They are extra plump and juicy this morning." He lifted the plate's cover off, waving it slightly so the aroma hit her square in the face. "Or would you prefer some eggs?" He raised another cover. "Oh, dear. I am afraid they are a tad runny. I shall have a word with Cook directly. Or do you prefer them this way?" He tilted the dish for her inspection.

Sophia stared at the slimy, pale yellow eggs and took a deep breath, trying to hold off her nausea. Unfortunately, the smell of ripe kippers did worse damage than anything she might have seen. Clapping a hand over her mouth, Sophia ran from the room.

She did not return for another four hours, and then only for a taste of weak tea before retiring directly to bed.

Sophia was awake. Her head had ceased pounding, her mouth no longer felt stuffed with muslin, and she was completely and totally awake.

And bored.

Too bad it was the middle of the night. Still, she could not force herself to remain in bed one minute longer. She had to go in search of something to do.

Never again would she touch strong drink, she vowed as she sat up in bed. It thoroughly disrupted a body's natural rhythms.

With a sigh of disgust, Sophia pulled on a wrap and wandered downstairs, not even bothering with a candle. She knew her way, and the moon shone bright enough to cast pale shadows through the house.

She wandered about, noting that her friend Lydia's letter still lay unopened by the front doorway. The two had mended their breach, but since Lydia's engagement, the girl's letters were filled with the joys of romance and plans for the upcoming nuptials, not to mention unending speculations about wedded bliss. The very thought of reading another such correspondence filled Sophia with dread—and an aching loneliness that spurred her feet onward.

Finally, deciding she might find something else to read, she meandered toward the library, even though the idea did not truly appeal to her. She did not want to spend her time with some dusty old tome. It was a pity the house was so quiet with everyone asleep.

She had meant to find a taper and scan the book titles, but the darkness was too appealing, the shimmering slivers of moonlight through the windows too mystical. She went to the glass, pushing aside the curtains until a soft expanse of trees and lawn glistened before her.

"Beautiful."

Sophia spun around, shocked and secretly thrilled by the rich masculine voice behind her. She knew immediately who it was. The major had plagued her far too much, day and night, for him to be absent now. This only seemed appropriate.

She spotted him quickly. He reclined in the shadows, his leg propped before him, his rugged features barely discernible through the shadows.

"I thought the household asleep," she said.

"The household, yes. Me? No. Not when such nighttime visions wander so freely about."

Sophia felt her face heat at the clear admiration in his voice and was grateful for the darkness that hid her features. She ought to go upstairs, she admonished herself. It was not right for any gentleman, much less the major, to see her attired in only her nightrail and wrap. But more than that, she was old enough to know what could happen alone in the dark with this man. It had been intimate enough sitting at his bedside in the hospital in the bright light of day. And the other night, drunk . . .

She should go back to her bedroom, she told herself. But she did not. Instead, she pulled her wrap tight around her body and settled into a nearby chair. After all, she was a free woman, one who made her own decisions. If she liked, she could do whatever she wished with handsome men in the dark.

"I know why I am about so late," she began, surprised by the husky quality of her own voice. "But why do you sit here in the dark? Does your leg pain you?" She found herself terribly concerned. "Has the fever returned?"

"My leg is healing, and I was merely thinking." His voice was low, his words easy, langorous, but she recalled their conversations in the hospital when pain slurred his speech and fever made his voice thick and raw. Just the memory of that time had her starting out of her seat.

"If you are ill, I shall send for a doctor at once."

He forestalled her words with a low chuckle. "My ailment cannot be cured by any doctor." He set aside an empty brandy snifter. "Do you wish to know of what I was thinking?"

She did not answer. His voice had trapped her, mixing with the moonlight to weave a spell of dark magic around her.

He leaned forward, pulling himself out of the shadows. "Of Spain and war," he murmured. "Of death and angels of mercy. Of you."

She shivered, drawn to him even as she kept a firm grip on the edges of her chair. She closed her eyes, determined to end his strange hold on her, but that only made the memories more clear, the pain more real. "Do you know what I remember?" she rasped. "I remember sitting like this—in the dark—when you were in the hospital. I told my mother I was going to a musical soiree, but instead I went to you." She stood up, needing to pace away her agitation, but there was nowhere for her to go. So she simply stood, staring into the dark shadows near his shoulders, her words continuing without her willing them. "I remember the smell of blood in the air, the coppery taste of it and the moans from the nearby beds. But mostly, I remember you. I remember listening for your breath, holding my own until I heard yours." She felt a tear slip down her cheek. "Do you know how guilty I felt? Each time you drew breath, I thanked God you were still alive, and yet I knew I was only prolonging your suffering. I knew you would die. We all did."

"But I did not," he said firmly. Loudly. And there was power in each word, enough to ease the ache in her chest, but not take away the fear that it would happen again, the terror that another fever would claim him, that another wound might kill him. Then he stood, his body large and whole before her. "Do not think of it, Sophia," he said. "It is over."

She shook her head, knowing that it would never be over for her, despite his new found strength. She would always remember those days by his side. That last night in the dark. "I had to leave the hospital," she continued. "I could not be out all night." How she wished she had defied convention. How she wished she had ignored the risk of scandal and spent the night by his side. Then she would have known he lived. But she hadn't. "In the morning, they told me you were dead."

" 'Tis over," he repeated. He touched her then. He reached out and stroked her chin, lifting it until she met his dark gaze. "Think of something else," he urged as he stepped closer. "Think of last night. Of how we kissed."

He made to pull her into his arms, but she shied away, just as she shied away from those memories. She had been drunk, her reason gone, but the experience remained burned in her thoughts. His caresses had seared her skin. His kisses had set her blood afire. And all her resistance had melted away. "I remember that you left," she snapped, using the words to cool the heat he created. "You said I disgusted you, and then you left."

Again he reached for her, and she turned away, choosing to look out the window. Her gaze roved the moonlit night, but her senses focused behind her. On him.

"I have not left," he said. "I am here." He set his hands on her shoulders, and she tensed, half in fear, half in desire. "I want to have children with you, Sophia."

She bit her lip, startled by his sudden shift in topic and distracted by the strange longing his words produced. When she had decided to take the life of a spinster, she had mourned only one thing—that she would never have any children. It was still an ache, one that caught her unawares at times. Times like now, when a man's words conjured the most appealing of images: babies that looked like the major. Little boys with dark curly hair and a mischievous twinkle, and little girls with an impertinent tilt to their smiles.

"I want to marry you," he continued. "I want to make you my wife and bring you to my bed. I want to spread your golden hair across my pillow and kiss you until your skin glows with passion." Her body tensed with a new hunger, one she could not recall having experienced before. His words were as frightening as they were exciting, and she did not know what she should do or how she should respond.

"You—you should not speak so to me," she stammered.

"Then go, for I will not stop."

Sophia pressed her palms flat against the cool windowpane, using it to steady herself. But, before the temperature could do more than sensitize her hands, he pulled her back against him, pressing her intimately against his broad chest.

"You are different," she said. "You seem . . ." She hesitated, searching for the right words.

"Determined? Forceful?"

"Stronger," she corrected, her body growing inebriated by the word. He seemed so powerful that despite her determination to resist him, she wondered what it would be like to lie in his arms. To feel his force surrounding her body, holding it, invading it.

"I am tired, Sophia. I have played at butler long enough." His words were almost harsh, but his caress was sensual, warming her, molding her to his will. "I should return to London to see if my post has been approved. But I will not leave without you."

She could not answer. Not with him touching her, her back pressed intimately against his broad chest. She could not think other than to turn to face him, shifting so she could feel the width of his shoulders and brush her fingers along the rough cut of his jaw.

"Sophia?" His voice deepened, sounding unsteady as he caught her hand, holding it in his firm grasp. She could not respond except to rise up on her toes, seeking his kiss.

He did not deny her, though she felt his muffled groan as a whisper of heat, tantalizing as it feathered across her mouth. Then he claimed her lips, his touch as fevered as before, as hungry and as demanding. She matched his tongue stroke for stroke, knowing finally the passion spoken of so often by poets. Unlike last night's drunken exploration, these kisses seemed more pure, more intense because the only intoxication came from the major himself. From his touch. And her desire. Together.

It was a heady sensation, and it filled her with a giddy excitement. She was in his embrace, feeling his arms around her, encircling her, and drawing her tight against his body. For a moment she did not think, too absorbed in the wonder of his kiss.

Then he ended it, pulling her away from him, his hands firm on her arms. "You *will* marry me." It was not a question, and she let her head drop back as she looked up at the ceiling.

Her breathing was ragged, and she still felt drawn to him, the hunger he inspired in her all but overwhelming her. But for all her newly discovered passion, her mind was wholly clear—for perhaps the first time in her life. "I . . . I like kissing you, Major," she said, shocked by her own brazen behavior. "I wish to do it again. But I will not marry you."

He stared at her for a moment, then his eyes grew wide as her meaning finally became clear. "Sophia . . ." he said, and the sound was more growl than spoken word.

"No," she said again. But still she remained in his arms, stretching forward, seeking his kiss.

Angrily he set her aside, crossing to the brandy decanter on the opposite side of the room. He stood there, the crystal held in his fist, but he did not pour. Instead he glared at her. "By Heaven, why are you so stubborn?"

"I could ask you the same thing," she responded. "Why do you insist I marry you? For duty? For England?" Her voice rose as her emotions outstripped her control. "You do not respect me. You said so yourself. Why would I marry you?"

The major set down the decanter, shifting until he faced her directly, his arms crossed over his chest. "It is merely the thought that you would value yourself so little as to wish to . . . to . . ." He shifted awkwardly as he searched for a word.

"To kiss you?"

He straightened his shoulders, and Sophia wondered for a moment at his odd expression. "Yes. To . . . kiss me without marriage."

"I am a free woman now, Major. I can kiss any man I choose when I choose."

"You are still unmarried. It is not appropriate behavior—"

"I am a spinster. If I am thought fast, then no one is hurt but myself. I have no dowry, no prospects, and I no longer care about gossip. I will not become married merely to satisfy your notions of propriety or anyone else's. I will never again dance to society's tune."

He stared at her for a long moment, and Sophia did her best to remain resolute. It was imperative that he read her determination in every line of her face and body.

At last he bowed, his movement as formal as it was stiff. "Very well, Lady Sophia," he said in his coldest servile voice. "If there is nothing further, I shall retire. Morning comes early, and I would not wish to be remiss in my duties."

Sophia blinked, surprise making her step forward. "But you cannot mean to remain as our butler?"

The major merely raised an eyebrow, and Sophia folded her arms in disgust.

"You *cannot* be serious. Think, Major; it is insupportable that you will be forever underfoot, kissing me at nighttime, then serving me tea in the day!"

His expression did not change, but Sophia felt his sudden amusement, as if he had laughed out loud.

"Why are you so stubborn?" she exclaimed, belatedly realizing she echoed his very words back to him.

He merely shrugged. "You keep repeating the word freedom. I have lately come to realize that perhaps you are like a soldier on furlough, drunk on his own independence. You wish to try everything, including . . . kissing. I suspect you will grow bored in time. You will soon find life as empty as it was in London. Then you will turn to me."

Sophia felt her jaw go slack at the arrogance of the man. "You intend to be forever underfoot until such time as I grow bored? But, that is ridiculous!"

"It was successful tonight."

"Nonsense!" She was fervent in her protest, but suddenly she feared he was correct. She had left her bedroom intent on finding something—or rather, someone—and the thought made her even more irritated. "I will not marry you out of boredom!"

He merely sketched a mocking bow, telling her without words that he would wait and see. Watching him, Sophia knew her first moment of true worry. He was a strong man, and for some unknown reason, she had been drawn to him from the very beginning. Even in his sickbed, she had been anxious for him, coming directly to his side nearly every day of his recuperation.

How many times had she wondered at her own behavior? How many times had she tried to explain away her strange attraction to this arrogant, bull-headed man? And so she knew he was right. If she allowed him to remain in the house, forever around every turn, she had no doubt she would eventually capitulate. The man was simply too fascinating for her to hold out against him forever.

"Very well," she said, grasping at straws. "I shall make a bargain with you. If you agree to leave this house, to remove yourself immediately, I . . . I will consider your offer. I will allow you to court me. But, if in three weeks' time I have not changed my mind, you must leave Staffordshire immediately."

The major frowned, his expression pensive. "You will allow me to be your exclusive companion for three weeks? For every outing, every excursion?"

Sophia nodded. "But they must be my choice of excursions, my decision as to our destination."

"Of course. I shall be pleased to accompany you wherever you wish to go."

Sophia nodded, a plan already forming in her mind. "You will cease to function as our butler, and you must swear, on your honor, to leave the county if my answer is still 'no' at the end of three weeks."

He did not hesitate. "I swear."

Sophia took a deep breath, feeling a sudden elation. "We have a bargain?"

"We do," he said. Then he smiled, his brown eyes lit by the silvery caress of the moon. "I regret to inform you, Lady Sophia, that I am unable to continue as your butler. And I shall be pleased to call on you tomorrow at exactly two in the afternoon."

Sophia shook her head. "Aunt Agatha and I intend a trip to the milliner's. You may come the next day. At noon."

He bowed to her, his own expression smug. "Very well. Noon in two days. Good night, Lady Sophia." Then he left the room.

Sophia watched him go, her smile slowly fading as the door slipped shut behind him. She wished he had remained, sharing kisses with her to seal their agreement. But that was foolishness, she told herself. And that was exactly why she had insisted he depart. Because she was much too vulnerable around him. She might want to give a kiss, but he would want so much more. . . .

At least in public, there would be no illicit kisses, no lingering caresses, no hunger for an unknown something that came alive whenever he was near.

Three weeks would be over in no time. Then, at last, she would be rid of him. The thought left her strangely sad, but she ignored it as something else struck her.

Remembering their conversation, Sophia realized that the major had agreed exceedingly quickly. There had been no hesitation in his voice. No reluctance in his demeanor. Could he already be tiring of her? Was this his way of retiring gracefully from the field?

Panic clutched at her heart even as her mind told her this was exactly what she wanted. Then she remembered his smile and the devious twinkle in his eyes. He had agreed to her proposal with such speed, as if . . . As if he had a plan of his own.

Sophia groaned. Of course he had a plan. What military man did not have a plan of some sort? Well, she decided, she would just have to devise a scheme of her own. Something that would put the major off her entirely. Some excursion that would shock him down to his regimented toes.

And she knew just the outing to do it.

Chapter Seven

"The cockfights? You wish me to take you to a cockfight?" Anthony stared at Sophia, his thoughts reeling.

When she'd first suggested their bargain, he believed he had won. She merely wished for the formality of a courtship before accepting their marriage. Now, he saw that she once again intended to dissuade him.

But Anthony had not survived war in Spain without his own fair share of stubbornness. He would allow her this wild outing—if only to show her what a vulgar display a cockfight could be. He knew with certainty her first glimpse of the event would be enough to send her scurrying home.

Lady Sophia was much too refined for so coarse an event.

"Very well," he said with a short bow. "Do you know of one we could attend?"

"Absolutely," she said with a radiant smile. "Mary tells me there shall be a fight today. There is a pit behind the butcher's home. Do you know where that is?"

Anthony nodded, feeling the movement pull at the taut muscles in his shoulders. "I know the place," he said curtly. Then his gaze traveled the length of her light rose walking dress, admiring her lush curves and remarkable features. "You might wish to change your gown. The field can get quite muddy."

Sophia smiled, her laughter rich and full. "Oh, no, Major. You shall not delay me today. If I took the time to change, I am certain the event would be over before we arrived."

"There is plenty of time yet," he responded evenly, but she merely shook her head.

"I am determined, Major. You cannot fob me off."

Anthony raised his eyebrows. "I had no such intention," he responded with complete honesty. "I am breathless with anticipation to view your reaction." He reached out and brought her hand to his arm. "This *is* your first cockfight, is it not?"

Her laugh sounded a bit forced, and for a moment, he thought she would lie to him. Then she shook her head. "This is indeed my first fight, but I have been anxious to view one since I overheard Geoffrey in alt after attending his first. He was most enthusiastic."

"Most young men are," he responded dryly as he stepped toward the door. "You are quite sure you do not wish to change your gown?" he repeated. "That rose is wonderfully attractive, but it is also . . ." He paused a moment, searching for the right words. "Your beauty makes you somewhat conspicuous."

She turned to him, and he distinctly saw a twinkle of mischief in her eye. "Do you wish me to wear something brown, nondescript, perhaps rather shapeless, and overly large, so as to disguise my appearance?"

"That would be the, uh, more prudent course," he answered. "The women who attend these affairs are not at all . . . of your sort."

"What would you know of my sort?" she responded archly. "I am a spinster now. I can go wherever I wish."

"As long as you are unmarried," he responded softly, "you shall never have the freedom you crave. You shall always require an escort, especially if you intend to frequent events such as this one."

She turned abruptly, and he saw anger in her eyes, but he could not tell if her ill humor was directed at him or her situation. They both knew that even as a spinster, she had restrictions on her behavior.

"A lady can always find an escort," she finally said.

"Can she also find a child to hold or something to fill the hours other than meaningless and coarse distractions?"

Sophia did not respond except to turn her back on him and walk regally to his waiting curricle.

Anthony watched her go, frustration making his shoulders heavy and his leg ache. She had done it again. He had resolved to be urbane and civilized, agreeing to whatever she wished without so much as a blink of his eye. Yet, despite his much vaunted self-control, they were already at daggers drawn.

Very well, he decided. He would exercise his self-mastery. He could afford to be patient. He would take her to the cockfight. When she ran sick from the sight, then he would have his victory. She would know her country diversions were as meaningless as the civilized ones of London. In the end, she would turn to him.

She would.

With a sigh that felt like a call to arms, he jammed his hat on his head and moved to join her on the curricle seat.

* * *

Sophia could hardly keep from squirming, unsure whether she should feel elated or humiliated. When she had first conceived of attending the cockfight, it seemed the perfect choice. Not only was it a scandalous thing to do, but she truly wished to attend such an event.

But planning to fly in the face of social convention was entirely different from actually doing it. As more than one gentleman lifted his quizzing glass to inspect her, Sophia was hard put to sit still. Suddenly she wished she had indeed put on a shapeless brown cloak as the major had suggested. But there was nothing for it now except to brazen her way through.

The major brought their curricle within distant sight of the center area while Sophia occupied herself by looking about, trying to see everything except the haughty stares of other attendees. There were vehicles of every sort, from flashy carriages to dirty, broken-down wagons. She recognized gentlemen who frequented *haut ton* ballrooms next to tradesmen and footmen. They all made their way to the tiered seating surrounding a sand pit. And though Sophia could see the wealthier patrons sneer behind their gloves at the lower classes, she saw the same eagerness on everyone's face.

And the same shock as the major pulled his curricle into place.

"They are all staring at me," she whispered to him.

"I did try to tell you that ladies, even spinsters, do not attend cockfights."

Sophia mustered a polite smile for an elderly gentleman who had courted her in her second Season, but her words were for the major. "I have noticed women of all classes enjoy vulgar amusements," she said more tartly than she had intended. "Think of all the *ton* who attend hangings."

He turned to her, and suddenly, Sophia felt the weight of his keen gray eyes. "Have you ever had the desire to attend a hanging?"

She could not repress a shudder. "No. Absolutely not."

His smile was slow in coming, but it relaxed his entire body, showing her how truly handsome he was. And how fully sure of himself, for in that moment, Sophia realized her mistake. By coming here, she had meant to show him that she was vulgar and uncouth, but her response showed him all too clearly what she thought of most bloody sport.

Sophia ground her teeth in frustration. Why could she not guard her tongue around this man?

"Shall we find our seats?" she asked coolly.

"If you wish."

"Of course." And with that she allowed him to assist her out of the curricle.

His hands were warm where they touched her, but Sophia refused to think of it. She was attending her first cockfight, she reminded herself sternly. Now was not the time to think of how large and strong Major Wyclyff's hands felt where they held her arm.

They crossed the field together, coming to the tiered benches in good time. But as the major helped her to a seat, Sophia could not help but notice how those around her seemed to react to her presence. The men were outraged, some even muttering curses under their breath. As for the women, they were too intent on attracting the men to do more than glare occasionally at her.

To add discomfort to humiliation, the major settled close beside her, his manner protective. "We may leave, if you like. I understand there is a lovely drive along the creek."

She stiffened, feigning surprise, though inside she was tempted. "How could you suggest such a thing?"

"Because I can see you are uncomfortable, and I have no wish to ruin our afternoon together because of this nonsense."

Sophia shifted, turning to face him so that his body did not press so closely against hers. "I have told you, I will not be ordered by society or by you. I have chosen to attend this event, and stay I shall."

His sigh was heartfelt, and Sophia felt his broad shoulders move with the sound. She was being willful and stubborn, she knew, but he would just have to accept that. This was the new Sophia Rathburn. And she attended cockfights.

The event began with little preamble. The butcher, who apparently owned most of the roosters, walked into the center of the sand pit. After a brief introduction, he began listing the bloodlines of the first two opponents, who were being carried into the ring in the arms of their handlers.

The butcher continued, his voice ranging easily over the noise of betting, while the two handlers turned their backs on each other, rocking back and forth as the heads of their huge roosters stuck out from beneath their arms.

"Why do they do that?" she whispered, leaning into the major to be heard.

He shifted, allowing her to settle closer to him, and she was too interested in his answer to keep herself from pressing into his solid form. "To excite the birds," he said into her ear. "See how they eye each other?"

Indeed, the birds seemed to be glaring at each other even as they were swung closer and closer.

"Set your birds!" called the butcher, now safely out of the pit.

The handlers dropped the roosters, then rapidly scrambled out of the arena. At the pit's center, the fowl began circling, eyeing each other with murderous intensity. All around, the crowd cheered and yelled, goading the animals on.

"This is exhilarating," Sophia gasped, leaning forward in her seat to see more. "They are such stately creatures. I had not thought how proud they could look." Sophia watched with rapt attention, the crowd's excitement stirring her blood. The noise, the tension, even the heated press of bodies—the major seemed closer than ever—intensified the atmosphere.

Suddenly one bird lunged at the other, and, as if on cue, the crowd erupted into a cacophony of noise. Nearer to the ring, betting seemed to increase a hundredfold, as the birds, those beautiful, stately creatures, suddenly attacked each other in a mindless fury of violence.

"Oh, my word," she whispered, her eyes widening as she took in the sight. Feathers. And blood. All surrounded by cheering, sweaty, bellowing men.

The stands swayed beneath her, but Sophia barely noticed. She was too mesmerized, too horrified to turn away. One bird lunged, gouging deep into the gullet of the other. Blood poured out of the open neck wound. Yet the wounded bird continued to attack, aiming for the head of his opponent. With a fierce peck, the cock lost an eye, a bloom of red appearing on his stately feathers. And all around her men cheered for more.

Sophia pressed her hand against her mouth, trying to keep her nausea at bay. Then she felt Anthony press nearer beside her, firmly twisting her, drawing her face from the sight.

Suddenly, she was gripping his arm, screaming into his face. "Major, they . . . they are *fighting!*"

"Yes, Sophia. I know." His voice was gentle, but it was no cure for the sight she had just seen.

"Anthony, they are tearing each other apart! And the men are cheering."

"Yes, I know."

How could he be so calm? He must not truly comprehend what was occurring. She clutched his lapels, shaking him as she tried to make him understand. "But they will kill each other!"

"Likely only one will die, Sophia."

"Anthony!" she cried, but the weak sound simply merged with the screams all around her.

The major pulled her close, drawing her into his arms as he spoke softly into her ear. "What did you think a cockfight was?"

"I did not think . . ." Sophia swallowed, struggling against his chest. She was no match for his steady warmth, and with a shudder, she finally surrendered. "I guess I had not thought too thoroughly through what it would be like—only that it was scandalous, and I had never been." She took a deep breath. "It is a horrible, brutish sport."

"Yes."

"These men are savages to watch such a thing."

She felt his shrug, but he did not disagree with her. After a moment he rose, clambered down, then pulled her out of the seating and down against his side. "We will take that drive now." It was not a question.

Sophia walked with him, silently matching his measured tread. Her emotions had settled somewhat, but the sound of the cocks screaming and the men cheering still pounded in her head. It was not right. Those beautiful animals should not have been forced into such barbarity.

Lord, it was almost like London, where Society took sweet young girls and threw them into the vipers' nest of the *haut ton*. Before long, the girls either became vicious fighters, meting out social death to their competitors, or they became victims. It was not right here, and it was not right there, either.

It had to be stopped. Sweet, beautiful creatures should not be forced to brutalize one another. It was hideous, and it had to be stopped.

But how?

She glanced sideways, watching the major. She could appeal to him, but likely he would not help her. He was a man, after all, and she had only to look around to see what men thought. And he'd only shrugged at seeing her horror. Still, she thought perhaps to ask.

"Major . . ." she began.

He turned immediately to her, his expression attentive.

"Shouldn't we try to, um, stop this somehow?"

He frowned down at her, his expression gentle. "I know you are upset, but truly, roosters are dumb creatures, bred for this. And if it amuses these men, keeping them from other bloody sport, what harm is there in it?"

Sophia stiffened. "Harm? Why, harm to those beautiful birds!"

The major chuckled, tucking her more tightly against his side as they navigated past a heavily laden wagon. "They are roosters, Sophia. Chickens. The same birds you have eaten at table."

Sophia pressed her lips together, realizing the futility of arguing. He was seeing things logically, refusing to censure something that entertained his fellow men. But this was not killing animals for food, for sustenance to strengthen the bodies and minds of families or children; this was killing for sport, and she detested it.

He was watching her closely, no doubt waiting to see if she accepted his pronouncement. She smiled at him, simply to reassure his mind. Unfortunately, he was not satisfied and continued to eye her suspiciously. But he could not watch her all the time, and so she waited patiently for her opportunity as they headed back to the major's curricle.

She knew just what to do. Indeed, she had decided upon it long before, perhaps the very moment she saw those imperial birds first lunge at one another. She would save the poor creatures whatever the cost.

She got her opportunity quickly.

In front of them, two curricles were set very close together in a long line of conveyances. The only way through was in single file. In short, the major had to release his proprietary hold upon her arm. Smiling, he gestured for her to go first, and for a moment, she hesitated, wondering at the wisdom of her choice. He would be very angry with her when it was all over.

A loud roar from the crowd overcame her fears. Another rooster had obviously just met its death. She had to prevent any more from being so brutally slain. Before she could lose her nerve, she looked away, toward some nearby trees, a smile of welcome on her face. As expected, the major followed her gaze. While he was distracted, she quickly gathered her skirts and slipped away in the opposite direction.

She did not have much of a lead on him. In fact, barely two seconds into her mission, she heard his commanding shout: "Sophia!" She did not hesitate, but headed straight for her destination. She had spotted it a few moments before and knew just where to go.

"Sophia, come back here!"

Amazing, she thought as she dodged through the audience's parked vehicles. The major's commands could carry even over this riot of noise. That voice must have served him quite well in battle.

She slid past the last of the wagons, only to arrive at a sea of bodies—gentlemen who had been unable to find a place to sit. They were pressed quite close, but Sophia was undaunted. Pushing forward, she jostled more than one of them.

Then disaster struck.

Trying to wiggle past a portly man who smelled of garlic, Sophia stepped on something slick, belatedly realizing it was a nearby gentleman's boot. It was the matter of a moment, but as she teetered, she grabbed the nearest item of clothing to steady herself, only to discover it was the unfortunate gentleman's cravat.

And that she was strangling him.

"I say—" he exclaimed with the last of his breath.

Sophia gasped at the man's bulging eyes, quickly dropping his cravat as she stumbled against his chest, both knocking him down and the last of his air from his body.

"Oh, goodness. I am terribly sorry," she said as she fumbled for purchase on the murky ground.

Fortunately for them both, strong arms pulled her up and off her poor victim. She did not have to turn to know that it was the major who had just saved her from no doubt killing the poor man.

"Sophia, what do you think you are doing?" he practically bellowed into her ear.

She flinched, but her focus was on her victim, who was only now regaining both his breath and his equilibrium. It took less than a moment to realize that he was not a man at all, but a youngster who had at one time been starry-eyed with devotion during her third Season.

"My goodness, Thomas!"

"Lady Sophia!" he sputtered, his eyes once again widening with horror. "What are you doing here? You must leave at once!" The young man reached forward, obviously intent on dragging her bodily away.

Of all the nerve! Did every man in England believe he could tell her what to do? Jerking away from his outstretched arm, she managed to evade both Thomas and the major, who was being pushed from behind by another rapt attendee.

"I say!" That was from Thomas, clearly shocked by her show of spirit.

"Oh, do not be a nodcock," she snorted as she pushed past. "Let me through!" But they were closely pressed, and Thomas's slim arm managed to capture her waist.

"Sophia," growled the major. He had fought his way to her and was clearly nearing the end of his patience.

"You cannot remain," interrupted Thomas as he rose to his full height. His quizzing glass found one eye, and he stared down at her through it. "Think of the scandal.

No honorable women come here. Why, what would your mother say? And think of Geoffrey. It is within his rights to beat you. He is the head of your family, you know."

Sophia glared at her captor, her anger rising with every self-important, arrogant word the witless fool uttered. Beside her, she heard the major groan, but she was not to be distracted.

"How dare you try to dictate to me, Thomas—"

"Really," he continued without even pausing for breath. "You should have married me. You obviously need guidance. And this person . . ." He turned his quizzing glass up on the major, as if Anthony were an insect. "He obviously is not capable of controlling your odd sense of humor. What would your brother do, do you think, if he were here?"

"This, no doubt," grumbled Sophia. She pulled back her fist as far as the crowd allowed, then swung as hard as she could—just as Geoffrey had taught her.

She watched with satisfaction as Thomas's head snapped back with the force of her blow. She caught him completely off guard, and he stumbled backward before landing flat on his behind. All about them, the audience turned their heads and gasped, craning their necks to ogle Thomas.

Sophia merely lifted her chin and continued on her way, moving as quickly and regally as possible before the crowd opened enough to allow the major through. But all the while, her blood was singing. She had finally showed one overweening popinjay exactly what she thought of him. If only she could accomplish the task she had now set for herself with as much success. Then she would truly feel alive!

Sophia arrived at her destination a few moments later. Compared to the rest of the area, this particular corner was unusually quiet. The wagons and carriages were almost orderly where they were parked, each holding anywhere from one to a dozen roosters in blanketed cages. Nearby, a row of boys had their backs turned as they strained to see into the cockpit.

Sophia approached the nearest wagon and its unfortunate cargo. It broke her heart to see such noble creatures caged like this, awaiting their turn to die in the sand pit.

She did not hesitate, knowing that at any moment the major would descend upon her. The boys at the fence were also potential hindrances. Right now they were too preoccupied to notice her, but that could change at any time.

She stepped up to the first cage, a blanketed wooden crate with a simple latch. Uncovering it revealed a large, dark bird. A very large, dark bird with bright eyes. It fussed and fluttered about its cage.

"Oh, you poor thing," she said softly. "Do not worry. I shall set you free."

With a quick flick of her wrist, she released the latch. She did not wait to see the creature escape. There were trees nearby; it need only flutter a small way before gaining its freedom. Pleased, she turned her back on it, uncovering and opening cages up and down the line as quickly as she could.

"Shoo!" she cried, as she opened a woven reed basket. "Go!"

She had freed perhaps a dozen creatures before she realized something was amiss. She had been so intent on her task, she had attributed all the noise to the nearby crowd. Suddenly, she was certain that the bird cries and screams were coming from nearby. They were very loud.

" 'Ey now!"

Sophia glanced up to see several boys turning around, their expressions a mixture of anger and horror. Following their gazes, she finally looked behind her and became thoroughly amazed by the sight.

She had thought that once freed, the birds would fly into the surrounding countryside like any other intelligent beasts. Unfortunately, these creatures did not seem at all intelligent. They were not escaping.

They were fighting.

In a huge mass of feathers and claws, they were attacking each other.

"Oh, my," she whispered, somewhat overwhelmed. "This is not at all what I intended." There was nothing to do but give the birds a little more direction. She began waving her arms at the creatures. "Fly free, fly free!" she cried. Sadly, far from responding to her urging, they merely became more excited, tearing into one another with renewed fury.

To make matters worse, the roosters caged on a nearby wagon were becoming highly excited by the mayhem. They began screeching and clawing, and Sophia watched with a mixture of awe and unease as first one, then two, then four of the birds clawed their way out of their baskets to join the massacre.

"Cover your eyes! Cover your eyes!" The major's command carried easily over the chaos, but Sophia could not understand his meaning. Did he think her too delicate to view such a sight?

And what a sight it was! Everywhere she turned there were birds fighting. Blood and feathers flew like fall leaves. Men, young and old, waded into the mess with their hands over their eyes, as if it were too horrible to see. It was at that moment that she noticed one of the birds was focused on her.

He was a large, mean-looking creature with a gaze that seemed to pierce right through her. Really, she thought, he looked quite like the major had just a moment before. "Shoo!" she said to it, gesturing it to the nearby trees.

To her shock, the beast lunged for her. Fortunately, she was as quick as the fowl, and she managed to raise her arms, knocking him away. Even so, she felt the hard glance of his beak and was gratified to realize she had the minor protection of her gloves.

"You brute!" she scolded, still trying to motion him away. "I am rescuing you, you idiot!"

But the bird had no interest in freedom, and it lunged for her again. She would have jumped backwards, but that would have put her into the thick of the battle behind her. Instead she tensed, intending to catch the bird and throw it to the trees.

Really, how could these creatures be so stupid?

All of a sudden, she felt strong arms around her, forcing her aside. It was the major, of course, interfering just when she was about to get the situation under control.

"Get in the wagon!" he cried as he turned to her attacker.

She had no choice. There was nowhere for her to go as man and bird circled one another.

"Really, Major. It is just a rooster. You need not be concern—Oh!"

It was only now, safely perched above the central fighting area, that she saw the danger, realized her mistake. These were fighting birds, trained since birth to kill one another. All about her, they fought, attacking even their handlers, who waded about with their hands over their eyes.

"Cover yer eyes, miss!" bellowed a boy from the side. "We train 'em to attack the eyes!"

At once, Sophia understood. These birds had powerful beaks. One peck to the face, and a person could lose his sight. Yet there was the major, his eyes steady and vulnerable as he faced off with the meanest, ugliest rooster of them all.

"Oh, dear," she moaned softly.

As she watched, her breath suspended in fear, the animal lunged at him. He had, in fact, adopted almost the same stance as she had only moments ago, waiting for the bird to come to him. The only difference was that he had stripped off his coat and held it out in one hand. He was also leaning forward, as if daring the fowl to attack. When the bird finally lunged—directly at his face, of course—he neatly knocked it flat, then wrapped it in his coat. The bird struggled viciously, and Sophia had no doubt Anthony's attire would soon be ripped to shreds, but by then the major would have the bird safely re-caged.

He was safe.

She breathed a sigh of relief, startled by the intensity of her emotion. But she did not dwell on it as she gazed over at the rest of the battle. Whereas the major had been quite magnificent, others did not seem to have his prowess. One youngster in particular was getting the worst of two birds.

She did not hesitate. Now that the major had shown her how to contain the creatures, she had absolute confidence in her ability to perform the task. Grabbing a blanket out of the wagon, she waded directly into the center of the fight, heading for the poor boy.

Fortunately, the nearby cocks were too busy fighting each other to notice her. She arrived at her destination relatively unscathed. Unfortunately, as soon as she readied herself to grab one of the birds, the blanket was unceremoniously ripped from her hands.

The boy, cut and bleeding, had grabbed it from her and buried himself in the heavy material. The birds, of course, immediately lost interest in the nondescript lump of fabric, especially since her bright, rose-colored gown was much more attractive.

Sophia was now faced with not one but two birds, and she had no blanket at all.

Then the oddest thing occurred. As she tensed, watching both creatures, all her senses seemed to enhance. She could see, hear, smell, even taste, everything with absolute clarity. She studied the two birds before her, noticing their every ruffled feather down to the silver spikes at the end of their feet. She was aware of the creatures behind her still fighting each other and their handlers. She even somehow felt the major, rushing forward to protect her.

In the distance, she heard the cheers and jeers of the crowd, now abandoning the cockpit to encircle this larger melee and bet on its outcome. Not a single one of them was joining in to help. In fact, they only seemed to be encouraging the mayhem.

Suddenly, Sophia was completely disgusted with the whole affair—from the stupid birds who would rather fight and die than be free to the gambling-crazed men, from the major and his silly marriage stratagems to the bloody boy who had grabbed the blanket out of her hands. She had done wrong by trying to free the cocks.

The situation was completely and totally ridiculous. She would not fight these stupid creatures. Neither would she waste her time on the rest of the men so fascinated with the sport. She would wash her hands of the entire, idiotic lot.

So deciding, she straightened, turning her back and walking away.

She did not even care when the two birds pursuing her sighted one another and began fighting. She was merely thankful that she would not have to confront them in her determination to get away.

"Sophia!"

The major's bellow once again held the clear note of command, but she ignored it, as usual. She merely continued plodding on toward his curricle. He would join her as soon as he finished dealing with the birds. It was unnecessary, of course. Eventually, the stupid roosters would either be killed or be too exhausted to fight. Then the handlers could pick up their remains. They should all do as the boy had done and simply hide until the mess was finished.

But there was no reasoning with men.

Chapter Eight

Mayhem. Complete and total mayhem.

Anthony shook his head as he held open a cage for a newly captured rooster. All about his feet lay the strewn wreckage of the fight. Feathers floated in the air, carcasses lay abandoned, and angry squawking abused his ears. Though most of the roosters had been captured, a few still fluttered about, looking for something to attack while, safely off to one side, the cock owners loudly bellowed for restitution. Surrounding it all stood the spectators, all laughing so violently they could hardly stand.

Taking in the amused crowd, he felt his lips twitch. The situation certainly sparked one's sense of the ridiculous. But some of the boys sported real wounds, and worst of all, he was haunted by the image of Sophia standing vulnerable and alone in the middle of the battle.

A shudder ran through his body, but he suppressed it. Sophia was safe now, sitting regally in his curricle. His task now was to remedy the situation. Unfortunately, some things remained impossible even for a major of the Hussars.

Looking about, he mentally counted heads in the crowd. Over a hundred at least, with more arriving every second. Without a doubt, this chicken battle would soon entertain listeners throughout England. No one could keep this event quiet.

A surge of real fear clutched at his throat. What would this do to Sophia's reputation? Would she be destroyed? And if so, would he lose his diplomatic appointment with her as his wife? He needed a woman of spotless repute, and Sophia no longer fit the bill. But the thought of throwing her over barely entered his mind. He would not give her up. If he lost his appointment, so be it.

Grimly, he focused his mind on the present situation. He could not save her reputation. The damage was already done. But perhaps he could use the situation to force Sophia's acceptance of his suit. Then, assuming he still had his appointment, he could take her to India where all this nonsense would be forgotten.

But how?

He turned, scanning the crowd for the man nominally in charge: the local magistrate. He wasn't hard to find. Baron Riggs stood in the center of a screaming group of cock owners. All were loudly calling for a hearing, and the baron was offering to officiate at the local alehouse. If Anthony didn't intervene soon, Sophia would soon be hauled into a common taproom, spend the afternoon being jeered at, then wind up in gaol.

Anthony set off, jingling his purse as he went, praying the baron was a bribable man. If not, Anthony's plan would create an even bigger problem.

"Baron Riggs!" he called, pitching his voice to carry over the crowd. "I wonder if I might have a word with you?"

The portly man turned, a glower on his ruddy face. "Who are you?"

"Major Anthony Wyclyff of the Eighth Hussars, sir. Could we speak?"

The baron's expression softened slightly, though not nearly enough for Anthony's purposes. "Are you responsible for this disaster?" he demanded.

"Yes, sir, I am." He meant to say more, but his words were cut off by shouts from the crowd.

"No, 'e weren't!"

"It were that girl. That *lady*!"

"She's over there! Sitting like to tea!"

Anthony raised his hand, doing his best to quiet the crowd. Eventually, the cries settled enough for him to make his plea. "I wish to discuss restitution," he shouted. The pronouncement had its desired effect. The various owners surged forward, only to be forestalled by the baron, a greedy light in his dark eyes.

"Make way, gentlemen. Make way. This man is a Hussar. He could cut you down with one glance. Make way."

Reluctantly, the aggrieved men fell away, allowing the baron to step forward. Anthony met him halfway, and though there was precious little space for privacy, together they managed to create a tiny circle for discussion while the crowd watched with impatience.

"Now, then," boomed the baron, but Anthony cut him off.

"Sir, I am afraid I am guilty of lying to you just now. I was indeed *not* the one who released the roosters from their cages."

The baron pulled back, ready to begin a loud protest. Clearly the man enjoyed an audience, but Anthony did not allow him to speak. Instead, he pressed a coin into the man's hand.

"Indeed, sir, this debacle was created by a tender-hearted young lady of the *ton*. Lady Sophia Rathburn, daughter of the late earl of Tallis." He had no compunction disclosing Sophia's name. No less than a dozen people had seen her release the birds. Her name would come up eventually. A moment later, the Baron confirmed Anthony's reasoning.

"Yes, yes. I thought I recognized the accused."

"Then I am sure you understand the need for discretion." He pressed another coin into the man's hand.

"You cannot think I would simply excuse this happenstance," protested the magistrate as he pocketed both coins. "A crime has been committed! The peace disrupted!" His voice was again rising to overly loud proportions.

"Of course, of course," agreed Anthony. "But you cannot simply bring a gently reared lady up on charges. And certainly not in a common taproom." Another coin disappeared into the baron's meaty fist. "Perhaps there is someplace more appropriate? Someplace more befitting her station?"

The baron frowned, confusion clear in his pinched expression. "I suppose my drawing room is rather large . . ."

"Excellent!" beamed Anthony as he slipped a few more coins into the baron's pocket. "But must you truly bring her up on charges?"

The magistrate glanced meaningfully at the crowd around them, the first sign of true reluctance on his face. "I cannot see how to avoid it," he answered in an undertone.

"Nor I," agreed Anthony truthfully.

"However," the baron continued, his hand meaningfully open, "We both know she won't spend time in gaol."

Anthony kept his hold on his purse tight. "On the contrary, I would like her to."

"What?" gasped the man, his thick jowls quivering in outrage. "I cannot gaol the daughter of an earl!"

Anthony took a deep breath. Indeed, what he was

about to do went against the grain in so many ways. But he had little choice. The sooner Sophia wed him, the better for everyone involved—most especially her. Indeed, this was the only way to save her reputation.

"Well," Anthony said slowly as he eyed the magistrate. "Do not gaol her, exactly. But perhaps you could detain her for the night. At your manor?"

The man gaped at him, his eyes bulging in shock. "But why, man?"

"Because I have taken responsibility for this event. I, of course, would have to be detained with her."

It took less than a moment for the man to grasp what Anthony wanted. "But you would ruin her!"

Anthony grinned. "Not if she married me in the morning." He dropped his entire purse into the magistrate's hand. "Certainly you understand that some courtships require more drastic methods than others."

The baron stared down at his palm, and for a moment, Anthony despaired that he had overplayed his hand. Glossing over a few dead chickens was one thing. Anthony was asking the man to help him ruin the daughter of an earl.

The magistrate looked up, his expression subdued. "I suppose you wish it to be as public as possible then."

Doubt once again surged through Anthony. Could he subject Sophia to such humiliation? One glance at the angry crowd dissolved his guilt. Sophia would suffer no matter what he did. The matter was already public, her name already bandied about. Neither he nor the baron could change that.

"Public trial or not," he finally said, "the damage is already done."

The older man did not seem to hear, his thoughts centered on the hearing's outcome. "I cannot sentence her to a bedroom," he said. "That would seem too much like a garden party." Then he smiled, and Anthony's purse disappeared into his now-heavy pocket. "But I have a priest's hole in the wine cellar. . . ."

Anthony nodded. "Then I shall leave it in your most capable hands."

"Are you sure you're all right?" the major demanded. "Sophia, do you know what could have happened? Lord, do you even know what will happen now?"

Sophia did not answer. Indeed, her entire body seemed encased in ice, so much so that she could barely think, much less respond. Besides, she was too weary with the whole situation to argue. Unfortunately, their difficulties had only just begun.

They were currently lumped into the back of a wagon being unceremoniously escorted to the residence of the local justice of the peace, otherwise known as Baron Riggs, who had been present at the fight. Sitting across from her in the conveyance was the local constable, a dour old man with a face wrinkled into a perpetual frown. Behind them followed everyone who attended the cockfight, rich and poor alike, all trooping to the baron's residence for her trial.

Not a one of them, from the baron down to the poor boy she had rescued, cared that she had been acting on humanitarian instincts. To a man, they were annoyed that she had ruined their sport. Everyone, that is, except Percy. Strangely enough, Lydia's fiancé had come to the country for sport—and had won a bundle betting on Sophia emerging alive and unscathed from the fight.

"I knew you could do it, Sophia," he prattled as he walked beside the wagon. "Not a one of them knew you had so much bottom! Can't say as I did, either, except that I couldn't bet against you. Not with yourself and Lydia being so close."

"Glad I could be of service," she responded dryly.

"Sophia!" snapped the major, and her attention returned to him. Naturally, Percy took that opportunity to drift away, abandoning her to the major's tirade. "They are taking you to trial. This will be gossip fodder for the entire country by nightfall."

She shrugged, feeling her mind and body slow, turning sluggish. She recognized the feeling—the chill that distanced her from everyone around her. Indeed, it was this very demeanor that had earned her the appellation "the Ice Queen."

Odd how she had not felt so cold since the major's return to her life.

"Sophia?"

She blinked, startled by his worried question. "I beg your pardon?"

"You *are* hurt! Where? Is it your head?"

"Apart from one peck, none of the birds paid the least attention to me. I am completely whole." Which was more than she could say for the major. His shirt was in tatters, revealing tantalizing glimpses of smooth flesh beneath. He had cuts along both his arms and a rather ugly gash along his cheek. For a moment, concern overrode her annoyance. "How is your leg? Does it pain you? I could . . ." She was imagining rubbing it as she had in the hospital, but her voice trailed away at his glare. Apparently the major did not want her touching him, and Sophia relapsed into a stoic silence.

Thankfully, the entourage soon reached the baron's house. The baron dismounted first, puffing up his chest with importance as he preceded everyone into his hallway. Cockfights were apparently quite a passion for the man, and he had acted quite indignant while supervising her arrest.

The constable climbed down next, all the while keeping a gimlet eye upon both herself and the major. Other men gathered around them, literally surrounding the wagon in case she or Anthony chose to make a run for it. Which was a ridiculous notion. With all the bodies squeezing forward to gawk at her, Sophia barely had room to breathe, much less attempt an escape.

She merely stood and allowed the constable to assist her to the ground. The major followed directly after, stepping to a spot behind her right shoulder, as if trying to shield her in some way. As they began to move toward the baron's entryway, she felt him wrap his arm around her, pulling her into his protective embrace. Any other time, she would have resisted his solid support. As it was, she had no energy to persist, her mind and body too frozen to do more than shrink into his side.

Moving inside, she felt him stumble slightly, his limp obvious now that she was pressed so intimately against him. She reached out, guilt creeping past her defenses. After all, she was the one who had begun this whole escapade. The major should not suffer for her actions.

"You need not protect me, Major," she offered softly. "You are much more injured than I, especially with your hurt leg."

"If ever a woman was in need of a keeper, Sophia, it is you. Good God, when I think of what could have happened!" His voice was haggard, his anger palpable, and when she looked up into his eyes, she could see fear lingering there. Fear, apparently, for her safety.

"Perhaps now you understand why I worry about your leg," she said. She had spoken softly, but she felt the impact of her words for his entire body stiffened. Meeting his startled gaze, she knew without a doubt that he understood her meaning. Some fears lingered despite all reason. She would always worry about his health, just as he would always feel horror when he recalled this afternoon's work.

The thought was oddly warming, as though it bound them together in some way. But she had no time to contemplate it as events once again overtook them. They moved into the baron's main reception room. Gentlemen crowded about them, pushing into the front hallway. The constable drew both her and the major to the center of the room, then glared fiercely at them before stepping back. A small circle of space opened up around them, and Sophia took her first deep breath in twenty minutes. Beside her, the major straightened, but he did not release her.

The baron took great time opening the chamber's windows to their fullest extent. All too soon, each opening became a disconcerting wall of eager faces as people who could not find space in the main room moved around to peer in through the window enclosures. At last, he raised his hand and waited in pompous glory for the citizens of Staffordshire to become silent. It took a long time.

When a modicum of peace reigned, the baron turned to Sophia, addressing her with his booming voice.

"Lady Sophia," he began. "You have caused quite a scene and hundreds of pounds' worth of damage this afternoon. What have you to say for yourself?"

"Merely that cockfighting is an uncivilized and repulsive sport where the ridiculousness of the event is matched only by the stupidity of the birds and their audi—"

"Sophia!" That was the major, releasing her as he pushed forward. "Perhaps you had best let me speak."

"Yes," agreed the baron in stern tones. "Major Wyclyff, are you responsible for this sharp-tongued woman?"

"Certainly not!" Sophia exclaimed. But when she made to move forward, the major cut in front of her, neatly blocking her out of any discussion. She opened her mouth to object, but the major began speaking, his forlorn look aimed at the baron.

"You have hit upon the very problem, sir. The young lady refuses to wed me. If we were married, I might have a bit more say in her choice of entertainment. As it is," he said with a sad shrug, "there is little I can do but follow along and mitigate the disaster."

Sophia was shocked. How could he bare their dispute to the world like this? How humiliating! The crowd roared with laughter, alternately cheering the major and jeering her. And rather than silencing the audience, the baron encouraged them. Obviously relishing the attention, he first smiled at the onlookers, then shook his bald head sadly at the major. "A quandary indeed," he said ponderously.

A quandary? Sophia thought in shock. This . . . this spectacle was a quandary? She felt her hysteria grow as she looked about. How had she come from a London drawing room to this, being the center of a display that would likely be talked about for generations to come?

Her only hope was that the major would somehow end this situation. She had meant to rely on herself but was frankly at a loss. She turned to him, hoping for a miracle, only to feel her spirits sink.

The major's expression was blank, totally devoid of feeling or expression. It was the exact look she herself had worn when she could stomach no more, when she had despised London so much she'd turned and walked away without so much as a backward glance.

The major looked like that right now. And she could not blame him. Actually, this was exactly what she wanted, wasn't it? She wanted to prove herself so vulgar that he would immediately get himself off to London to find some young debutante far removed from cockfights and the threat of gaol. Didn't she?

Sophia bit her lip. It was done now. All she could do was pray that this business finished quickly, while she did her best to maintain as much dignity as possible.

The room settled as the baron raised his hand for silence. He appeared about to make some official statement, and Sophia could only breathe a sigh of relief.

Perhaps it would be over soon. With luck, next would come judgment, and without nearly the vulgarity she might have expected from a public trial.

"Ahem," began the baron.

But at that moment a burly man suddenly pushed forward, dragging a dead bird into the room. "An' wot about me cock? He cost me three p a day just to feed, an' now he be deader than me Uncle Joe." The rooster landed with a dull splat at the major's feet. In fact, the major had to dance backward a step just to avoid it.

"Yer Uncle Joe woulda fought better!" called someone from the crowd.

The burly man stiffened and began shouting back at the other, his bellows containing words Sophia had never heard before. Rather than puzzle them out, she decided to take matters into her own hands.

"Please, gentlemen! I will pay whatever restitution is necessary," Sophia called, trying to establish some sort of order. How she would find the money for it, she did not know, but she would manage. Incredibly, the men completely ignored her, more intent on arguing than fixing anything.

Unfortunately, her pronouncement was heeded by everyone else in the room. The excitement was deafening as owner after owner shoved their way forward.

"Me bird was a champion!" cried a woman in a shrill voice as she tossed another dead cock onto the floor.

"An' mine—"

"An' mine—"

Sophia flinched as the bodies of the roosters were piled one by one at the major's feet. He looked like he was dancing a jig as he tried to avoid being spattered by bird after dead bird.

It was at that moment that Sophia began counting the number of dead fowl littering the floor. Goodness, there was no way she could have released so many animals in those few short moments. It took less than a minute for her to realize that some of those birds had been recently killed. Why, one was even a hen!

They were killing new birds just to claim recompense!

"This is outrageous!" she cried, but she was silenced by both a roar from the audience and a wave of the baron's meaty hand.

"Those who wish restitution shall present themselves forthwith," cried the baron.

"Wot?"

"What he say?"

"Line up and present your claims!" bellowed the baron.

It was as if the Red Sea had parted only to be forcibly pressed into a ragged line aimed at the baron. The entire town scrambled for a position in the raucous assembly. Three fistfights broke out over line disputes, while bird after bird continued to pile at her feet. It looked as if it would take the whole of the dowry she no longer had just to pay for all the claims.

"Just so as we all maintain our dignity," whispered Sophia sardonically to herself, her face burning with mortification.

The baron, at least, appeared equally appalled by the stampede of people. He quickly raised his hand, then waved it at the constable. "Er, present your claims to Virgil." Again the line shifted in a mad scramble toward the dour constable, but this time, they had to stumble through those who had begun to brawl.

Sophia closed her eyes, unable to bear the sight.

"Lady Sophia!" She opened her eyes at the baron's angry tone. "I shall hold you directly responsible for any damage to my house."

"You cannot be serious!"

"I am. As for you, Major Wyclyff, am I to understand that you do not approve of ladies attending cockfights?"

"Approve? Absolutely not." Anthony's response was so

crisp that Sophia half expected him to salute. Except this time when she looked closely at his face, she saw the distinct twinkle of amusement. Gone was his blank facade, replaced by a reluctant humor.

He actually found this situation comical?

"If you were to wed the lady," continued the baron in his booming voice, "would you prevent such an event from happening again?"

"Absolutely!" he said, then the major turned and grinned at Sophia. "And most definitely."

Sophia felt her jaw go slack, finally understanding the baron's direction of thought. Was he thinking of forcing them to marry as part of her punishment? Was she to be married as a public service? "I protest!" she cried. "I will marry no man, and certainly not one who thinks he shall have the least success in preventing me from going wherever I see fit."

At this pronouncement, the crowd exploded into a frenzy of catcalls and jeers. She was nearly bowled over from its sheer volume.

The baron merely shook his head, as if she were a lunatic. "She is quite shrewish," he said to the major. "Do you truly wish to have her?"

Anthony turned, leisurely inspecting her from the top of her tangled hair to the bottom of her mud-stained hem, much to the delight of the crowd. Sophia stiffened in outrage, but there was little she could do while the major was providing such wonderful entertainment for the locals.

"This is horrible of you," she hissed at him.

He merely grinned, then spoke to the baron and the eager crowd. "It *is* quite a quandary," he said, his eyes twinkling with deviltry. "Perhaps we should be thrown in gaol for the night. That might teach her a lesson. Let me see if I still wish her afterwards."

Immediately the room echoed with cheers, liberally

peppered with crass remarks. But it was the major's bawdy wink that was the final straw for Sophia. She stepped forward, outrage making her hands clench in front of her. "Do not be ridiculous! What of my reputation? I shall be completely ruined." What was he thinking, sending her to a common prison? Ladies were not treated this way! And why was the baron looking pleased by the suggestion?

Anthony lifted his shoulders in a casual shrug. "I thought you cared nothing for your reputation, my dear. That is, after all, why we attended the fight in the first place."

"But . . . but I shall be spending the night—"

"In gaol, my dear," boomed the baron. "Lady Sophia, I hereby find you guilty of . . . of disrupting the peace and a very fine afternoon of sport."

"Sport!" she exclaimed. "Where is the sport in watching dumb animals murder each other?"

The baron continued as if she had not spoken. "As for you, Major Wyclyff, you shall accompany her. Appear before me in the morning to tell me of your decision."

"But you cannot do this," sputtered Sophia.

Unfortunately, no one paid her the slightest heed and, from the unholy glee on Anthony's face, she knew she would get no help from him.

"Come along, my dear," boomed the baron as he came up beside her. "It is this way."

"But—"

"Silence, or I shall make it two nights."

Sophia had no choice but to quiet. The baron placed a hand on her arm and neatly helped her step over the dead birds still on the floor. The major was left to follow at his leisure. The crowd shifted before them, and their ribald comments made her face burn. Soon, Sophia found herself in front of a heavy wood door, which the constable took great ceremony to pull open.

"Here?" she asked.

"Of course!" responded the baron congenially. "This is our gaol!" Then he leaned forward, dropping his voice to an undertone. "It is the only lockable room in the house."

"But . . . but it is a wine cellar!"

"Naturally. I am quite sure you will be comfortable there," he said with a broad wink. Then he turned to the major. "There is a priest's hole just off the main chamber down there, and I trust I shall not have to lock the both of you in so that you don't drink all of my wine?"

If possible, Anthony's grin grew even wider. "Absolutely. Of course," he added with a wink to the crowd, "cockfighting is very thirsty work. I am sure the lady will wish a drop or two. She has been known to imbibe on other occasions."

Sophia gasped at his crude reference to her earlier attempt to disgust him with inebriation. "How dare you!" she cried. "You know quite well—"

"Yes, yes, my dear," he interrupted. "I am sure you need not elaborate."

"Of all the vulgar . . ." It was at that precise moment that Sophia spotted her rescue. There, trapped between the butcher and the baron's poor confused-looking wife, stood Percy, clearly torn between amusement and horror. If the major would do nothing to help her, then surely she could convince her friend's betrothed to assist her.

Pushing away from the baron, she stepped toward him. "Percy!" she cried. "Help me! Do something!"

The boy started, obviously surprised to suddenly become the focus of the crowd's attention. To add to his shock, he was roughly pushed forward by the butcher, then jostled about until he stood directly in front of the baron.

Still, much to Sophia's relief, Percy had enough wits about him to begin an earnest plea on her behalf. "I say," he began, "this is not at all the thing. Sophia is good *ton*, after all. We can't have her tossed in gaol."

Sophia closed her eyes, feeling a headache begin to pound in her temples. This was not quite the learned argument she had hoped for. Nevertheless, the baron did not seem to mind. He cleared his throat to study the boy.

"And just who might you be?"

The young man straightened his shoulders, meeting the baron's look with calm distinction. "Percy Fitzgerald, Lord Waverly." The effect would have been just what Sophia had wanted, if his voice had not cracked on his title.

"Another suitor, sir," added Anthony in a dry voice.

"Throw 'em all in together!" called someone in the crowd.

"An' see 'oo comes out standing!" added another.

"Now, now," bellowed the baron. "I will have no bloodshed in my wine cell—I mean, in my gaol." He turned his heavy stare on the boy. "Is that what you wish? Do you want to join them down there?"

Percy blanched, his cheeks becoming the color of his fine lawn shirt. "In there?" he squeaked. "But Lydia will have my ears for it. Not to mention Mother." And, with that, he hastily backed out of the room. Sophia watched his departure with a sinking heart while the crowd lambasted the boy for such a lily-livered display.

"Very well," bellowed the baron over the din. "Down with you." He gestured Sophia toward the rickety stairs descending into the dark cellar. She did not move at first; instead she stood watching the baron clap the major on the back and wish him the best of luck. But then the crowd began pushing in, and she had no direction to go but down the stairs. The major followed quickly after, making no attempt to hide his grin.

Once they were inside, bit by ponderous bit the door closed behind them, settling into place with an echoing thud that easily cut off the bawdy comments of the crowd.

The only light was from a candelabra that had been thrust into the major's hand.

Sophia watched it all happen with a brittle kind of detachment. She was now locked in for the night with the major. Her future was over. Her reputation destroyed. Her dreams of a quiet spinsterhood forever shattered.

And there was only one person to blame.

Major Anthony Wyclyff.

After all, he was the one who had truly begun this entire debacle. If he hadn't been absolutely insistent that she marry him, she never would have thought to go to the cockfight in the first place. Neither would she have been drinking or kissing, for that matter. None of the last dreadful, wonderful, bizarre week would have happened.

And that thought made her very, very confused, twisting her emotions into a tangle of conflicting feelings. It was all too much for her, and so she took refuge in anger. Pinning the major with her coldest stare, she practically hissed her words at him: "You are quite the most odious man alive," she fumed. Then she turned her back on him and flounced the rest of the way down the stairs.

Anthony watched Sophia stomp away in high dudgeon and could not suppress a grin. Finally, he had done it. It had taken a cockfight of gargantuan proportions, a bribable baron, and gaol, but he had finally gotten into an excellent battle position. He'd broken through Sophia's cool reserve.

Good lord, she had punched that overweening viscount in the face! She had been a magnificent, avenging fury descending on that stuffed popinjay! Now, that glory seemed to follow her even into this dank cellar. He watched her cross the narrow room, glaring at inoffensive bottles, her back as rigid as an iron pike.

She was furious with him.

Fortunately, he knew it was only a tiny step from fury to passion.

He could not have been more pleased if she had declared she would wed him then and there. But he knew it would take a good deal more persuasion to get her to that point. And now, he thought with a grin, he had all night to persuade her.

"Shall we see what accommodations our illustrious baron has provided?" he called cheerfully.

"I hold you directly responsible for this turn of affairs."

"Me?" he cried with offended dignity. Actually, he cared not the least whom she blamed for the situation, just so long as she remained at his side. Tonight. And always. "I was not the one who chose to level a peer of the realm. Nor was I the one who thought cocks bred for battle would be better off roaming the countryside."

"I did not think the birds were so stupid!"

"You did not think at all!" Anthony felt his cheery mood dim at the memory of Sophia in the middle of all those frenzied roosters. For as long as he lived, he knew he would recall his worry for her safety. "Sophia. Are you sure—"

"I am completely whole," she snapped, somehow knowing what he was going to ask.

Watching her skirts swirl as she spun away, Anthony relaxed. Sophia's spirited display reassured him that she was unhurt. If only he could reassure her about his leg and health as easily. He had caught her many anxious glances, especially whenever she saw him limp.

"And stop grinning at me," she snarled from where she leaned against a wine cask. "If you think for one moment—"

"Are you thirsty, my dear?" he asked, hoping to distract her from her temper.

"No!"

His smile became more of a smirk, as he took in her

posture and fiery pride. "You are absolutely magnificent," he said, and he meant it. Before she could find a scathing retort, he lit a new candle from a stack he found on a nearby shelf, held it out for her to take, then raised his candelabra to illuminate their surroundings. "So, should we see what our dear baron has provided for our incarceration?"

She huffed, holding out her candle with clear disgust. "It makes no difference whether this is a pig's wallow or a king's palace; I am still quite angry with you."

"I know that, my dear, but I, for one, would prefer to make the pig's wallow as much of a palace as possible." Holding out his light, he began inspecting the cellar.

The room was long and thinned into more of a passageway because of the long racks of bottles stored here. Apparently, the baron enjoyed wine. There were racks and racks of various vintages all along the wall, with more than a few empty spaces from what the baron had already consumed. Anthony spotted brandy and port wine and all manner of drink.

He stepped forward, bringing his light closer as he noted the enormous variety of offerings; then his attention was drawn to one side as Sophia sighed heavily and wandered away down the passageway. He let her go, knowing she needed time to cool her temper. It took at least ten minutes before he heard her gasp.

"Oh, goodness," she said, her voice clear despite the distance between them.

"Is there some difficulty?" He moved quickly toward her, anxious for her safety. This had been a clever plan, but he did not want her getting hurt.

"Not for me," she answered. "But then, I suppose you have slept in worse. Still, I cannot say I envy you tonight's accommodations."

Anthony made it to her side, at last able to understand her comments. As the baron had promised, the passageway ended in a rather austere room, no doubt once used as chambers for a servant or priest. Sophia was looking at a rather dismal straw tick mattress that drooped in the middle of a narrow bed. It was the only item of furniture in the room.

"It will not be comfortable," she admitted, "but it will be better than letting you stand all night on your leg."

He looked around the filthy little room, wondering at her words. "As you said, I have slept on much worse in my life. But where do you expect to rest?"

Sophia merely shook her head. "I am too angry to sleep at all tonight," she said. Abruptly, she stuck her head back into the passageway then looked at him. "But, this is appalling. There is not even water to clean your wounds."

Anthony felt his smile return. "Gaol is not intended to be comfortable."

"It does not have to be repulsive, either."

He did not answer, not wishing to disillusion her. He had only once been incarcerated. In Spain. And it was not an experience he cared to remember. Compared to that, this was indeed a king's palace.

The mere memory of that place was enough to make him feel tired. With a sigh, he set down his candelabra, stripped off the tattered remains of his coat, then set that down on the straw tick. He sat atop it with an audible groan.

As expected, Sophia's attention immediately turned to him. "Are you ill, Major? Feverish? Perhaps we could end this farce if—"

"I am quite healthy, if a little tired."

His words apparently did not reassure her. Inserting her candle in a sconce on the wall, she knelt in front of him, her hands trembling slightly as she touched his knee. "Is it your leg?"

"That and perhaps a dozen other minor injuries."

She swiftly rose to her feet. "Then I shall call the baron at once. He will get a doct—"

"All I require is you." With a quick shift of his weight, he caught her wrist and gently pulled her down to sit beside him.

"Major! If you are ill—"

"I merely wish to speak with you."

"But a fever . . ." Her voice trailed away as she pressed her hand to his forehead. He allowed her to do it, allowed her to reassure herself that he was fine. He did not speak until he heard her sigh of relief.

"You see," he said softly, "I am fine. Please, Sophia, can you not sit and speak with me?" He held his breath waiting for her decision, but in the end, she nodded, shifting to sit by his side, her rose skirt settling softly about her.

"Very well, Major," she said calmly. "What do you wish to discuss?"

He leaned forward, trying to capture her hands, but she remained steadfastly out of his reach. In the end, he leaned back watching her expression carefully. "Your fears for my leg. Sophia, why do you worry so?"

"I thought you understood by now." She paused, scanning his face. When he did not respond, she beetled her eyebrows in a clear frown. "Major, why were you so upset when I released the birds?"

"Because you could have been severely hurt . . . blinded or maimed—"

"Well, *you* died."

Her soft words silenced his anger, allowing him to understand her message. If he felt terror at just the memory of Sophia in danger, how much more pain would he feel if she had nearly died? Did she feel so much horror whenever she looked at him? Did every sight of him remind her of his supposed death?

"But I did not die," he said for what seemed like the hundredth time.

She pushed up from the cot, frustration making her movements short. "You refuse to understand."

"Because you refuse to see me as whole!"

She stopped, turning toward him so that the candlelight fell full on her face. And in that moment, he saw true fear on her face, a terror that seemed to engulf her. But then it was gone. He watched in amazement as she shuttered her expression, closing it down until she stood as if frozen solid.

Why was she so set on remaining afraid? he wondered. What did she risk in believing him healthy?

He had no answer, and soon she was speaking again, her words soft, her body held excruciatingly rigid. "I do not wish to argue."

"Nor I," he returned.

They regarded one another in silence. And in that stillness, he studied her, seeing why she had been called the Ice Queen. Whenever the woman felt threatened, whenever anyone or anything veered too close to her pain, she froze—inside and out—refusing to feel, refusing to be touched by any other soul.

He could not allow her to remain like this. Not with him. But how could he melt through her reserve? How could he reach her?

"Please sit down," he asked softly. "It hurts my neck to forever look up at you like that."

She wanted to refuse. He could see the wariness in her eyes. But Sophia was too tenderhearted to cause him any pain, even a simple crick in his neck. Slowly she came forward, finally settling herself on the edge of the cot. Then, before he could think of something to say, she began speaking, her voice cool and composed.

"It occurs to me that I have not thanked you for your assistance with the birds. I realize I might have been severely injured." She turned to look at him, and he read sincerity in her eyes. "Thank you, Major, for your help."

A peace offering, he realized, and he responded with all the chivalry in his soul. "It was my duty and my honor, Sophia."

She relaxed slightly, a rueful smile touching her lips. "And now we are incarcerated like common criminals. Small thanks for your heroic deed."

"Your appreciation is thanks enough," he said with absolute truth. Indeed, he would brave a thousand demonic chickens if it meant another night with her at his side. But he could not say so to her. Indeed, he was startled by the vehemence of the thought.

Rather than dwell on his unruly emotions, he chose instead to look out into the wine cellar. "Perhaps we could get something to drink. I am afraid I find myself quite parched."

He started to fit task to word, but she stopped him with a single raised hand. "Please, allow me. It is the least I can do after you stopped that huge brute of a rooster."

"There is no need—"

"I *want* to." Then she was gone into the passageway, and he could do nothing but lean back and enjoy the highly pleasurable experience of having Sophia attend to him. It was not that she had never assisted him before. She had, in fact, been most supportive during his early stay in the hospital. But somehow this seemed different. Today, she seemed motivated not out of an abstract pity or concern, but by simple desire. She wished to help *him*.

That would have made up for the cuts and bruises from a dozen cockfights.

She returned quickly with a fine brandy. "Is this acceptable, do you think? I do not know what one serves with fleas and dust."

"Normally," he said with a teasing smile, "port is called for in such circumstances. But I believe the Prince Regent once claimed a preference for brandy."

She smiled in pleasure at his sally. "Well, I am glad we

shall be upholding the royal custom. Especially since we have no glasses."

He reached out, taking the bottle from her hand, managing to extend the movement into a soft brush across the back of her hand. "Then, from the bottle it is," he said cheerfully, his happiness having more to do with her blush than any drink.

"The baron left a tray at the top of the stairs," she admitted with a shy glance. So saying, Sophia slipped from the room. Anthony counted the seconds until she returned. He was at a hundred and four when she stepped back into the room, a large tray with bread and cheese in her hands.

"A veritable feast," he said, though his eyes were on her.

Again, he saw her skin tinge with rose, but she covered beautifully, setting the tray between them and sitting on the straw tick. Digging into the cheese, bread, and, of course, the brandy, Anthony felt surprisingly hungry, and he was gratified to see that Sophia appeared famished as well.

They made quick work of the repast, eating in companionable silence. More than once, he caught her speculative gaze on him, but she quickly looked away each time, and he was left to wonder at her thoughts. As he'd expected, she hadn't held on to her ire for long, and even now she seemed to be relaxing in his presence. Her icy reserve was melting, warming with each moment of friendly companionship.

She didn't even object to their vulgar method of drinking directly from the bottle, merely tossing him a rueful smile before imbibing. And, in the end, he was grateful that she was adaptable in her standards.

All in all, things were looking up, and he was happily anticipating the night to come when Sophia at last gave him a clue as to her thoughts. His hopes began to sink.

Chapter Nine

Sophia busied herself brushing bread crumbs off her fingers, but her thoughts were elsewhere, on the virile man beside her on the bed. She sighed silently to herself. There was no other way to describe Anthony besides virile. Even his limp did not diminish him in her eyes. It certainly had not prevented him from rescuing her back at the cockpit. Nor had it prevented him from tirelessly engineering the chaos that plagued her since she'd quit London.

Still she could not help but worry about him. What if he pushed himself too far? What if—

She ruthlessly cut off her thoughts. She would not dwell on that when there was something more important to address—the coming morning. "Do you think there is any way to save my reputation?" she asked, her voice unnaturally loud in the small room.

The major did not hesitate. "Apart from marrying me?" he asked.

She nodded.

"No."

She bit her lip, then lifted the tray off the pallet, placing it on the floor. Would she truly be forced to marry the major? she wondered. If so, how would she feel about that?

Apparently, his thoughts ran a similar course, for he voiced the sentiment aloud: "Would it truly be so horrible a fate?" he asked curtly. "I am not a monster. In fact, I know no other man who would become a butler, fight trained cocks, and go to gaol all for the sake of being caught in a parson's mousetrap."

She carefully moved the now empty brandy bottle to the floor, delaying the moment when she was required to answer him. Privately, she hoped that somehow she could delay the entire coming argument, but one glance at his set face and she knew he would press for answers—now, before she could order her jumbled thoughts.

She made a desperate attempt to delay: "Do you truly wish to discuss this here?"

"No," he retorted hotly. "I do not wish to discuss this at all. I wish to be happily on my way to India. But I wish to do so with my wife by my side."

She felt her hands clench into fists, her anger already overwhelming her restraint. "Then pick some peagoose debutante and be done with it, Anthony! By Heaven, I tire of this argument. Why do you insist on *me?*"

She meant to move away, but she was slow, the brandy having affected her more than she had at first realized. He easily caught her hand, drawing it toward him. "Because you are a lady, Sophia. In every sense of the word. And only a lady can represent the Crown as it should be represented."

She jerked her hand back, folding it tightly against her chest. She truly didn't know what she had wanted him to say. Certainly, she had expected no less. He valued the coolness she had shown in the hospital, saw through the crazy things she had been doing lately. He admired all the things that she hated about her life. Those were the reasons he wished to wed her.

She felt tears prick her eyes and hastily blinked them away. "I am no lady, Major. Have you not seen as much, yet? Does a lady get drunk? Does a lady go to cockfights? Does a lady sit in gaol drinking wine from the bottle?"

"Yes. She does if she is you."

Suddenly, she could not look at him anymore. She could not stare him in the face, see his earnest expression, and still remember that he wanted a Sophia that did not exist. She had destroyed that cold, reasonable woman. She pushed herself up from the cot, pacing the tiny room with short, angry steps. "You make no sense."

"Then we are of a pair," he responded. "Neither do you."

Sophia turned and stared across the tiny cell at him, her spine straightening out of habit. She was tired and more than a little woozy from the brandy, but she would not sit down. The only place to sit was on the bed.

With Anthony.

And she could not do that. He had the oddest effect on her senses. He could be overly commanding and stubborn to the bone, but when she was with him, she forgot all those things. All she could think of was how wonderful it felt to be in his arms, to feel his hands touching her.

He leaned forward, as if to enact the very embrace she was imagining. "Sophia . . ." he began.

"I shall return the tray to the top of the stairs," she suddenly stammered. "There is no reason to attract rats by leaving the cheese here." And, with that, she snatched up the tray, grabbed her candle, and fled.

The task took only a moment, but she lingered at the top of the stairs for considerably longer. The baron had left a new tray, this one holding a water basin and cloth. She studied the items, using the time to think, time to sort out her conflicting emotions.

This was most unlike her. Since the major had come into her life, she had run harem-scarum from one scandalous action to another. It was frightening to her how wild she had become. What had begun as a simple symbolic ritual had ended in gaol.

And yet she could not regret it. She felt alive for the first time in her life. When she was with the major, she saw everything more vividly, lived more fully. Why, even her arguments were more passionate.

Perhaps that was the key. Passion. Who would ever think to associate such a word with Sophia Rathburn, Ice Queen? Not her London peers, certainly. Only Major Wyclyff.

But passion was a foolish emotion, as she knew too well. She would not succumb to it, heading pell-mell into ruin and despair as her mother had. She would remain cool and collected, her mind focused on the necessities and no more. In such a manner, she could survive this night. As for the morning, she would deal with it when it came.

With that thought firmly fixed in her mind, she returned to the tiny priest's hole.

"I found this at the top of the stairs," she said calmly, showing the major the new tray. "The baron must have thought of us. You can clean your wounds now."

Anthony did not move. He remained as he was, semireclined on the bed, his injured leg stretched across the mattress.

"Truly, Major, some of those cuts are quite deep. They should be washed."

He nodded, but she could see something strange in his eyes. "You seem quite composed, Sophia," he commented.

" 'Resigned' is perhaps the better word," she corrected

as she set the new tray on the floor beside the bed, then refixed her candle in its sconce. "I cannot change what comes tomorrow. I can only resolve to meet it with dignity and aplomb."

"You have become the Ice Queen again—refusing to feel, moving through your days without being touched by anything."

Sophia flinched even though that was exactly what she had called herself moments before. "I am reserved, Major. And—"

"Dead?"

She glanced up, her eyes narrowing in anger. "You are trying to goad me into an argument."

"I am trying to break through your reserve, Sophia. You cannot freeze me out. I *will* reach you one way or another."

She stared at him, trying to remain calm and distant, but inside she trembled. She very much feared he was correct. She would never be indifferent to him, no matter how much she tried. And the very thought terrified her, though she could not say why. "Your wounds, Major," she said coolly. "They need tending."

He nodded. "Of course," he agreed, then groaned loudly as he leaned over toward the water. "Perhaps you could assist me in the task. I find my leg pains me greatly this evening."

"Of course," she said, unable to deny him aid as he struggled to shift positions. He sighed audibly as he fell backward, and Sophia became alarmed at the thought that his leg might fare quite poorly in this damp cellar. "Perhaps I should call the baron. If your leg—"

"I will not cry craven at the thought of spending a night in a wine cellar." His voice was forceful and hard, but Sophia persevered.

"Truly, Major, it is folly to let pride stand in the way of your health. Pride will not stop your pain. Pride will not heal your leg or prevent a fever. In fact, I am persuaded that pride is the most useless of all emotions."

"Really?" He opened his eyes, and Sophia felt pinned by the sharpness of his stare. She knew what he was suggesting. He thought that it was her pride that kept her from the altar. She would disabuse him of the notion.

"My pride has nothing to do with my decision to remain unwed."

"Then it is perhaps stubbornness that keeps you to your course without reason?"

"You are the original irresistible force, Major. Only an immovable object can stand against you." But even as she spoke, Sophia shifted awkwardly, uncomfortably aware that his implication might be correct. She might very well have spent so much time fighting with the major that she'd neglected to think of herself or even her future. After all, she was in gaol with him, her reputation sure to be in tatters.

"Come," she said, pushing the thought away. "Let me tend your wounds."

He nodded again, then began stripping off his shirt. Sophia scrambled back in alarm, one minute looking at torn and bloodied white linen, the next minute faced with a broad expanse of golden skin atop rippling muscles.

"What are you doing?" she squeaked.

He paused in a most disconcerting position, one that showed all his glorious muscles to wonderful advantage. It was not until he spoke that she noticed his grin. "You cannot expect to wash my wounds through fabric."

"Er, no," she admitted through a suddenly dry throat. "Of course not. Carry on."

"Believe me," he said in a silky undertone, "I intend to."

Sophia swallowed, unsure how to proceed. There was so much skin . . .

"Perhaps you should start with my back."

"Uh, yes. Perhaps I should." She watched as he turned over, thinking what now faced her was a much less intimate beginning, especially since his eyes would be on the floor instead of her many blushes. But as he at last settled, she saw the error of her thoughts.

She had not thought a man's back a sensual thing, but there, spread before her, was the broadest expanse of masculine physique she had ever witnessed. Unable to stop herself, she reached out and stroked his golden skin, watched in fascination as the muscles rippled in response.

Good Lord, he was magnificent!

Then, almost without thought, she let her fingers trace a jagged scar that started just below his right shoulder blade and slashed down his side. She marveled at the length of it, shuddering at the thought of the original wound.

"This must have hurt terribly," she said softly. "But now it is merely a jagged pink line."

"Yes." The word sounded breathless, almost as if it were a groan.

"Major?" she asked, alarmed. "Are you in pain?"

"Oh, yes," he groaned. "As much as a man can be while lying on his stomach."

"Then, I will call—"

"No!" The force of his exclamation nearly raised him off the bed.

"Ah," she said, guessing at his meaning. "You are afraid that the washing will hurt. But I must tend to your cuts before they fester." She leaned forward, touching him gently. "You are a brave man to face such pain without complaint."

"Yes," he agreed, his voice excruciatingly dry. "A very brave man."

Sophia nodded, though she did not understand his tone. Then, with an unsteady hand, she wrung out a linen cloth before gently applying it to the major's deepest cut.

He flinched only slightly at her touch, then seemed to relax as she tried to wipe away the tiny flecks of dried blood.

"They are not so bad," she said. "I do not think any will scar."

"They would not dare," he responded with a forced laugh. "Not after your tender ministrations."

Sophia softened despite herself. "You always say such outrageous things while lying in a sickbed."

"You bring out my sense of humor. You always have." His voice was low and thoughtful, and Sophia paused in her work to consider his thick, curly hair.

"I thought I brought out your anger, your sense of command, and your masculine bullheadedness."

"Those, too." She could hear his smile in his words, and she could not help returning the gesture. It was a pleasant sensation to enjoy the major's company without fighting him.

"I have missed this," she said as she wrung out the linen.

"What?" He raised up on his elbows, but she pushed him back down.

"Talking without arguing. We have not truly done it since the hospital."

"I used to measure the seconds until you would return. I would start out at eighty-two thousand, eight hundred, and count backwards."

Sophia's hand stilled on his back. "You cannot be serious. My visits could not have been nearly so important."

Anthony turned and focused a serious gaze directly at her. "I assure you, they were."

She hesitated, her hands poised in midair because she did not know what to do with them. "I spoke with many injured soldiers. I am positive none of the others counted the seconds to such precision."

He raised a single auburn eyebrow, and she swallowed

nervously. Why did he have such a powerful effect on her? When she started to look away, he stopped her, catching her chin between his fingers.

"Did you speak your true opinion of high society with the other soldiers? Did you tell any of them that young Lord Blakesly made your flesh crawl? Or that you longed to visit Italy one day?"

Sophia bit her lip. No, she had not confided in anyone but the major. "It appears I spent too much time with you. I should not have spoken of those things."

He rolled over completely, turning so that she faced his naked chest. "Perhaps you spent too little time with me. I am just the person to hear your dreams."

"I have no dreams," she answered automatically. Then she paused, startled by her own words. When had that occurred? When had she given up all the daydreams she had enjoyed as a child?

"Perhaps I could help you find some new dreams, Sophia. And we could achieve them together."

Sophia looked away, her mind in turmoil. "I thought your dreams were of England and India and a dignified wife by your side," she said stiffly.

He shrugged. She was not looking at him, but she could feel the movement through the cot, and through her entire body. "We were speaking of what *you* want."

She turned, this time quite able to meet his gaze. "It seems strange. We have never spoken of what I want except when you are lying down."

"That is because you are forever running or barring the door to me when I approach you standing up."

"That is not true!" Sophia stiffened in outrage, though inside, she knew he was correct, which made her even angrier.

"Then let us test it," he proposed. "I shall stand, and you will tell me everything you desire."

She smiled. In truth, she could not help it. It was such

a delightful image, him standing at attention while she poured out her heart to him. Worse, she knew he would do it. But she feared what she might say to him. She stopped the conversation by pushing him back down with a firm hand. "You will remain horizontal while I clean your wounds."

His groan startled her, and she wondered if she had used too much force. "Major!" she cried. "Have I hurt your back?"

He shook his head, his expression rueful. "No. Your washing has helped. But I sustained many more cuts on my front from that damned—" He stopped, then hastily corrected himself. "From that ill-tempered bird," he amended. Then he caught her hand with the wet cloth and firmly drew it to a gash on his chest. "Please. I believe this needs your attention."

She looked down and almost wished she had not. Their hands rested together on his breastbone, the water from her cloth trickling across the curve of his ribs to become lost in the slight dusting of dark curls on his abdomen. She felt her breath catch and lifted her gaze to his face only to be enmeshed in the heated depths of his eyes.

Without words he began to move her wrist, guiding her hand across the muscled planes of his chest. Her mouth felt dry, and she licked her lips only to hear him catch his breath, his chest rising as if in anticipation of her touch. If she closed her eyes, she was sure she could feel his heart beating. Or was it her own that pulsed so?

She tried to pull away, but he stopped her, holding her imprisoned until she had to press her other hand against him for balance.

"Why do you fear me, Sophia?" he suddenly asked, his voice low and rich.

Looking at him in the candlelight, she wanted to run away but knew he would not release her. In the end, she met his gaze as calmly as she could. "I do not fear you," she said, but her voice trembled, and he smiled at her lie.

"I *know* why," he whispered. "It is the same reason you came to my sickbed every day, spending longer and longer—"

"I did not!"

"You did. Remember, I counted the seconds."

Sophia had no response, and so he continued, his voice as relentless as it was persuasive. "Because I make you feel. I do not accept your cool ivory smile or your brittle porcelain nod. I do not allow you to fob me off with pleasantries or socially acceptable responses."

"Which is merely another way of saying you irritate me."

"Yes! And I excite you. Admit it, Sophia; have you ever in your life been so angry, so happy, so vibrant except when you are with me?"

No. She could not say anyone else made her feel the way he did. No one else could make her breath quicken from across the room as he did. No one else could touch her and make her heart pound in her breast.

"Kiss me, Sophia."

She hesitated, unsure. But even as she waited, he drew her closer, without touch, without anything more than the magnetic compulsion of his eyes.

"Kiss me," he urged, and she felt her elbows bend, her face lowering toward his.

"No!" She turned away, trying to run from the room, but he did not release her hand. He still held it pinned against his chest, the warmth of his body seeping through the cloth covering it.

"Sophia—"

"I cannot!"

"Why?"

Why? It was so simple a word, and yet it demanded too full an answer.

"Why, Sophia? You must know I will not release you until I have an answer."

She looked back at him, her sight already wavering from tears, but she saw the resolution in his face. Then she was speaking without wanting to, the words tumbling heedlessly from her lips. She did not know where the thoughts came from, but even as she uttered them, she knew them to be the truth.

"When I am with you, I lose control of myself! I no longer recognize who I am. I cannot control my thoughts or my actions. You anger me as no one else ever has. It is because of you that I have become drunk, gone to a cockfight, and now . . ." Her voice trailed away.

"And now you want to kiss me."

"Yes."

"So why do you stop yourself? Why do you hold yourself apart? From me, from the world, from everyone?"

She lifted her free hand into the air in a gesture of futility. "You can know of my family and still ask me that?"

He frowned, his grip suddenly relaxing on her hand. She used the moment to pull away from his disturbing touch, but she did not leave him. She knew he would continue to harass her all night until she told him it all. So, she stumbled through the words even though they tore at her like brambles.

"Have you heard the stories of my father? My mother loved him to distraction. He was handsome and impetuous and full of what she called *le joie de vivre*."

"The joy of life," he translated.

"Yes." She took a deep breath. "But after they married, he did not reserve his . . . joy for his wife. He . . ." She took a deep breath. "He wenched. He had dozens of mistresses who demanded the most expensive baubles to maintain their interest. He spent my mother's dowry on diamonds for his other women. And when her dowry disappeared, he gambled what was left of his inheritance trying to find enough money to buy one more precious stone to please one more lady fair."

"How do you know all this?"

Sophia shrugged. "It is common knowledge, and I was in London for five Seasons. Time enough to hear all the gossip. But what was worse by far was to see my mother. Despite my father's whoring, she still adored him. But without money for fine clothes or expensive airs, she could not compete with the lures of London. He came home less and less, and my mother became wild in her own ways. Rather than try to curb his recklessness, she began to spend money as freely as he. After all, he would run through it soon enough. She decided to spend it while she still could."

Anthony pushed up onto his elbows, his dark eyes steady and sad. "But who managed the estates? Who cared for you and your brother?"

"We had a steward and a nurse for as long as we could pay them. After they left, Geoffrey took over the accounts. I learned my sums at his knee. When I grew, I cared for the household while he tried to manage the rest. We learned early that there was no time for emotion, that there were penalties for losing control."

Anthony took a deep breath, and when he reached forward to caress her cold cheek, Sophia did not move away. "And when your father died?"

She shrugged. "No one cried except my mother." Which told it all in one short sentence.

But he was not done. He continued to press her as he caressed her arm. "But, I am not your father. I do not gamble or whore or spend money recklessly. What has that to do with us?"

"You merely fight in wars."

"Not anymore," he said firmly.

She raised her brows, challenging his declaration.

"Then you would not go to whatever wild land, perform whatever task—dangerous or not—that the Crown demanded of you?"

He stiffened. "Of course I would. It is my duty—"

"To leave your wife and children alone at home, abandoned?" She shook her head. "Gambling and defending the Crown are different, Major, but the end is the same. Your wife shall be left to fret and manage as best she can without you. To wonder if you will come back."

"I intend to take you with me to India, Sophia," he said softly.

She almost laughed. "To be abandoned in a foreign country is ten times worse."

"Sweet heaven, Sophia, I have no intention of abandoning you at all, in India or anywhere else. Have I not already proven that?" His outrage echoed in the spare room.

"These were merely games, Major. My aunt wanted to test you, and so you became our butler. I wished to become outrageous, and so we ended up in gaol. Games, Major. They are nothing compared to a lifetime of waiting by the window wondering when a loved one will return." And in what condition, she added silently.

"So you have been testing me," he said. Surprisingly enough, he did not seem to be angry, merely pleased that at last he had solved the puzzle.

She looked away, ashamed to admit to the truth. She had not thought she would torture a suitor to test his constancy, but that was indeed what she had been doing. "I did not mean to," she admitted. "But it seems I have."

He reached out, grasping her chin and pulling her back to face him. "I have not abandoned you, have I? Indeed, here I am sharing a gaol cell with you." His thumb caressed her cheek. "Sophia, I will not leave you alone in India. Neither will our children ever have to care for themselves as you and Geoffrey did. I want you by my side. Always. Wherever the Crown sends me, you shall go as well. Whatever I do, you shall stand beside me. I would not have it any other way."

She looked at him, wishing she could believe him. Indeed, part of her did trust his words. Her mind told her he was an honest man, speaking his heart clearly and openly. But life had a way of interfering. Indeed, her father had died the one time he intended to keep his promise, had fallen off his horse on the way to her birthday celebration. "You would not *intend* to abandon me," she said.

"I came back from the dead because I swore I would. Doesn't that demonstrate the power of my promises?" He wiped away a tear she had not realized was slipping down her cheek. "You are thinking too much, Sophia. For once in your life, relax and trust someone else."

"Trust is not easy to come by."

"I think I have earned a little," he said, dryly gesturing at his gashed body. "These were, after all, earned on your behalf."

"Yes," she said, a smile easing some of the stiffness in her body. "Perhaps you do deserve something." And with that she leaned forward with the wet cloth, intent on cleaning away the blood on his face. But as her fingers found the cut, her gaze found his eyes, and then his lips.

Before she realized what she was doing, her eyes closed and her lips found his.

Their kisses had always before been born of anger and frustration, their passion nearly bruising in its intensity. This time was different. It was slower, sweeter, and infinitely more stirring. Perhaps it was because she felt in control. She could pull away at any moment, but she did not. Instead, she allowed herself to relax into his touch, exploring the changes in his lips, feeling the textures of his face until at last, she opened her mouth.

He teased her with a skill belied by his ragged

breathing, and Sophia found herself responding to him, wanting things she never thought possible. Emotions and sensations swirled through her in a confusing kaleidoscope that she could not sort through.

In the end, she stopped trying, learning to merely enjoy without thought or restraint.

"Oh, Sophia," he moaned as his hands traveled across her body, neither drawing her near nor pushing her away. Instead, he tantalized her, stroking first her neck, then her shoulders and arms, until Sophia was startled to discover his hands on her breasts. It felt natural somehow, the warmth of his palms pressed against her there, as if he weighed her, shaped her, and, most wonderful of all, found her infinitely pleasing.

The thumb of his right hand rolled over her nipple, and she gasped aloud at the shock of sensation that burst across her senses. Yet she did not pull away, but continued to kiss him. She felt his groan of delight reverberate through their joined lips, and then he spoke, his words seeming to caress her as intimately as his hands.

"Oh, Sophia, I have wanted you forever. Please, do not leave me now."

"No," she answered softly, her words coming too fast for her to examine them. "I shall not leave you now."

She felt his hands move. Indeed, she felt all of him, his hands, his lips, and his body. When her dress loosened about her, she was not surprised. Her body was quivering like a taut bow, and all she could think was that it felt wonderful. All of it was so wonderful.

She was not sure what to do, which at one time would have worried her. But not now. Not when his kisses seemed to drain her of all thought. His hands tugged at her clothing, and she found herself helping him, shrugging out of her dress, raising her arms as he removed her chemise, even rolling onto her side so he could pull off the tape that bound her stockings.

The candles were flickering as she felt her breasts spill free of their restrictions, but she saw his eyes glow with hunger. Then she felt the most amazing delight as her naked flesh pressed against his chest. He was warmth and power and triumph, and all she wanted was to suffuse herself with his strength. To feel him wrap around her, to press against her, to be within her.

She heard him groan, the sound both a demand and a question, but she had no answer. Her only thought was to touch him everywhere. She ran her hands over his body, caressing and feeling him as best she could. She tugged at his clothing without realizing what she did.

He placed his hands over hers, stilling her. "Sophia, we should not . . ." he said, but she quickly kissed his words away.

"Don't speak," she whispered.

"But honor demands—" He would have said more, but she stopped him with another kiss, while her hands at last worked his breeches free.

When she raised herself off his lips, she whispered into his ear. "I don't want words." Into her mind flashed an image, that moment in her ritual when she'd flung away her corset, the hated restriction lifting high into the air before it disappeared forever.

How much more liberating was this? How much more freedom could a woman desire than to feel a man stroking her breasts, pressing her down into a cot while he murmured sweet words of wonder into her ear? The major was doing all of those things to her and more. He was taking her breast into his mouth, suckling there while she writhed in delight. He was stroking her thighs and making her feel things she didn't know she could.

Then there was no more thought, only glorious sensation as his naked legs brushed up and along the inside of her thighs. She arched against him, aching, hungering, needing something she could not name while he kissed her face, her neck, her breasts.

"Sophia," he moaned. "My Sophia."

Then his hands slid lower, pulling at her waist, settling on her hips. Her legs were spread and he positioned himself between them. Looking up into Anthony's eyes, she saw such emotion that she could not speak. But he did. He had one last word for her. One word that echoed throughout the room.

"Mine."

Then he thrust into her.

She felt herself stiffen. One thought flew through her mind. It wasn't phrased in words, only in a fleeting glimpse of panic born of the pain. But then it was buried in a glorious tide of other emotions, wondrous sensations.

She felt him move, sliding inside her, filling her, making her larger, bolder, stronger with each powerful stroke. Soon she was pushing toward him with each of his thrusts, her staccato cries a distant echo of the need that clamored within her.

Something was happening. Something was building. Something she wanted was right there, and yet still out of reach. He continued to thrust into her, through her, like lightning, flashing fire and beauty with every push. He was bringing her to that thing she wanted.

It was right there.

Soon.

Now.

Joy!

Chapter Ten

Anthony woke quickly. It was an old army habit he found hard to break. Every morning he woke instantly, his senses alert, cataloging his every impression as his mind sorted them into a coherent order.

He lay on a straw pallet in a dank, musty gaol. His back hurt and his leg ached, but he was filled with a wondrous contentment that warmed him inside and out. And that, no doubt, was due to the single sensation that overrode all of his other senses: the feel of Sophia, pressed intimately to his side.

He opened his eyes and turned carefully so as not to disturb her. He saw nothing. There was no light, their candles having long since burnt out. But still, in his mind's eye, he saw it all as clearly as if daylight illuminated the room. Her skin would be like fine porcelain, but it was warm, not cool. Her face would be relaxed in sleep, her golden hair spread like a halo around her. Her lips would no longer be kiss-swollen, but perfect dusky rose bows that would forever tempt him to forget reason, honor, everything so long as she was his.

Last night, he had meant to resist her. His goal had been to tempt her, not take her. But now that the deed was done, he could not regret it. Indeed, how could he ever regret something so beautiful it had literally overwhelmed him?

She had been like a living flame in his arms. He always knew that when he finally coaxed her into releasing her rigid control, her passions would surprise him. But last night he had been more than surprised. Thunderstruck was a better word. Astounded. Enraptured.

She had been incredible.

And he loved her.

Anthony leaned down, about to drop a light kiss on Sophia's forehead, when his last thought returned full force.

He loved her.

He froze.

He loved her?

His hand trembled, and suddenly he collapsed backward on the pallet. Of course. Why had he not seen it before? He had told himself he wanted to marry her because of her lineage, her regal carriage, and because of the damned wager. Because she would be a significant asset in the foreign service. Because he'd been grateful for her visits during his convalescence. Because he had long since guessed at the passion that simmered underneath her cool exterior, which meant they would have lifelong enjoyment in their marriage bed. Because he found her wonderful and beautiful and . . .

Love?

He had not even considered that.

He lay beside the woman he would marry, suddenly aware that he adored her.

The thought was so stunning, so literally breathstopping, that he could hardly believe it.

He curled up behind Sophia, drawing her deeper into his arms. He wanted to tell her, could not wait to share the news with her. But the words would not come. The thought was too new, the feelings too potent to express. He would find a way to tell her. A special, romantic moment to reveal himself. For now, he would be content to hold her, to feel her luscious body pressed against his own.

He loved her.

Smiling to himself, Anthony slept.

Sophia awoke slowly, her body languorous, her thoughts slowed by a rosy contentment that seemed to pervade her every pore.

She was happy.

The sensation was so odd, she forced herself to wake fully and examine it. As her consciousness pulled together into intelligence, sensations began to flood her thoughts—some remembered, some actual.

She was undressed, her body uncomfortable in small ways, but mostly, she felt warm and cozy, enfolded by a man—by Anthony. The room was completely dark, but last night, there had been candlelight as the two of them . . .

Her body flushed with the memory as she felt both stirred and horrified by her actions.

They had made love with glorious abandon.

She had surrendered. She had traded in her goal, her dream of freedom, for one night of bliss in his arms. And such bliss! Never had she imagined lovemaking could be so amazing, so full of everything wonderful and joyous.

And yet, now it was morning, and her breath caught in her throat as the ramifications of last night slammed into her. They had *made love*. She was a tainted woman.

She had no choice but to marry him. And in that marriage she would lose everything.

Suddenly shaking, she scrambled out of bed, frantically searching for her clothing, her heart beating painfully in her chest. Anthony—No, the major. She must think of him formally. The major sat upright. She could not see him, but she heard his muffled gasp and the creak of the bed as his weight shifted.

"Sophia?"

"Do not light a candle!" she cried.

"But—"

"Do not!" She was on her hands and knees, patting the floor as she tried to find her clothing. But it was nowhere to be found. Nowhere! "Oh, where are my clothes?" she cried.

"Right here," came his disembodied response. "Right at the foot of the bed."

She scrambled forward only to bang her shin painfully. The major no doubt would have cursed a blue streak at the sudden bolts of pain, but she merely clenched her jaw.

"Sophia? Are you all right?"

She felt a hand touch her face, and she recoiled instantly. He had touched her last night with such tenderness, done such marvelous things to her body. Sophia bit her cheek, slamming down equally hard on her wayward thoughts. She could not remember those things he'd done if she wanted to be free. She would not remember.

"Sophia!" His voice was becoming alarmed. "What is the matter?"

"N-nothing," she gasped as she finally, miraculously, found her dress. "I . . . I merely knocked my shin against the . . . the . . ." She could not even say so simple a word.

"The bed?"

"Yes."

She heard him shift again, and she scrambled backward, away from the pallet, her dress clutched against her breasts. He had touched her last night. He had kissed her.

"Let me light a candle. There are a few we have not burned."

"No!" Her voice echoed in the chamber, reverberating back to her until it finally faded, leaving a harsher silence than before. "I . . ." She took a deep breath. "Please, allow me to dress myself first."

"But sweeting, I saw all of you last night." His voice trailed away, the note of hurt clear.

She let the silence remain, uncertain what to say. Uncertain, even, what to think. Last night had been . . . Had been . . . It had been everything and more, and yet she could not shake this feeling that she had surrendered, that she had given up everything to the major. There was nothing left for her but endless years as his wife, following him around the world like a lapdog. Worse yet, she might be left alone in England to stare at the walls, counting the lonely hours until his return.

She swiftly donned her gown, the rustle of fabric loud in the stillness.

"Are you suitably attired?" the major asked, his voice dry with sarcasm.

"Yes."

"Excellent." She heard the harsh brush of the lucifer and then the steady glow as the taper caught. And there stood the major, bathed in its warm light. Unabashedly naked.

"Major!"

"Last night you called me Anthony."

Sophia swallowed, willing herself to look away from his glorious form.

He crossed to her, lifting her chin, urging her to meet his gaze. "Sophia, what is it? Why are you acting this way?"

"I . . . I . . ." What could she say?

"You are crying!" She felt him brush away the tears, but for the life of her, she could not understand where the moisture had come from. She never cried.

"Uh . . ." Why could she not think of something intelligent to say?

"Are you hurt?"

She blinked, wondering to what he referred. Then she recalled the momentary pain of last night, the breaching of her maidenhead. "N—no. No, I am fine."

"But then—"

"Please. Please, stop. I need to think." She spun away from him, intending to escape down the corridor, but he caught her, holding her wrist tightly.

"Do not run from me, Sophia. Please. Not today."

"But—"

"Not this morning." His voice was hard and laced with a pain she could hear even through her own conflicting riot of emotion. She swallowed and nodded. Then, slowly, he released her.

They stood there, staring at each other. She was rigidly stiff, her muscles clenched so tight she thought the slightest movement might shatter her. And he, still naked, stood poised as if ready to fight, to spring to attack or defend at a moment's notice.

Into this tense silence came noise from above. Sophia lifted her head, her gaze drawn to the ceiling where the sound of many feet shifted and moved.

"They will be coming for us soon," said the major, his voice curiously flat.

She nodded. "I—I suppose you will tell them we must marry."

He lifted his chin as if daring her to disagree. "Yes."

She swallowed, and something within her gave way. It was as though a spring wound too tight finally broke, leaving her fragmented and disjointed. Her knees went weak, but suddenly he was beside her, helping her to sit on the edge of the bed.

"We will marry then," she said dully. "I cannot refuse. Not after last night." She pressed her hand against her lips, remembering, then abruptly, she shrugged. "You said yourself there was no other way to save even a modicum of my respectability."

She looked up at him, her emotions almost entirely drained, but as she gazed at him, she saw his jaw clench in anger. It was only then that she realized he had not joined her on the bed. He stood above her, glaring at her as though she were evil incarnate.

"Major?"

"My name is Anthony," he ground out.

She nodded. "Anthony, then."

Dropping to his knees before her, he searched her face with his eyes. "Why do you fight this, Sophia? Why is marriage to me so terrible a fate? You were not unhappy in my arms. Last night—"

"I know what we did last night," she interrupted.

"So, why do you look so stricken? Is it because of my leg? Am I that repulsive to you?"

Sophia shook her head, words forming on her lips without her conscious volition. "You are not the least bit repulsive. Even burning with fever, almost dead, you were the most handsome man I ever met."

"Then what is it?"

She looked down at her hands, wondering if she could explain. "You have stripped me of all control in this matter. I refused you the first time—"

"You agreed in the hospital!" he interrupted.

"I eased a dying man's mind. I had no idea you would recover. And then, when I explained it all, you invaded my household as my butler. I refused you again, and we ended up in gaol."

"That was your doing," he snapped.

"Yes, I had a hand in it. But you have known from your first moment in Staffordshire that I had no wish to marry you. Yet here I am, despite all my intentions, about to become betrothed. It is exactly what I feared."

"What? To marry a man who—" He cut off his words abruptly, and she wondered what he was about to say. Instead he finished, "Who would care for you, cherish you for the rest of your life?"

"A man who would strip all control from me. Who will make my decisions and force me to go his way whether I wish to or not. And then . . ." She cut off her words.

"And then what?" he demanded.

She didn't continue, but he did, guessing correctly at her thoughts.

"You still think I will abandon you. You think I will tire of you, leaving you alone." He dropped down on one knee. "You trusted me last night."

She looked away, shame making her cheeks burn. "I suppose now I am a wanton to boot." Her words were for herself, but he seemed to take them as a physical blow, recoiling from her. She looked at him, wishing she could make him understand. "I am not angry with you," she said. "You are correct that I have created my own problem, so to speak. Now I must accept the consequences."

"Made your own bed, and now you must lie in it?" he asked dryly as he regained his feet.

She felt her cheeks flame. "Well, yes."

"So you see marriage to me as your punishment."

She took a deep breath. "You are putting a meaning on it I do not intend."

"Am I really?" She could hear the anger in his voice, but even so she could not deny his words. He had forced this situation on her, and now there was no help for her anywhere.

She looked away.

"Sophia." His voice was raw, but his intonation was flat, and his every word still held the note of command. "I have never forced myself on any woman."

"I never said—"

"And I will certainly not take an unwilling bride."

"But—"

"Listen to me!"

Sophia obediently shut her mouth.

"I will ask you for the last time. Forget thoughts of your reputation, of the people upstairs, of everything. Simply search your own heart. Do you wish to marry me?"

"No."

The answer came out quickly, a reflex before she could stop it or even hear the part of her heart that said something entirely different. And then, when she did hear it, it was too late.

"Very well." The major walked stiffly away, pulling on his breeches with crisp, military efficiency.

"Major?"

"Do not be concerned, Sophia. I will not bother you again."

"But—"

He spun around, his eyes glaring at her through the gloom. "I said, do not be concerned. I will take care of everything." And with that comment, he suddenly stooped down and grabbed their bottle of brandy and raised it like a club.

Sophia gasped, unsure what he meant to do. She did not move away, knowing he would not hurt her, even when he brought the neck down with shattering force against the side of the bed. She flinched at the sound that was deafening within their little room. Still, it did not totally overcome the loud rumble of the people upstairs.

"They will be coming for us soon," he reminded her curtly.

Sophia nodded, her eyes still on the jagged bottle in

his hand. "What do you intend to do with that?"

With his eyes still fixed on hers, he turned the cut edge toward himself. Sophia slowly stood, unsure and worried. His face was so hard, as if he steeled himself. Then, to her horror, the major quickly slashed the cut edge across his chest. Blood welled up along the wound, bright red even in the muted candlelight.

"Anthony!" She jumped to him, grabbing her skirts to staunch the blood.

"No!" he said firmly, grabbing her hands and roughly pushing her away. "Let it bleed."

"But . . ." Tears burned in her eyes.

He took a deep breath, and she watched the cut well rich red down his shirt. Sophia bit her lip. It was a physical ache to see him hurt and not be allowed to help him, to touch him.

"Please," she whispered. "You are bleeding."

"Aye," he agreed. Then, suddenly, he pressed the bottom of the bottle into her hand. "Hold on to that as if your life depended on it."

"Anthony—"

Another voice interrupted them, calling out from the other room. "Come on up, you two. We's all waitin' t' 'ear." It was the constable, come to take them upstairs. Faster than Sophia thought possible, the elderly man rounded the corner to the bedroom, and all opportunity for private conversation was lost.

"Major," she whispered.

"Get me out of here," he snapped at the constable, "and away from that she-devil."

Sophia bit her lip to hold back a sob. If the venom in his voice had been real, he could have poisoned the whole of Staffordshire. As it was, she seemed to be the only one who shriveled inside. She looked to the major, but he had already turned his back on her.

She did the only thing she could, what she always did

when she hurt. She simply closed her mind to the pain, drew herself upright, and stared down at the world through a numbing wall of bitter cold.

She became the Ice Queen.

The major preceded her and the constable up the stairs, and Sophia was forced to watch him limp along, practically dragging his weak leg while his arm held tight to his bleeding chest. She did not know if he was truly in pain or merely exaggerating his injuries as part of some devious plan. Whatever the reason, there was nothing she could do about it.

He had made it clear she was to say nothing to him at all.

Sophia should not have been surprised by the bawdy comments that followed them as they entered the baron's front room, but she was. How could so many people have so much interest in her affairs? Good Lord, the room was even more packed than the day before! And this time, there were as many women as men.

She and Anthony were led to the same spot they had occupied yesterday, in the dead center of the cheering, jeering mass of people. Fortunately for her own piece of mind, she saw Aunt Agatha immediately, standing on the near edge of the mob, a tranquil spot of beribboned lavender. Unfortunately, her relative looked pale and nervous as she literally shredded her favorite lace handkerchief. Still, the dear lady managed an encouraging smile that Sophia did her best to return.

Then it was as if everything occurred to someone else, and Sophia was merely a distant spectator, watching a play.

"Well, Major?" boomed the baron rather abruptly. "Have you come to a decision? Will you wed the lady?"

"Absolutely not!" he said, his voice carrying loudly to the back of the room. Then he straightened, giving the baron a clear view of his bloody chest and hand.

There was a moment's stunned silence, then the room erupted into sound as seemingly a thousand voices all debated and cursed and laughed at them both. In front of them, the baron was clearly taken aback. "But . . . but . . ." he stammered. "But she is a lady, and you have spent the night with her!"

Anthony stepped forward as he turned toward the crowd, giving everyone a good look at his bloodied shirt. "And what good did that do for me? She held me off with a damned broken bottle! This morning, when I thought to catch her unawares, she cut me!"

The response of the crowd was nearly deafening. The women cheered Sophia's courage while the men laughed uproariously at Anthony's plight. It was not until Sophia realized many were staring at her that she remembered the broken bottle still clutched in her hand. She would have dropped it then and there, except one look about her told her that she had best keep it handy. Some of the men looked fit to be tied.

"Ye mean a major o' 'Is Majesty's army can't even diddle a woman?" jeered a man to Sophia's right.

Anthony stiffened, taking one angry limp forward. "She is a hellcat with her skirts nailed to the floor. A whole battalion of the Hussars could not prevail against her."

The entire room erupted after that remark, but Sophia could only cringe at the derision in his voice. She understood his plan now. Anthony was trying to save her reputation as much as possible. She had told him that she had no wish to marry, and he was now doing his best to give her that opportunity. At the cost of his own honor and reputation.

She could not have been more touched.

Yet there was nothing she could do to thank him except stand clutching a broken bottle in the center of a screaming mob. Meanwhile, the baron was moving forward, grabbing on to Anthony's arm as he spoke.

"Do you mean to tell me that the lady is still pure?"

"A glacier could not be more pure!" spat the major.

Sophia flinched—inside. Outwardly, she merely straightened her shoulders. She understood his intentions, but that still did not keep his words from inflicting pain. She had never wanted to be the Ice Queen, but somehow she always seemed to return to that persona.

"Well," sputtered the baron as the furor died down. "I suppose that is all, then. You are free to go, Lady Sophia," he added with a rather confused bow.

Sophia did not know how to respond. She was still too numb from the entire experience to comprehend it all. But then Aunt Agatha was across the room and enfolding her in a mass of ribbons and furbelows, and Sophia was burying her face in the woman's arms.

"Aunt Agatha," she whispered, unsure whether it was a sob or a cry for help.

"Hush, dear, we shall sort this out later. Come along now."

But before she could leave, the other occupants of the room had to clear from the area, and they showed no interest in doing so. Sophia was forced to stand ramrod straight as she listened to one after another coarse man make vulgar comments about her person.

"That 'un's as cold as a witch's tit, she is."

"Aye," cackled a woman. "Have t' be t' refuse the likes of 'im! 'E can come to me bed whenever 'e likes."

Sophia heard the words as distant rumbles, whispers of nonsense that could not touch her. All she had to do was stand still, her expression distant, her body regal. That was all. Soon, it would be over.

Except part of her did hear. Part of her heard everything and remembered similar words voicing the same sentiment, only phrased more politely. Jeers spoken in

London about the Ice Queen. The cold woman without a heart. The frozen witch best left alone.

She had thought to escape, but the words had followed her. Just as the major had.

She could not escape. Would never escape.

Except for one night, one glorious night when she had been alive and fulfilled, and joyously, wondrously happy. The night she had spent in Anthony's arms.

But now that was over, and there was nothing left. She had no intelligence to rescue her. No ritual to redeem her. No man to love her. So she did the only thing she could.

For the first time in her life, she willed herself to faint.

Anthony heard the jeers. Indeed, how could he not? He maintained his pretense of being offended, a thwarted suitor. It was an easy role to play, since he was indeed thwarted.

He told himself that he had made his best attempt to win the lady. He had done all that was humanly possible, and still she had refused. Some events God did not intend, and apparently his marriage to Sophia Rathburn was one of them.

So he told himself.

But the memory of last night still burned in his mind. He recalled her passionate kisses, her ardor, her undeniable hunger for him. She did not feel indifferent to him. She could not.

And yet she did.

He had lost. And at the same time, he'd lost a thousand guineas and his diplomatic post. Anthony clenched his jaw. It was time to return to London. He could lick his wounds in peace there, perhaps save his career. No doubt he could find some insipid girl to wed, then be off across the water to India.

Without Sophia.

The thought was a bayonet wound, piercing and deep.

Then he heard it. It was only one of many ugly comments, but this one stuck in his mind.

"Wait a couple o' months an' we'll see 'ow pure she is. 'Er belly'll be round, you mark my words."

Sophia's belly round with his child?

The thought was both glorious and terrifying all at once. He turned to Sophia, wondering if she had heard the comment. He noticed her unnatural pallor, saw her stiffened spine and haughty expression. What was she thinking? Was she as flustered as he? Excited at the thought of carrying his child?

He did not have to wait long for an answer.

Within moments of the woman's words, Sophia fainted dead away.

Chapter Eleven

She woke with a cool compress across her forehead. She felt warm and comfortable, but a strange ache of emptiness seemed to surround her. She didn't want to examine it, but instinctively curled away from the thought. The feeling. From everything.

"Come along, dear. Wake up."

It was Aunt Agatha. Which meant she must be in her own bed. Indeed, when she finally, reluctantly opened her eyes, Sophia saw the familiar pink curtains illuminated by the same afternoon sunshine that filled her bedroom every day in Staffordshire. But somehow, it did not seem like home. Though the featherbed and Aunt Agatha's smiling face seemed familiar, they appeared much too cheery for her mood.

She rolled over and buried her head away from the brightness, away from the forced beauty. Away. She would never come out again.

"You might as well roll over and look at me because I am not leaving until you do."

Sophia stiffened at the reproving note in her aunt's voice. "I am not at home, Aunt Agatha. To anyone. Even you."

"Too bad," her aunt snapped. "This is my home, not yours. Now, you will speak with me or I shall be forced to tell all those people downstairs that you will see them directly."

Sophia shifted, poking her head out from under the pillow. "People? What people?" Could it be Anthony had changed his mind?

"Friends of yours, so they say. From London. Come to comfort you in your hour of need."

Sophia winced. "Come to gawk, you mean."

"Yes." Sophia could hear the disgusted note in her aunt's voice and most heartily agreed with the sentiment. But it did not prevent her aging relative from speaking in an excessively stern voice. "Now, will you talk with me or shall I bring them upstairs? A Countess of Ashbury seems most anxious, as she is your dear, dear friend."

Sophia groaned into the mattress and wished she could hide in it for the next decade. "Lord, not Drusilla. Anything but Drusilla."

"She is quite determined."

Sophia waited, but her aunt would not comment further. Neither did she leave. Eventually, Sophia had no choice but to push herself into a sitting position and regard Agatha with a dark look. "You have not invited them to stay, have you?"

"Nonsense. We have only enough room for two guests. The rest have taken up lodging at the Stag's Heart Inn."

Sophia almost asked who had been fortunate enough to manage an invitation to their house, but then she stopped herself. There was not a soul she wished to see.

Even were it the King of England himself, she would tell him she had the migraine.

"Talk, young lady."

Sophia searched her aunt's face for a glimmer of sympathy, some weakness that would allow her to delay this moment of reckoning. But there was no quarter in Agatha's expression, and Sophia sighed, knowing she would not get any peace until she gave in. She folded her hands primly in front of her and eyed her aunt. "Very well. What do you wish to discuss?"

"Exactly what happened. And in great detail. I trusted the major, you know. He seemed quite smitten with you. I cannot believe this betrayal. I am most disappointed with the man. Most disappointed. Now, tell me, what exactly did happen?"

Sophia blinked at her aunt. "What makes you think that it did not happen exactly as the major explained this morning?"

Agatha folded her plump arms, her expression bordering on the insulted. "I am not a peagoose, Sophia. The major does not strike me as a man who lets a simple piece of broken glass keep him from what he wants."

"But—"

"And I have never seen you hurt anything so much as a fly, much less a man. You could never have cut the major, no matter what he did."

Sophia did not know whether to be offended or not. "My virtue was threatened," she said in stiff accents.

"Piffle."

Sophia stared at her aunt, but the woman glared right back. And, in the end, it was her aunt who was stronger. Sophia crumbled, her spine sinking back into the pillows as she released a heavy sigh. "You are right, of course. I have never been so frightened in my whole life as when he cut himself."

"But *why* would he do it?"

She blinked, suddenly appalled to feel tears slipping down her cheeks. "He did it to save my reputation," she whispered. And then Sophia Rathburn, Ice Queen, began to cry in earnest.

The sad truth about tears is that as much as one might wish, one cannot sustain that level of heart-wrenching emotion for long. Especially when one is of an analytical bent and has absolutely no idea why the tears are flowing so freely. Or so Sophia told herself before a half hour had expired. Though she had never in her life cried so long or so hard, eventually the tears stopped, and she was left drained, exhausted, and no more enlightened than before.

"What is wrong with me?" she asked her pillow.

"You do not know?" responded Aunt Agatha. In truth, Sophia had not even realized the woman was still with her. She wanted to be alone with her misery. But then she felt her dear aunt's hand gently pat her shoulder, and Sophia had to admit she was grateful for her presence. She needed insight, clarity, from an older and wiser woman. So she turned, looking up at the person she most adored.

"Tell me what to do," she whispered.

Agatha's hand slipped from Sophia's shoulder to gently pat her niece's cheek. "You think on it, my dear. I am sure it will come to you soon enough."

The odd note in her aunt's voice prodded Sophia into finally reaching out. She grasped her aunt's arm, tugging on it in her desperation. "Aunt—"

Gong.

Both women started at the sound, but it was Agatha who sighed, her lavender ribbons fluttering in dismay. "Oh, dear. There is the dinner gong, and I am not even dressed appropriately."

Sophia clutched her aunt's arm even tighter. "But—"

"Hush, now," the older woman said as she gently disengaged her niece's fingers. "It cannot be helped. All those wretched guests will just have to accept me as I am. After all, I did not invite them here."

Sophia blanched, her tears momentarily forgotten in a wash of shame. It was not only her own life in such chaos. She had managed to thoroughly disrupt her aunt's once-peaceful home as well. "I am so dreadfully sorry for all this mess."

Aunt Agatha blinked; then her eyes began to twinkle with a mischievous smile. "Nonsense, my dear," she exclaimed as she rose from the bed. "This is the most entertainment I have had in years. In fact, no doubt most of the county feels the same."

Sophia could do no more than groan, but her aunt absently patted her shoulder before moving to the door, her ribbons trailing away behind her.

"Try to rest," Aunt Agatha called over her shoulder. "All will look better tomorrow."

The morning dawned disgustingly beautiful. Sophia's first admittedly cowardly thought was to hide in bed for another week at least. Unfortunately, she knew her aunt's unwanted guests would not leave until they had actually discussed her trauma ad nauseam. Therefore, for the sake of her aunt's limited means, she rang for Mary and made herself get dressed.

Forcing herself to leave her room, however, was almost beyond her abilities.

Fortunately, Drusilla was at hand to push her the rest of the way.

"Good morning, my poor dear," the shrew exclaimed as she burst into Sophia's room. "Ah, I see you are dressed already. Good, good, though I am afraid that shade of blue is not quite right for your face. It brings out the smudges under your eyes. Ah, well, never mind. We are late for breakfast, and you will just have to do. Besides, after what you have been through, it is no wonder you look fagged."

As she spoke, Drusilla pushed Mary aside and toured the room, picking up this and that, inspecting everything as she moved. Sophia merely stared at her, noting that the woman's dark hair was a perfect complement to her flawless skin. The two had come out together, and once another debutante, Amanda Wyndham, had disappeared, Drusilla and Sophia had constantly fought for the status of reigning beauty.

At first, Sophia had not cared a whit. In fact, she would have been happy to relinquish the spot to anyone, but Drusilla had been grasping, manipulative, spiteful, and every other wicked name she could think of. By the end of the first month, Sophia had entered wholeheartedly into the rivalry.

But then Drusilla married brilliantly, and Sophia began to see the emptiness that filled the London ballrooms. Drusilla had obediently begun breeding, and Sophia had commenced the retreat into herself that earned her the title Ice Queen.

Now, five years later, she could hardly care what Drusilla or anyone else thought of the color of her gown. In fact, she could hardly believe she had ever thought Drusilla worthy of a second thought, much less a rivalry.

"Good morning, Drusilla," Sophia said wearily as Mary began brushing out her hair. "You look pretty as always."

Drusilla stiffened, her gaze narrowing. "Pretty? My dear, one does not call a married woman pretty."

"Hmm? Oh. I am terribly sorry. You look divine." She purposely made her voice flat and weary, hoping Drusilla would take the insult and leave. If she was truly lucky, Drusilla would be so insulted, she would flee Staffordshire entirely.

Contrary to the bone, Drusilla chose instead to supplant the maid at the dresser. "Goodness, you cannot wear your hair like that. Whatever possessed you to cut it so short?"

"It was part of a ritual."

Drusilla paused. "A what?"

Sophia merely shook her head, too tired to explain.

Suddenly, Drusilla was all hands as she fussed about. "Go, go," she said as she waved Mary away. "Let me do it."

The maid hesitated, but Sophia nodded, allowing her to escape. She would not, however, allow Drusilla to touch her blond curls. The shrew might take scissors to them. "I think I shall wear it down," she said as she rose from her chair.

"No, no!" cried Drusilla as she pushed Sophia back down. "We mustn't leave just yet. Please, sit down and tell me all about it."

Sophia merely blinked at Drusilla's reflection in the mirror. "About what?"

"Why, what happened at Baron Riggs's! Did Major Wyclyff attack you? Did you truly defend yourself with a wine bottle?"

"Drusilla—"

"You must know that you have been my dear friend for years. Surely you realize we can discuss anything!"

Sophia allowed herself her first smile in days. "Of course I realize exactly what I can tell you, my dear. But, right now, I am absolutely famished." And with that she straightened her gown and made for the door.

"Wait!"

Sophia did not wait. The threat of an intimate tête-a-tête with Drusilla had her descending the stairs and walking into the breakfast parlor in record time.

Even so, she took a moment to steel herself to confront more than one overly curious guest as she crossed into the sunny room. What she had not prepared herself for was the sight of the major, calmly eating eggs at her breakfast table.

"Anthony!" The exclamation was one of shock, and she instantly regretted it. With one word, she had informed everyone in the room that she and the major used Christian names. And there were a lot of people at the table who were gossips.

Just inside her peripheral vision, she counted five of her London "friends." She noted Percy immediately. No doubt he was the reason for her current overabundance of visitors from London. Beside him sat Miss Lydia Smyth—his intended—and her mother. Next to the older woman sat Drusilla's husband, and beside him sat Reginald Peters, Lord Kyle, her neighbor and sometime good friend. Aunt Agatha fluttered near the sideboard, looking less than well.

Sophia barely spared them a thought as the major stood up from his chair.

Sweet Heaven, she had forgotten how good he looked in his uniform. His shoulders never seemed so broad, his carriage never so impressive as when he dressed for the occasion. Add to that the warm sun that seemed to bathe him in a special golden aura, and he was truly magnificent.

She wanted nothing more than to step into his arms and tell him without words just how handsome a man he was. But she could not do that. Indeed, she could not seem to do anything but stare at him. She knew every curve of his face, every muscle in his body—intimately. And yet all she could do was take it in again, filling her hungry eyes with the sight of him.

"Lady Sophia," he said stiffly.

She blinked and swallowed.

"I apologize for intruding on your breakfast in such a way."

"I am afraid we insisted, Sophia, dear," drawled Lord

Kyle as he came leisurely to his feet. "Can't starve the man, you know. Especially when he came most particularly to speak with you. And in all his colors, too."

"Oh, do stop, Reg. You are beyond boring today."

Lord Kyle blinked, startled by her curt tone. Sophia was a bit startled herself. She had never snapped like that at anyone in her life. But she did not have time to dwell on it as her thoughts all centered on the major.

If only she could think of something to say instead of gaping at him like a fish. But her body seemed unwilling to perform the simplest of tasks. She stood stupidly, staring at him, reading his body as she might a Minerva novel. She took in the way he favored his injured leg. She noted the tight set to his shoulders and the lines of fatigue that creased his face. He must not have slept well last night.

Perhaps he had been plagued by the same memories she had.

At that thought, her face began to flush, her entire body burning with . . . with . . . what? It was part embarrassment, part something else. Something she might label longing or pleasure—or perhaps hunger.

She was not ready to think such thoughts, so she merely swallowed and locked them away. After all her years in London, she was quite adept at the process.

Then Anthony spoke, his rich voice low and husky even as he obviously strived for a formal tone. "Lady Sophia, I wonder if I might have a word with you in private."

"Absolutely not!" cried Drusilla as she stepped forward into the room, placing possessive hands across Sophia's shoulders. "The dear girl is much too distraught to spend *any* time with you, much less time alone. I am afraid whatever you have to say must be said here. We are, after all, Sophia's dearest friends. She has no secrets from us."

Sophia did not so much as blink. She merely glanced

behind the major at the broad expanse of garden and lush greenery just outside the window. Without a second thought, she shrugged Drusilla's hands from her shoulders, then moved for the outside door. "I believe I shall take a walk," she said firmly. "Major, you may accompany me, if you wish."

"But my dear," came Lord Kyle's amused drawl, "do you not fear for your virtue?"

"I shall simply cry out. I am sure I can count on you, my dear friends, to remain within earshot." She made sure the sarcasm fairly dripped in her voice but did not take the leisure to remain and view their reactions. Still, she managed to get a glimpse of Percy's flushed face as she swept from the room.

As expected, the major followed after. As soon as she was out of the room, she moderated her pace so that he could catch up to her.

"Anthony—" she began.

"Not until we are outside."

She nodded and pressed her lips together.

Though she did not say anything, her mind was whirling. Yesterday, she had thought him completely out of her life, and yet here he was again. Rather than feeling annoyed at the intrusion, she was unaccountably cheered. It was a truly odd sensation, and one that she would have to examine more closely later.

They rounded a bend decorated with Aunt Agatha's clematis, and Anthony stopped walking and turned to address her. "I shall make this short."

"Anthony—"

"I realize you have as little wish to speak with me as I with you, but it occurred to me that I made an error in judgment yesterday."

Sophia blinked. Did he mean when they made love? Or when he publicly swore he wanted nothing to do with her? Oh, why did her thoughts insist on whirling when all she wished was for some clear thinking?

Heedless of her turmoil, the major took a deep breath and continued. "Have you thought that perhaps you might be with child?"

Sophia gasped. "A child!" The words came out as a startled whisper, but it seemed to echo in her mind. A baby? The major's baby! Her hand found her belly and she bit her lip, not knowing what to think. On the one hand, she felt an overwhelming sensation of terror. To be pregnant would upset all her carefully laid plans of a peaceful spinsterhood. Which was what she wanted, wasn't it?

On the other hand, he was speaking of a tiny child to cherish and raise. What could be more joyful? Especially if it was a little boy who looked like his father, with dark brown curls and a twinkle of mischief in his eyes.

"I see you had not thought of this." The major's tone was curt, effectively damping much of Sophia's enthusiasm.

"No," she said slowly. "It had not occurred to me."

"Well," he continued, his voice excruciatingly dry, "I have had all night to ponder the possibility."

So, Sophia thought sadly, he had not been tormented by the same erotic dreams as she.

Before she could think of an appropriate comment, Anthony took her by the arms, swinging her around to face him fully. "I will not allow my child to be raised as a bastard."

Sophia felt herself straighten with horror. "Absolutely not!" No child of hers would be so branded.

The major nodded, as if he had expected as much. "Very well. Then we will be forced to wed." He did not seem at all pleased by the thought, and Sophia found her spirits sinking dreadfully fast.

She frowned, staring hard at him, wishing she understood his thoughts. Unfortunately, the major was as unreadable as ever, so she eventually turned away, curling her hands protectively over her belly. "Are we not getting ahead of ourselves? There is nothing to suggest I am with child." Nothing but a tiny flutter of hope quivering within her.

"When should be your next course?"

She blushed at such frank speech, but it did not stop her from answering. "Two weeks. Or perhaps a little sooner."

He nodded, the movement as crisp as a salute. "A fortnight it is, then."

She looked up, squaring her shoulders as she faced him fully. "What do you mean?"

"I have some business in London, but I shall keep my man here. You may contact him at the inn whatever occurs."

Sophia took a hesitant step forward, then stopped, uncertain what she was doing. She had believed her thoughts in turmoil when he appeared this morning, but that was nothing to what she was experiencing now. She felt completely lost in a world that would not settle for one minute.

"Sophia!"

She had not even realized her knees had weakened until he was beside her, gently guiding her to a stone bench. When she felt the solid granite beneath her, she looked down at her hands and spoke to them, focusing on the tight clench of her fingers rather than the man to her left. "I am sorry. It is just that everything moves so fast. I cannot seem to catch my breath."

"I know what you mean," he agreed dryly. Then, with a tenderness belied by his gruff manner, he touched her face. His fingers were callused where they caressed her cheek, but Sophia could not imagine a gentler touch. "You were correct," he said. "We are rushing things. Many go months, even years, without conceiving a child."

There it was again. The word. Child. His child. She began to smile, looking up into his handsome face. "We are worrying overmuch. In two weeks, we shall see that there was no cause for concern."

He stiffened, and she felt his withdrawal though she could not understand the reason. There was no time to ponder as he abruptly straightened and looked to the sky. "It is time I left," he said.

She understood his underlying meaning and felt her hands tighten reflexively, as if fending off the thought. But she could not ward it off. "You are going to London," she said. "You will be looking for another wife." Though the words felt leaden in her mouth, she worked hard to keep her voice light.

"No." He shifted so that even her downcast eyes could see his formal stance. He might have been facing a court-martial for all the stiffness of his carriage. "I shall not look yet. Not until we know for sure."

She let her gaze drift away, seeing the glorious beauty of the summer that surrounded her, knowing it would pass too soon. "The fall Season should start in a few weeks. Perhaps you should think of attending—"

"In two weeks, Sophia. I will think on it then."

She pressed her lips together, knowing he was right. Neither of them could progress with life until they knew what their night together had cost them. She glanced up at his set face. "What shall I do for two weeks? How can I just pretend that nothing has happened?"

Anthony shrugged. "Enjoy your friends."

"They are not my friends!" she snapped. "They are merely here to find fuel for gossip."

He glanced down at her, apparently startled by her sharp tone. "Then send them away."

She sighed. "What would be the use? The gossip will follow wherever I go. Sending them away would only make things worse."

He shifted, his expression suddenly very cold. "I care nothing for what you do, Sophia, so long as you tell no one what truly happened."

She frowned up at him. "Not even Aunt Agatha?" How could she go though these next two weeks without even one confidant? One friend?

"No one, Sophia. No one must guess. If they do, your reputation will be ruined and you will be forced to marry me. You do not want that, do you?"

She bit her lip, then finally stammered the response he seemed to expect. "No, I do not wish for that," she echoed hollowly.

"Then we understand each other." With that, he spun on his heel and left.

Chapter Twelve

Sophia remained where she was, staring at all the summer glory, her thoughts on tiny baby faces, little knitted booties, and sweet, sticky kisses.

"Do I detect from your smile that the major is gone?"

Sophia looked up as Reginald, Lord Kyle, stepped around the greenery. She had not heard him approach, but then she had not heard much of anything beyond the sound of the major's heavy footsteps as he departed. "Hmm? Oh, the major has left for London." She could not keep the depression from her voice.

"Then you are well rid of him."

Sophia did not wish to answer. Her thoughts about the aggravating man were too confusing to focus on. She would much rather think of babies. But she could not do that with Reginald here. "Is there something you wanted?" she asked stiffly.

"Why, merely to see if all was well with you. You have

been gone so long, we began to wonder if the major had spirited you away."

"After publicly denouncing me yesterday? I think not." Her words were heavy, her mood soured with the thought of the entire wretched incident. And now he was gone to London. Soon to find another wife.

"You know," Lord Kyle commented as he took her hand, "I have always stood by you as your friend."

Sophia turned to look at him, a sudden urge for honesty overcoming her usual tact. "No," she said softly. "I had not known."

Lord Kyle stiffened, as if her comment startled him. "Ah. Well, I have. I would like to think you could trust me to assist you, if necessary."

"Hmmm," she answered, her response noncommittal.

"Sophia," he began again, "I have always had the greatest admiration for you. I would not wish the major's schemes to harm you. Please, if you are in some sort of coil, I will do all I can to help you unravel it."

Sophia stood slowly, taking the time to look for the first time at her longtime acquaintance. His black hair and chiseled face were handsome in the dark, brooding way considered fashionable. His clothing was immaculate, his attitude one that reflected wealth and refinement. In short, he was everything the forthright and militaristic Major Anthony Wyclyff was not.

She ought to be attracted to the man. But for some odd reason, she was not. "We have been friends a long time, Reg," she finally said. "But I am not in a coil right now, thank you."

"Then why are you sitting here, staring at the plants? Why have you been attending cockfights and spending nights in gaol?"

"Night, Reg. One night." She took a few steps forward, wandering aimlessly through her aunt's garden. Naturally, he fell into step beside her, too tenacious to be dislodged so easily.

"No matter," he returned. "The entire affair is scandalous in the extreme and most unlike you." He grabbed her arm, turning her to face him. "Why, Sophia, you are the epitome of refinement. My sister is constantly harping on her children to act more like you."

"Oh, Lord," gasped Sophia. "Pray do not make me your model. Not only am I most unfit, but the poor children would hate me within seconds."

He shook his head. "Nonsense. You are everything I consider acceptable."

Sophia twisted in his grasp, her jaw growing slack with astonishment. "Reginald," she gasped, "are you proposing to me?"

For the first time ever, she saw Lord Kyle do something unfashionable. He blushed. It was a fiery red that seemed to burn in his cheeks. Then he released her arm as if she had scalded him. "Well, as to that," he stammered, "I actually considered it. But after five Seasons and your . . . um . . ."

"Lack of a dowry?"

"Your financial assets are not sizable enough. Your breeding is, of course, not to be questioned."

"Of course," she agreed, secretly amused by his unintentional double entendre. In actual fact, her "breeding" was very much in question. It *was* the question.

He continued, "If circumstances were a bit different and your recent scandal—"

"Enough, Reg," she cut him off with an absent wave of her hand. "I understand your position."

He suddenly frowned, once again hurrying to her side. "This is not going nearly as well as it ought."

"I have found that to be the case more and more," she commented, her thoughts still on babies, her feet wandering a twisting, curving path.

"Truly, I wish to be of assistance."

She took a deep breath, absorbing the floral scent in the air, the humid summer wind, even the feel of having a gentleman take hold of her hand, though he was not quite the gentleman she would have chosen. "Where did you go, Reg? You were my friend. My only friend, and suddenly, you were gone. We stopped talking about real things, we stopped really understanding each other." She could not keep the note of hurt from her voice.

He didn't respond at first, then when he did, he spoke haltingly as if searching for words. "I was not aware you needed me. Sophia, you have always seemed so competent. I cannot count the number of men who planned to marry you."

"Boys, Reg, they were boys. And it was because I was as fashionable as your cravat," she said, throwing a dismissive gesture at his dark blue necktie. "Easily picked up. Easily discarded." She stopped walking, turning to face him directly. "You were the only one who did not speak in trivialities, Reg. And then . . ." Her voice trailed away.

"Then I left."

She nodded. "And when you returned, you had changed. You became one of *them*, thinking of nothing but the cut of your coat."

She expected him to defend himself, to loudly proclaim the importance of fashion. Instead, his expression became undeniably sad. "I fell in love."

She gaped at him, startled beyond words. Of all the things she had expected him to say, this was absolutely the last on her list. She searched her memory for a name, a face, anything that would clue her in to the mysterious woman who had captured her friend's heart. Finally, a name clicked in place, bringing with it the memory of large brown eyes and a sweet heart-shaped face. "Miss

Melissa Grant, Blakesly's niece." Then suddenly she frowned. "She ran off with a Scotsman."

Reginald shrugged, becoming suddenly interested in the petals of a tiny pink flower. "Do not throw away love, Sophia. It is too easily lost."

Sophia felt her chest squeeze tight at his words, her heart beating painfully against the restriction. "I am so sorry, Reg," she whispered.

She lay her hand on his shoulder, noting the tension there. But then it eased away, carefully erased as he assumed the breezy attitude she had come to hate. "Ah, but I came here to assist you, my dear. Tell me what I can do."

She knew better than to press him for details of his romance. He would tell her when he chose and not before. So she simply took his arm, strolling about her aunt's garden while silence like a suspended breath reigned about them. Eventually, she spoke, wishing she could say more, but mindful of her promise to Anthony to remain silent. "I am not in a coil, Reg. I am merely waiting."

"Waiting?"

For a baby. She felt her expression shift into a dreamy smile. "I shall know in a fortnight."

He nodded, as if calculating the time. "Most of the scandal should die down by then."

Or rear up anew, she thought with a grin. "Two weeks and my life shall return to some semblance of order," she said firmly.

"Well, then," he quipped, suddenly extending his arm to her, "I shall endeavor to be vastly entertaining for a fortnight."

Sophia smiled, as she knew he expected. "Always that. If nothing else, Reg, you have always been entertaining."

At last in accord, the two began to stroll the grounds.

* * *

Life continued for Sophia, despite all her unwanted guests. Reginald kept his promise of being entertaining, but Sophia was too distracted to do more than smile politely when required. She did rouse herself to restrengthen her friendship with Lydia, which was easy enough: All she had to do was encourage her friend to chat about plans for a nursery.

Every once in a while, Sophia would catch Aunt Agatha giving her a significant look. She had no idea what those penetrating stares were meant to convey, and truly she did not care. She supposed her perceptive aunt might have guessed the truth, but Sophia herself was too happy to do more than smile and return to her thoughts.

It was all rather exciting, this wondering about a baby. She had already chosen names, had special clothing created in her mind, even outfitted an imaginary nursery. In her mind's eye, her boy child had grown into a man, entered the military, and come out as fine as his father. Her little girl had grown into a beautiful, vivacious woman who charmed the *ton* during a delightful Season. She had not yet chosen a husband for her daughter, but then again, there were so many suitors it was hard to pick just one.

But in all that time, she had not once given thought to the children's father or their life together—or so she told herself. Certainly, she thought of his smile, for she'd given it to both boy and girl child. She remembered his gentleness and gave that to her daughter. To the son, she gave his nobility, his stern character, even his firm jaw and military bearing.

As for her other thoughts, the ones that appeared at night . . . Well, they were certainly not her fault, and she didn't spend time thinking about Anthony during the day!

All in all, she told herself, the major was quite distant from her thoughts. She absolutely did not miss him. And she would never dream of wishing he were with her. Except perhaps in a distant corner of her mind that once in a while whispered an evil word.

Love.

That is a horrible thought, she screamed at that tiny part of her mind. She could not possibly love the major. Why, she had worked so hard to give him a thorough and complete disgust of her. He was in London, no doubt spying out the latest crop of beauties. She had all but thrown him there. She could not love the man. It would simply be too tragic.

That settled, she occupied herself with thoughts of their child and gave the other tiny corner of her mind no heed.

Until the day her monthly courses came.

It was there as clear as day on her unmentionables. A tiny spot, hardly worth mentioning. But she knew its significance. Knew her courses would follow.

And they did.

So, with a hand that shook with each word, she wrote to Kirby, the major's batman, who waited at the inn for her word. Her note was curt and to the point. It read:

"Apply to my mother regarding a potential bride. I am sure she can direct you to many who fit your requirements."

She signed it, gave it to a footman, then promptly fell on her bed and cried harder than she had done in all her life.

It was well after midnight when Anthony arrived at his tiny room in the Staffordshire inn, but despite the late hour, Kirby was still awake, holding the door to the room open, a small piece of parchment folded in his hand.

Anthony paused on the threshold, his heart beating painfully in his throat. "Is it . . . ?"

"Yes."

"Yes?"

"Er, no. I mean, I don't know."

"The hell you don't." Frustrated and anxious, Anthony grabbed the note, pulling it out of the unsealed envelope. He read it once. Then twice. Then a third time.

Cursing, he threw it on the ground. "What the hell does that mean?" he fumed. "A lot of nonsense."

Kirby wisely said nothing. Anthony glared at him nonetheless. Seeing that he could not provoke his batman, Anthony turned, heading back for the door. "I will talk with her myself."

"In bed?"

The major spun around. "What?"

"It is dark, Major. Will she be wantin' t' speak with you now?"

Anthony changed direction again and glared out the window at the dismal night. "No."

"Then, perhaps 'twill be better in the morning."

Anthony stomped back to his tiny room, unable to deny the truth. Sophia would be sound asleep right now, likely dreaming of a life spent alone in Staffordshire. Without him. Without his child.

It was enough to make him slam the door.

"Wake me at first light," he called out. The batman's reply was muffled.

Sophia woke with a splitting headache and dismal thoughts. She felt like a sodden lump of barren ground. The last thing she wanted to do was entertain houseguests.

Thankfully, most everyone had left. The gossip had died down, and with no expectation of anything new, Drusilla and her husband had taken themselves off. Similarly, many of their fellow vipers had packed up and left the county. Percy and his fiancée remained, sneaking time alone whenever Lydia's mother nodded off, and, of course, so did Lord Kyle, her most devoted entertainer. He had, in fact, been so pleasant that she could not ignore him as she had yesterday. It would be too rude.

She got out of bed and performed her morning toilette, although each movement felt as if it were through molasses.

"Ere, miss," said Mary, as she brushed out Sophia's hair. "Put this on your eyes."

Sophia accepted the cool cloth in silence, only now noticing how red and blotchy her face was from crying. Goodness, she could not appear before Reg looking like this. Not after two weeks of blissful peace. He would certainly guess something was amiss, and then it would be a small step to the truth, especially for such a bright man.

In the end, she resorted to her paint pot and the hope that the bright day would dim somewhat.

By the time she made it downstairs, she was already thoroughly disgusted with the day. So it was that, when she pushed open the door and saw the major calmly sitting at her breakfast table, she lost all sense of decorum.

"I do not know why I bother thinking of you as out of my life, Anthony," she snapped. "Every time I come downstairs, here you are." He looked up, his face carefully blank, and Sophia bit her lip. Good Lord, what had she said? "I . . . I do beg your pardon," she stammered, mortification heating her face. "I do not know what came over me."

"More animation than you have shown in a fortnight, is what," returned her aunt as she calmly buttered her toast. "But why you choose to come out of your stupor with acid on your tongue is beyond me."

Sophia turned and blinked. She had not even realized anyone else was in the room. Looking about, she saw not only Aunt Agatha, but Lydia, her mother, and Percy all staring wide-eyed at her. She would have said something, but she could think of nothing relevant or social or even civil. Instead, she turned back to the major, and the other people quickly faded right out of her thoughts.

Anthony did not look at all well, she decided. In fact, he looked rather haggard. His skin had a slightly gray cast, and his eyes seemed pinched, as though he were in pain.

"You have been riding again, Major." It was not a question. "A great deal, I wager. Really, can you not try to be moderate? You are recovering from a nearly mortal wound, and the strain on your leg—"

He did no more than raise an eyebrow at her, and she looked down at her hands in consternation.

"Sophia," he began, his voice chill, "I came to speak with you. If you have—"

"Good morning, all!"

Sophia squeaked in alarm and practically leaped across the table to avoid being hit by the door as Lord Kyle burst into the room.

"Oh, goodness, my dear, I had no idea. . . ." His voice trailed away as he caught sight of the major.

"Yes, Reg, apology accepted," she said in rather curt tones. Then she turned back to Anthony. "You were saying, Major?"

But Anthony was staring frostily at Lord Kyle and slowly drew himself upward. "I was saying that I came to inform you of my recent appointment to India, despite my bachelor status. It will be some time before I depart, but I knew you would be anxious to hear—"

"That you shall be leaving this portion of the globe," interrupted Lord Kyle. "I am sure Sophia is most relieved."

"Reg," snapped Sophia, "really, I can comment for myself." Except, of course, that she had no comment whatsoever. Her thoughts were consumed by a strange feeling of emptiness. And while everyone stared at her, waiting for her to say something, all she could do was look at Anthony and wonder what was wrong with her.

The silence dragged on.

Finally, she said the only polite phrase that came to mind. "I wish you all the best in your new appointment." Then she frowned, knowing that was not at all what she wanted to say.

"At Uncle Latimer's." That was Reg, but Sophia was certain she could not have heard him correctly.

"I beg your pardon?" Aunt Agatha asked, looking as perplexed as everyone else in the room.

"I was just thinking that we should visit my friend's uncle today. I believe we shall all fit in there nicely."

"I beg your pardon?" Lydia's mother asked. Her tones were frosty.

"Why, he used to be quite a one for the ladies, if I recall correctly. At the very least, it will be a diversion, what with him running the women 'round the table and all that." Then he winked at the major. "Why don't you come along, old chap?"

"I beg your pardon!" Percy spoke up. His tones were even more frosty, if a bit higher pitched, than that of his future mother-in-law.

"Well, the major is merely waiting to be shipped off," continued Reginald. "Deadly dull, waiting, you know. And here we all are, in the country. Why not pass the time with a visit to Uncle Latimer's?" He added in an undertone that was nevertheless heard throughout the room, "He is said to be quite insane, but I have been given to understand that is only a rumor."

Sophia took a deep breath, determined to stop this absurd farce before it went any further. "And why," she asked, her words clipped and distinct, "would you imagine that we should benefit from seeing that?"

He turned and fixed her with an amused glare. "Because, among the insane, one can act however one wishes without anyone thinking it odd. You are merely participating in the . . ." He waved a casual hand in the air. "The ambience."

"Reg—"

"And, you *do* wish the major to accompany us, do you not?" Lord Kyle asked, his dark eyes penetratingly intense. She returned the look, recognizing that there were more levels to his question than she cared to admit.

She looked back at Anthony, noting his expression was carefully blank, his manner stiffly formal. Two months ago, she would have thought him too rigid, but now she knew the truth about why. He was indeed reserved, but it was because he was hiding emotions that were perhaps too strong for safe expression. Underneath all that stiff formality, he was kind, tender, and exceedingly passionate.

And she loved him to distraction.

Sophia felt her breath catch in her throat. After a fortnight of suppressing that tiny corner of her mind which admitted her love, here it was again, clamoring in a voice too loud to be denied.

She was smitten with Anthony. It was not possible. It could not be possible. But it was.

The world began to spin and contort dizzily. She felt her legs go weak, and everything seemed to splinter before her.

"Sophia!" The major cried out, scrambling across the room to catch her and guide her to her seat. She just stared dazedly at him, her left hand going up instinctively to touch the worry lines etched in his face.

The world fell into order at the very moment his arms encircled her.

She loved him. Yet all she had ever done was fight him and cause him endless misery. Sophia blinked, her eyes suddenly awash with tears as he deposited her gently into a chair. What was she to do now? She had fought him for so long; he was likely sick to death of her.

"So, we shall all make a party of it, hmm?" exclaimed Lord Kyle in overly cheerful tones.

Sophia turned, her eyes seeking out her friend's. He met her gaze, his eyes steady, and Sophia experienced another moment of wrenching shock.

Reg knew. Good lord, the man had known she was in love all along. Sophia felt her chest squeeze tight as she saw the truth in his slow smile. Not only did he know her feelings, he was using this outing as a way to throw her and the major together. And in a neutral environment, no less. One where she and Anthony would be slightly less constrained.

It was so ridiculous that she nearly laughed out loud. Lord Kyle, fashionable fribble, was in truth more clear-sighted than she had ever been.

Gathering herself, she smiled. "Yes," she finally said, her voice steady. "Yes, I think that would be an excellent excursion. And of course the major must come along." She turned to Anthony, her smile as warm as she could make it. But as she looked into his shuttered expression, her hopes dimmed.

She was a fool to think that she could erase all the arguments, the nonsense that she had put him through. He did not love her, and probably never would. He had been passionate at the start, but whatever tender emotions he may have had for her, she had systematically crushed.

It was hopeless.

And yet, there was no time to change her mind: Lord Kyle had began discussing the arrangements for their trip with singular devotion and good cheer.

"Pssst! Reg!" Sophia peered around the corner of the hallway and motioned frantically to Lord Kyle. He noticed her immediately, of course. Indeed, how could he not when she was jumping up and down like a maniacal frog?

Still, he took his time, leisurely setting aside the newspaper and casually removing himself from his chair.

Sophia was tapping her foot in severe annoyance by the time he ceased stretching and had made his way to her.

"Really, Reg, I swear you would have stopped to eat had food been available!" she snapped when he finally made it to her side.

He winked at her and peered toward the dining room. "Has lunch been served yet?"

"Reginald, be serious!"

Lord Kyle merely folded his arms and grinned. "But, I thought it was my job to be charming and frivolous."

Sophia clenched her hands into fists and glared at him. "I swear, you make me want to hit you!"

"Oh!" he cried. "Please, I would not wish you to hurt your delicate hands on my muscles of iron!"

"You mean on your thick head," she muttered.

To her total disgust, Reginald burst into laughter.

"Reg!" She was near her wits' end. They were to leave for Uncle Latimer's home directly after the noon repast. The major had departed to change into more "appropriate" attire—although what one wore to a purported mental patient's home, she had not the slightest clue. Perhaps he would change into something drab; his uniform's bright colors and his handsome physique might be too stimulating for Lord Kyle's sick uncle. Heaven knew, she certainly found them exciting enough.

In any event, the major had departed, leaving her behind to listen to Percy and Lydia's insipid chatter and ponder the revelation that she was in love—all the while not revealing the fact to anyone. Which was enough to make any sane person go mad.

"Reginald, please," she pleaded. "I believe I am going insane."

"I know," he agreed with another grin. "That is precisely why I suggested the outing. You can have a look around and see if you like how the insane are cared for."

"But—"

"Come, my dear," he said as he neatly caught her elbow. "Perhaps we should go walking about your aunt's lovely garden."

Sophia nodded with a grateful sigh. She needed to speak with someone levelheaded enough to tell her she was confused, that she was not in love at all. She was positive that Lord Kyle was just the man.

Unfortunately, as soon as they made it outside, they met up with Aunt Agatha, who was pruning a flowering bush.

"There you are, my dear," called the sweet lady as she peered around a large purple blossom. "Are you sure you are well? You look a trifle flushed."

"I—" began Sophia.

"She has just discovered she is in love," Lord Kyle said with a laugh.

Sophia pulled back with a start. "Wha—"

"Well, I must say it is about time," interrupted her aunt. "Really, my dear, I had thought you were the intelligent one, but you have taken such a long time at this, I was beginning to think you a lackwit."

Sophia spun back toward her aunt. "I—"

"I could not credit it at first," agreed Lord Kyle. "But it is too obvious, and I am much too chivalrous to allow her to continue deluding herself—despite my desire to keep her away from such entanglements. They change one's personality. Of course, I have a vested interest in keeping the major and Sophia apart . . ."

Both Sophia and her aunt stared at Reginald.

"What the devil are you talking about?" snapped Aunt Agatha.

"Hmm? Oh nothing. Merely that Sophia is in such a muddle now, she has completely lost her composure.

Why, she was jumping up and down in the hallway just a moment ago."

"Indeed!" exclaimed Aunt Agatha as she peered anxiously at her niece. "Are you sure a trip to this Uncle Latimer's is appropriate?" She peered suspiciously at Lord Kyle. "Have you ever been there?"

"Never," responded Reginald with a shrug. "But lately I have heard certain rumors, and I have dawdled much too long on investigating. Indeed, that was why I came to this area in the first place." He leaned forward and spoke in a conspiratorial whisper. "I would have gone much sooner, but I was waiting for Sophia to resolve her affairs. Truly, Sophia," he added with a wink, "did you not realize that there were people waiting on you?"

That was the final straw. "Waiting on me!" She drew herself away from Lord Kyle and planted her fists on her hips, then alternated between glaring at him and her aunt. "You both knew I was in love, and yet you . . . you deliberately said nothing! How could you?"

"My dear," drawled Reginald, "I do not interfere in the private lives of my friends."

"You merely arrange assignations at the homes of the mentally ill," she returned hotly.

"The perfect place for lovers," he quipped.

"Harrumph!" Sophia turned toward her aunt. "But how could *you* know?"

"How could I not?" Aunt Agatha returned. "You two practically made love directly before my eyes!"

Sophia started. "I most certainly did not!"

"When you tried to get drunk, my dear. My, the two of you were dancing with such brooding intensity, I nearly had heart palpitations."

"We did not!" she exploded, though she knew her face was heating with a guilty flush. She and the major had indeed been dancing most scandalously.

Aunt Agatha threw up her hands in disgust. "Just because I snore does not mean I am asleep. Goodness, you would think I was blind, kissing that way right before my eyes."

"Your closed eyes," said Sophia sternly, trying her best not to remember the major's kisses. "I specifically saw that your eyes were closed."

Aunt Agatha pushed a trailing ribbon out of her eyes and gave an imperious sniff. "The sound is quite distinctive."

Sophia did not have an answer. Indeed, she was very sure she did not have a coherent thought in her head. All she could do was stare at her two friends in horror. "I came out to the garden for you both to tell me I am not in love, that I am merely confused. I wanted to hear that this is perhaps a temporary aberration in an otherwise sane world."

Reginald's grin grew even wider. "Well, that's exactly how I would describe love. Hence the trip to Uncle Latimer's."

"But—"

"Come, come, Sophia," said Aunt Agatha as she put away her gardening tools. "You must not upset yourself."

"Absolutely," agreed Reginald. "You do not wish to appear haggard during your seduction."

"Seduction!" gasped Sophia, spinning around to confront her friend. "Who said anything about a seduction?"

"Well, that is the point of this outing, is it not?" Aunt Agatha asked Reginald, calmly fitting her gardening basket onto her arm. "Although, personally, I would prefer a picnic."

Reg shook his head. "Not with that harridan around, Lydia's mother. She would see to it that everyone was miserable. No, this trip is much better, what with the beds and all."

"Beds!" squeaked Sophia.

Reg offered Aunt Agatha his arm, all the while speaking to Sophia. "Scores of beds at Uncle Latimer's. In that mausoleum, surely you can contrive to get into a compromising situation with the major somewhere along the way."

"But—"

"And then I shall arrive and shriek," put in Aunt Agatha. "He shall be forced to marry you!"

"An excellent notion," confirmed Reg. There were a few moments before they noticed that Sophia was standing stock-still, glaring at them as if they had both just suggested she kill Anthony. Then, as one, they both turned surprised expressions to her.

"Sophia?" they asked in unison.

"I do not want to marry him like that!"

Her aunt paused, disengaging from Reginald long enough to inspect a rose bush. "Like what, my dear?"

"I cannot force him. Besides," Sophia added with a sigh, "if he did not marry me after a night in gaol, I cannot see that a kiss in a bedroom will force his hand."

"Then take off your clothes," quipped Reginald.

"Or, you could take off his," returned Aunt Agatha from her position behind the roses.

Reginald frowned as he surveyed Sophia with a critical eye. "I am not quite sure she has the strength."

Sophia just stared, alarmed by the sudden mental illness of the two. Seduction? Kisses? Ripping off the major's clothes? She felt her face heat in memory. Well, perhaps—She ruthlessly cut off her thoughts. "I cannot seduce him. I simply cannot."

"Ah," sighed Reginald. "Pity. I would have liked to be the one to discover you." He waggled his eyebrows.

Aunt Agatha stood up, brandishing her shears. "Do not be such a lech!"

Lord Kyle merely shrugged.

"Be serious!" Sophia exclaimed, annoyed by her companions' good-natured bickering. "I am at my wits' end, and I have come to you both for help."

Her two companions frowned, each appearing to consider her options for this serious and weighty manner.

"Rip off your clothes," said Reginald.

"No, his," returned her aunt.

And with that, the helpful pair both wandered away.

Chapter Thirteen

Anthony stormed into the Stag's Heart Inn in an extremely foul mood. Kirby took one look at his face and found something else to do. Meanwhile, Anthony flopped down on his bed and began cursing, taking singular delight in exercising his vocabulary.

God, she had looked lovely. Between the dress and her flawless complexion, not to mention her exquisite figure, it had been all he could do to keep from hauling Sophia into his arms. Yes, he had noticed the slight puffiness around her eyes, seen the telltale signs of her trying to mark it with her paint pot. He knew she had been crying, but that only made it harder to keep from comforting her. From touching her. From loving her.

But then *he* had walked in. Lord Kyle, the handsome, stylish, perfect gentleman, who apparently had been visiting with Sophia for the last two weeks.

Had Kyle been the cause of her tears? Or was it something else? Anthony did not dare hope she cried for the loss of their child, the child who had never been.

Anthony rubbed his hand over his face, groaning in true unhappiness. She had not chosen him. She preferred to remain in the company of that fop.

He knew what was happening. Lord Kyle was no doubt spending every moment poisoning Sophia's thoughts in an effort to win his thousand guineas. The man apparently did not know that he had already won.

Sophia would never be his.

Well, there was one thing that was absolutely certain: He would not be accompanying her to any blasted house party. He had gone to her home to see that she was well. Her answer had been loud and clear. She was so well, she was entertaining handsome, rich young men.

He would be damned if he ever visited her again.

Anthony was raised from his dark thoughts by a discreet tap on his door.

"Come in, Kirby," he barked. "I will not kill you."

"Does that restraint apply to other guests as well?" inquired a cultured voice.

Anthony sprung to his feet and hauled open the door. There, standing like his worst nightmare come to life, was Lord Kyle, his expression as urbane and annoying as ever.

"Come for your guineas, no doubt," Anthony snarled. "You shall have them as soon as I contact my banker." And his father, as he himself had nothing close to a thousand guineas in his account.

"Actually," drawled the man, "I had thought to speak with you on another matter entirely."

"Perhaps another time. At the moment, I am in no mood for polite company." Anthony's voice was unnecessarily surly, but he could not restrain himself.

"I shall endeavor not to be polite."

At another time, Anthony might have smiled at that sally, but not now. And not with this man. He merely folded his arms across his chest and glared across the threshold at the intruder.

Lord Kyle gave a put-upon sigh. "We can accomplish our business out here, but I would much prefer to be private," he said. His voice was calm, but there was an urgency beneath.

Anthony considered. He would like nothing more than to keep the hateful gentleman out in the hallway, cooling his heels. But he had no idea how much the fop knew. Despite Sophia's promise not to tell a soul what had occurred between them, he could not be sure that Lord Kyle had not somehow wormed the truth from her.

And that was something he had no wish to discuss in public; no matter her rejection of him, Sophia's reputation was still of utmost importance. With a grimace of distaste he stepped back, swinging the door wide. "By all means," he drawled. "Let us be private."

Lord Kyle bowed slightly and stepped in, waiting calmly for Anthony to swing the door shut. When he had, Kyle turned and addressed him with a civility that turned Anthony's stomach. He would like nothing better than an excuse to punch the man.

"I shall endeavor to be blunt," Kyle began. "Am I correct in assuming that you do not wish to accompany us on our outing?"

Anthony frowned. He had not expected a discussion of this ridiculous excursion to a madman's house. "I intend to return to London posthaste." After all, there was nothing for him here.

"I would like you to reconsider."

Anthony raised an eyebrow, this time pushing aside his dislike of the other man to look closer. Beneath Lord Kyle's polished appearance and studied elegance, there was an intelligence that could not be denied. He appeared to be no more than a Jack-a-dandy, but Anthony could see determination in his stance, purpose in his eyes.

"What do you intend?" Anthony asked, his suspicions well and truly roused.

Lord Kyle shrugged, but the casual gesture did not fool the major for one moment. "As to that," Kyle answered casually, "I am not entirely sure. I have been asked to speak with my friend's uncle. Perhaps to make some inquiries into the situation there. There have been disturbing rumors of locked doors, angry fits. Guards of amazing brutality. It does not sound at all the thing. Not at all."

"Then why do you go?"

Kyle sighed as he took a delicate pinch of snuff. "I have already answered that, Major. I wish to investigate. Uncle Latimer was once a dear friend of my mother. I would hate to see him in a poor state." He paused, raising his gaze to Anthony's. "Of his own making or someone else's."

Anthony shifted, wondering if he truly comprehended the undercurrents here. "Do you believe this Latimer is being unlawfully restrained?"

Kyle shrugged. "I cannot say. I am merely intent on investigating." Suddenly the man's gaze sharpened. "Though I anticipate nothing untoward, I cannot be sure of Sophia's safety in this matter."

Anthony stiffened. "Then don't take her!"

"Unfortunately"—Kyle shrugged—"she is absolutely determined."

Anthony felt his hands ball into fists. "You must dissuade her," he commanded. "Good God, what kind of man are you to endanger a lady?"

"Sophia is no shrinking violet. She can care for herself." There was admiration in Kyle's voice.

"Aye, she can," Anthony agreed reluctantly. "But she is also young, inexperienced, and has a fiery and impulsive temper. She is both a lure and a danger in ways she cannot even conceive." He shifted his weight to a more aggressive stance. "I will not allow you to hurt her in any way."

Lord Kyle was silent as he appeared to study Anthony. His gaze was keen and penetrating, and Anthony allowed him to see his own absolute determination to protect Sophia in every way.

Abruptly, Lord Kyle nodded. "Very good. I can see that Sophia will come to no harm in your care."

"She has never been in danger from me," he growled.

Kyle responded with a slow smile. "Yes, I can see that. Too bad I did not understand that before I wagered my thousand guineas. Ah, well, you will come, will you not? To protect her?"

Anthony frowned, wondering if the man were as insane as his strange uncle. "I will do what I must to ensure Sophia's safety," he finally said, amazed by his own dogged stupidity. He ought to be in London dangling after some heiress. How many times would he court rejection at Sophia's hand?

"Sophia will not thank you for your interference," said Lord Kyle softly, breaking easily into Anthony's grim thoughts.

Anthony responded with a wry grimace. "She is the most independent female I have ever met."

"It is one of her charms."

Anthony grunted as he folded his arms. "Aye. And one of her greatest faults."

Kyle hesitated, but then he spoke, his words tentative. "Then you care for her?"

"Of course!" The very question was insulting, but even as he spoke, Anthony realized that there was more to Lord Kyle's question than was at first apparent. In fact, for a moment, he had the distinct impression that he was being interviewed as a father would question a potential son-in-law. He straightened his shoulders and stepped forward, a sudden suspicion making his eyes narrow. "Just what exactly do you intend for this outing?"

"Why, nothing more than a pleasant trip on a dull afternoon." Lord Kyle's smile became positively mischievous. "I vow it shall be most entertaining."

With that, he sauntered away.

Anthony wanted to hit something. In fact, he would have thoroughly enjoyed an hour or so pummeling a worthy target. Unfortunately, none was available.

As promised, he had returned soon after luncheon, ostensibly to join the outing. In truth, he had intended to dissuade Sophia from joining this particular excursion. He knew he would have to tread carefully. Two months ago, he would have simply told her she could not go, then done everything from barring the door to tying her down to keep her safe.

Now, he realized that such tactics were ineffective with Sophia. Not only would he infuriate her, she would no doubt find a way to cut through her bonds and climb out a window—just to prove that he could not control her.

As if he had any doubts.

What he had to do, he realized, was speak with her logically, sensibly, as an adult. That was where he had erred, he realized. From the beginning, he had tried to manipulate Sophia into what he wanted. First, he had played upon her sympathies, proposing from his deathbed. He had masked his fears of rejection by simply assuming that she would honor her promise. And when she had rightly refused to honor so ridiculous a proposal, he had tried logic and insane purportions of England and duty. What woman found that appealing?

When that too failed, he had maneuvered himself into her household and struck a nonsense bargain with her. Why, he had even bribed Baron Riggs to lock them in gaol for a night, believing that once Sophia succumbed to her natural passionate nature, she would be all too willing to marry him.

And see where all that scheming had brought him? Right back where he started, standing in her hallway, begging for an audience with her. Only this time, he feared that the situation was so bungled that she would not deign to even speak with him.

Yet, all he had learned did not matter, he decided. Whatever mistakes he had made in the past would just have to be repeated if he had no other options. He could not allow Sophia to risk her person on this mad outing. If he could not reason with her, he would simply have to tie her down and sit on her.

That decided, he continued to pace, waiting at the foot of the stairs for her approach. Unfortunately, she was making herself completely unavailable to him. From the moment he arrived at her aunt's home, she had disappeared into her bedroom, and that was the last he had seen of her. He had sent a message up, but there had been no response.

If he were still their butler, he could find some excuse to go up to her bedroom. Given his somewhat tenuous position as guest, he had no business on the upper floors at all.

That, of course, would not have stopped him, except that Bowen blocked the stairway with the efficiency of one of the major's own best foot soldiers. Short of beating the elderly retainer senseless, Anthony was stuck on the main floor.

She was avoiding him. There was no doubt in his mind. He was not blind to the tension that had permeated the room this morning, but he had thought it a product of his fevered imagination, a physical state due to lust, desire, maybe even lingering thoughts of his love. His unwanted love.

Could it be that she felt equally unsettled, and this was

her method of dealing with those emotions? But the very thought was insupportable. Sophia was not nearly so much of a coward. The truth was, she simply did not wish to be around him.

Which made the prospect of this excursion all the more grim.

Sophia twisted her hands beneath the folds of her skirt. She could not believe she was doing this—hiding in her room like the veriest toddler. She stared down at the major's note. He wished to speak with her directly regarding this potentially dangerous outing.

Clearly he did not wish her to go to mad Latimer's residence, but why? It did not matter. Truthfully, she had her own doubts about the trip. But Lord Kyle had been most insistent. It was important, he had stressed to her at luncheon. And Reginald rarely felt anything was important.

Still, she had not quite made up her mind. How could she go anywhere with Anthony until she decided what she would do? She had only just realized the true nature of her feelings toward him. But to go from such a shocking thought to Aunt Agatha's suggestion . . .

It was just too far a step, too fast. She could not possibly just tear off her clothes and seduce him. Could she?

Sophia glanced down at her serviceable yellow muslin gown. It was old enough to rip quite easily, but she could not do it. It would be too bold, too brash, too contrary to a lifetime of restraint. Besides, after all she had done to anger and frustrate the major, she sincerely doubted he could ever forgive her, torn clothes and offered heart or not.

And she simply could not humiliate herself by throwing herself at him.

But then she remembered how he had looked this

morning. He had been haloed by the sun, his regimentals sparkling, the power in his strong form obvious to anyone with eyes. She remembered the pinched lines about his mouth and eyes—lines likely due to pain from his leg and anger at the current situation. She recalled everything she loved about him and more, and knew that she had to try to reach him, to try at least to beg his forgiveness.

She glanced back at her door, seeing the major in her mind's eye. Suddenly, ripping off her clothing did not seem like so strange an idea. After all, he had not objected to just such an event not too many nights ago.

She resolved to try. But first she would need to find the perfect gown.

Anthony was still standing by the stairs when Sophia finally came down. The carriage was waiting and everyone was assembled to depart. Everyone, that is, except Lydia's mother, who had declared the outing too vulgar for her taste.

Anthony was actually pacing, working and reworking his thoughts on how to best approach her. His original plan had required time, which was now sadly lacking. As for tying her up, he could not very well do that with everyone else in the house watching. He would just have to rely on common sense and his forceful nature to get the message across.

Frankly, he had grave doubts that either would be of any effect at all. Which was his last thought before glancing up and seeing Sophia.

At one time, when he was feverish in the hospital, he had thought her ethereal, untouchable, an angel of mercy come from Heaven to minister to him. Looking at her now, he saw she was very much a thing of the Earth, a creature to be touched.

Good Lord, she was dressed for seduction!

Attired in light blue and gold, she should have looked

like sunlight in the sky. But instead of thinking of things celestial, he watched the round, full curve of her breasts and her lush figure. Her gown shimmered and moved in just the right ways and in places he longed to touch, to caress, to kiss.

Her hair was piled loosely on top of her head, as if the most casual wind would bring it tumbling down around her ears. Her face, usually radiant, seemed flushed and sensual. Then, to make matters worse, as he watched her descend, she nervously wet her lips. The sight of her tiny pink tongue electrified his body as if he had been struck by lightning.

"My, my, Sophia," drawled Lord Kyle from the side. "You are a surprise."

Anthony's spine straightened as he turned to glare at Lord Kyle. He noted the gleam of appreciation in the man's eyes, the ready and welcoming smile, and fury nearly overcame his restraint. How dare this fop look at Sophia that way! And yet, there was absolutely nothing he could do about it. Sophia was not his to command and never would be. His only hope for sanity was if he assured himself that for this afternoon, at least, she would be safe.

At home. Alone.

"Lady Sophia," he said curtly, "I wish to speak with you."

She turned and raised her eyebrow. "You do not wish me to go to visit Reginald's Uncle Latimer."

Anthony blinked, as startled by her perception as by her low, husky voice. "Uh, I believe—"

"Not my Uncle Latimer," Lord Kyle interrupted. "My friend's."

"Of course, Reg. How silly of me. And just who is this mysterious friend?" asked Sophia with a sweet smile. A smile that made a man think of mouths and kisses and illicit tastes.

"Sophia!" Anthony exploded.

She turned back to him, her eyebrows raised. Then, before he could speak, she opened her delectable mouth to address Lord Kyle. "The major believes this will be a most vulgar and potentially dangerous event." She descended the last of the stairs, reaching automatically for Lord Kyle's extended arm. "You did say Uncle Latimer had a predilection for chasing women around tables and all."

"So it was rumored," answered Kyle with a grin. Anthony noted that the man's eyes were fixed slightly lower than Sophia's face. In fact, his gaze seemed to be trained upon the stunning expanse of creamy white flesh left exposed by her ridiculously low-cut gown.

"Sophia," he growled. "This is unwise."

"Piffle," she shot back. "I am going." And with that she sailed past him on Lord Kyle's arm.

Anthony could only stare at her, his thoughts too tangled to sort, especially as his gaze focused directly on the gentle sway of her curved behind.

"Coming, Major?" asked Sophia's aunt as she came up behind him, latching her hands around his arm. "I must confess that this activity seems somewhat odd to me. I would much prefer to have a trained soldier along. Yet, if you feel too uncomfortable, I do understand."

Anthony looked at the sweet lady and nearly groaned out loud. He had no choice now. Even if he could physically drag Sophia from the carriage, it would still leave Percy's fiancée and Lady Agatha subject to Lord Kyle's strange scheme. Whatever was going to happen on this mad outing, he had no choice but to tag along, protecting the ladies to the best of his abilities.

"I would not dream of being anywhere else," he answered dryly. Calmly he took Agatha's hand and escorted her to the waiting carriage.

Chapter Fourteen

"What is the gentleman's full name?" asked Anthony irritably as they tooled down the rutted driveway toward the manor home that was their destination. He felt silly asking, but it was better than listening to Lord Kyle as he teased and cajoled smiles out of Sophia—fond, soft smiles like she had never given him. "We cannot call him Uncle Latimer."

"Oh, he does not mind," responded Lord Kyle with a wink at Sophia. "He especially enjoys being familiar with lovely ladies such as yourself."

Anthony felt his hands curl into fists as he imagined himself punching the man directly in the face. As it was, he barely restrained his curt tone. "His name, if you please."

"Lord Blakesly," answered Lord Kyle with a smile.

Sophia looked up, a frown pulling at her lips. "Blakesly? Have I met him? I have met the younger Blakesly and cannot say I care for him at all."

"Blakesly the elder had a sudden illness two years ago," supplied Lord Kyle. "Soon afterwards, he was put here to be cared for, and young Blakesly adopted the title. Some felt it was most premature, but then again, he is young and—"

"Impertinent?" interrupted Sophia. "That is what I most remember. Impertinent and boorish."

"You said," put in Anthony, his voice barely civil, "that he purposely stumbled so as to touch you in a most inappropriate way." His blood burned at the thought. But what struck him more was the look of total amazement on Sophia's face.

"You heard me say that?" she whispered.

He frowned at her. "Of course I heard it. I heard everything you said."

"But you were in hospital then. You . . ." Her voice trailed away as she remembered. "I thought you were unconscious."

He shook his head, stunned by how little she realized her importance to him. "I assure you, Lady Sophia, were I buried six feet under, I would still hear everything you ever say to me."

The silence that greeted his words was somewhat unnerving, but only because Sophia was quiet, staring at him as if seeing him for the first time. The others were less important, though some part of him registered the smug expressions on both Lady Agatha's face and Lord Kyle's. Still, his eyes were on Sophia, and it was she who lightened his mood with a soft smile.

"My apologies, Major. It appears I severely misjudged some things."

Just as he had misjudged her, he now realized. Stupid from the start, as one of his oldest lieutenants had been fond of saying. Why hadn't he met her and courted her in the usual way, right from the beginning? But there was no help for it now.

A moment later Miss Lydia Smyth, the boy Percy's fiancée, was speaking, and there was no more time to think. "I remember a different *on-dit*," she said softly. "Something about a girl. His niece, perhaps?"

"Ah, yes," returned Kyle coldly. "Melissa eloped. With a Scotsman."

Anthony looked up, surprised by the sudden anger in Lord Kyle's tone. The man's face had changed, too, closing down to become inscrutable. Clearly there was something more here, he realized, but there was little he could do to explore the issue as the man deftly changed topics. With an almost feminine gesture, Lord Kyle pulled back the carriage curtain and began pointing out at the scenery.

"Look, we are nearly there," he said.

Sophia leaned forward to see and nearly butted heads with Kyle as they both tried to peer outside.

"Oh, my, pardon me," she gasped.

"Not at all, my dear. Not at all," he responded congenially. Then, suddenly, all was as it had been moments before. Gone was the moment of rapport between Anthony and Sophia. In its place was that cheerful camaraderie between her and Kyle, creating a cozy scene that made Anthony grind his teeth in frustration. What on earth had ever possessed him to join this ridiculous trip?

The carriage at last pulled to a stop, and as they all tripped and stumbled their way out of it, Anthony remembered exactly why he had come. One look at the bizarre structure before him and all his military instincts went on alert. He was here, he recalled with grim purpose, to protect Sophia from whatever lived inside it.

"Oh, my," whispered Lady Agatha from his side. "It does look somewhat forbidding, doesn't it?"

Anthony could only nod. Lord Blakesly's manor was set in a beautiful meadow of classic pastoral charm. Unfortunately, the house itself looked like a dungeon drawn from the bowels of the earth by a cruel giant's hand. The stone was dark and solid, the windows shuttered, and the ivy so thick it appeared menacing.

Miss Smyth pronounced the place "delightfully odd" as she snuggled closer to Percy in mock terror. Sophia simply frowned at the dreary structure. Anthony barely restrained a groan, feeling as if he had fallen into a Grimms' fairy tale.

Lord Kyle remained unfailingly cheerful. "Come along," he said. "No doubt they saw us coming up the drive."

Indeed, someone had. A rotund, jolly fellow named Sween appeared at the door and introduced himself, exuding good cheer. He shook hands and bowed with all the joy of a preacher finding a new congregation. "My, my, what a surprise," enthused Mr. Sween. "Come in, come in. Always happy to have visitors."

Percy stepped forward to perform some initial introductions, but he didn't have the chance. Mr. Sween turned to address Lady Agatha with a suddenly sad expression as he reached out and patted her hand.

"Were you a particularly close friend of Lord Blakesly before his illness? He does so enjoy visits from the ladies he used to . . . um . . . pass time with."

Lady Agatha frowned, clearly taking a moment to comprehend his words; then her eyes widened in shock. "No! Of course not! I have never met the man."

"Ah," he said with sudden understanding as he turned to Sophia, clearly appreciating the charms exhibited so stunningly by her dress. "Then you must be—"

"You are misinformed," cut in Sophia in her most freezing accents.

Anthony could not help but smile. Though Miss Smyth and Percy seemed quite cordial to the man, doing all that was polite during an initial meeting, Sophia seemed decidedly on edge, perhaps a bit unsettled by Mr.

Sween's overwhelming enthusiasm. Whatever the reason, Anthony could only applaud such good sense. He, of course, had disliked the man from the very start. But then, he was beginning to notice that he disliked a good many men who fawned over Sophia.

Mr. Sween turned from one person to another, a slight frown of consternation on his face as he at last focused on Miss Smyth.

"Have *you* come to visit Lord Blakesly?" His tone was tentative, clearly noting Percy's proprietary hold on his fiancée.

Lydia dimpled up prettily. "I should adore meeting his lordship."

Mr. Sween's frown deepened as his gaze searched each of the three ladies. "I am afraid I do not understand. His lordship, as a whole, does not get visits from, um, gentlemen. If the ladies are not particular friends—"

"I am his friend, Mr. Sween," interrupted Kyle. "And I would like to see him directly."

"Oh." The man blinked a moment as he stared at Lord Kyle. "Oh! Then these are your—"

"My friends," Kyle answered congenially. Then, suddenly, he was smiling, his manner soothing as he began pushing forward toward the front of the house. "They wished to view some of Lord Blakesly's excellent art."

He slipped past the fat man with the rest of the party trailing behind. Mr. Sween turned an alarming shade of purple before rushing forward to block their progress. "It is not here anymore, unfortunately," he said. "We were forced to remove it from Lord Blakesly's environment. The, uh, fits. You understand." Then he dropped his voice to a low whisper. "I am afraid Lord Blakesly is not at all well today. His mood is somewhat unpredictable."

Kyle paused just before the threshold. "But, just a moment ago you said he would be happy to see the ladies."

Mr. Sween shifted awkwardly, clearly uncomfortable.

"Ah, well, you see, female companionship is something the younger Lord Blakesly allows his father. It makes him, er, it keeps him—"

"More manageable?"

Mr. Sween looked distinctly uncomfortable. "It eases his distraught mind. Gentlemen, on the other hand are . . ." His voice trailed away on an ominous note. "Please, perhaps you might come back another time?"

Kyle appeared to consider, but Anthony snapped. He wanted this excursion over. Also, with one look at Sophia's face, he knew she would not be satisfied until she understood exactly what was going on in this dark old manor. It seemed clear, for her safety, his best option was to force the investigation now, when he was here to protect her.

Stepping forward, he roughly pulled Mr. Sween to the side. "Are you suggesting, sir, that you and your staff are unable to protect us from Lord Blakesly's queer starts? Oh, dear, what will the young Lord Blakesly think? Has he hired men of so little competence?" He invested just enough derision in his voice for Mr. Sween to turn from a mottled red to a pale white.

"Oh, no!" gasped Mr. Sween. "I am quite capable of handling one old man, sir."

Anthony smiled. "Excellent. Then do bring us some tea and have his lordship brought to us directly." He paused, then added a sneer for effect. "After showing us to the front parlor, of course."

There was nothing left for Sween to do but give them a sickly smile and do exactly as he was bid. "Yes, of course," he said, bowing slightly. "How remiss of me. Please, do come in." But his movements were slow and reluctant as he opened the front door.

They followed in loose order, with Lord Kyle leading the way, the engaged couple next, then Lady Agatha and Lady Sophia. Anthony remained at the back, all his senses alert. It was an odd procession, and he was not used to this sort of anticipation when walking with ladies—an adrenaline rush very similar to that of battle. But then again, he was getting used to new experiences when accompanying Sophia.

The front foyer was completely in keeping with the exterior decor. Although some measures had been taken for comfort, on the whole it was a bare and dark chamber. Even the wood flooring was dull and cheerless, to say nothing of the cold grate and faded furnishings.

"As you can see, Lord Blakesly does not much worry about appearances," said Mr. Sween as he ushered them into a side parlor.

"The older Blakesly? Or his son?" asked Lord Kyle.

The butler did not answer as he busied himself with the ladies' wraps and hats. Meanwhile, Reginald tapped his foot impatiently. "Where is Lord Blakesly?"

"Hmmm?" asked Mr. Sween, obviously stalling for time. "Oh, ah, as to that, I am afraid he is napping right now. He is not at all well, you understand. But I am sure he will be glad of your visit. Yes, in fact, I am persuaded he will be in alt over it." The man bowed deeply to Lord Kyle. "You have done a good deed today. Thank you so much for bringing such cheer, but I fear it will storm tonight and his lordship will be most upset if I detain you past the prudent time."

Anthony stepped forward, his determination growing by the second. Clearly this man did not wish them around, and that made Anthony all the more curious as to what went on in this dark horror of a house. Still, he forced himself to smile at the obnoxious servant. "We have come all this way, Mr. Sween. Lord Kyle is a good friend of Lord Blakesly. I believe we will look about, wander around, so to speak, and hope that the man wakes before we leave."

"But—"

"Please be so good as to serve the ladies some tea."

"But—"

"Now." Anthony did not raise his voice. He knew he did not need to. The man was clearly a hired lackey, not used to defying orders. And indeed, after another perfunctory bow, Sween scurried away.

"Well," said Lady Agatha after the man had disappeared, "this is most unsettling."

Lord Kyle nodded. "I quite agree. Unfortunately, I must ask that we remain and, um, look about. If we scatter, then perhaps one of us could discover Lord Blakesly."

Anthony stepped forward. "Surely you would not wish the ladies to simply wander around? They would be much happier here drinking tea." He did not add that the women would no doubt be much safer as well. Whatever was happening in this household was likely not something he thought Sophia ought to see.

Before Lord Kyle could respond, Miss Smyth looked up. "Happier *here?* What nonsense! Why, we have come with the express purpose of assisting Lord Kyle with his mission."

Sophia had been looking through a window at the back garden, and she spun around, her face pale. "You cannot be serious!"

"To locate Lord Blakesly, my dear," said Lord Kyle smoothly. "That is all."

"Oh!" whispered Sophia, her complexion slowly settling into a rosy blush. "Of course. How silly of me."

Anthony narrowed his eyes. There was something going on in the room that he did not understand. Sophia had been nervous and edgy ever since she had descended the stairs in that dress. He had ascribed it to the unusual circumstance of having both himself and Lord Kyle together, but now he suspected something else was at work. Something with Sophia at the center. Something other than this mysterious business with Lord Blakesly.

Before he could demand an answer, Sween returned with tea.

"Excellent," exclaimed Lord Kyle, though the fare seemed particularly dismal. "We shall just wait now for Lord Blakesly to wake."

"As you wish," said Mr. Sween, and he bowed out of the room.

Sophia reached for the tea service, apparently intent on serving, but Lord Kyle stopped her. "Good God, Sophia, pray let us not drink that. Come, it is time for us to search for Lord Blakesly. If any of you find him, bring him to this room directly." Then he turned to the engaged couple. "Percy, you and Miss Smyth take the main floor. Lady Agatha and I shall take the top. Sophia, please join the major, if you would, on the middle floor."

"But—" Sophia's objection went unheeded as the others suddenly leapt to their task, obviously eager to set about their tasks. All too soon the room emptied, leaving her staring wide-eyed at Anthony.

He waited, his arms folded, for her to speak. She was not accomplished at subterfuge and would soon crack under his steady regard.

Or so he thought. Instead, he saw her rally her mind, put on a dazzling smile, and raise her arm to him. "I believe it is time for us to stroll a-about."

It was a marvelous performance. He might have thought his earlier judgment was in error, except for the fact that she stuttered on her last word. Clearly, something was in the wind.

"Sophia, what are you doing? What is Lord Kyle's game?"

She shrugged. "I have no idea, except for what you already know. He said he heard certain rumors and is intent on speaking directly with Lord Blakesly."

She placed her hand on his arm, and he felt it tremble

slightly. He covered it with his own, a fierce wave of protective instincts washing over him.

"I do not like this," he said darkly.

She gave him a nervous smile that in no way reassured him. "I believe the stairs are to the left."

Anthony sighed. It was clear she had no desire to speak with him about anything of consequence. He could feel the tension in her body. Her movements were stiff as they climbed the stairs. He supposed she would explain when she chose, and not before. Sophia had always been stubborn.

They reached the second floor landing in moments, only to view two rather long expanses of drab hallway—one to each side. They had no adornment at all. No tables. No famous art. Nothing except the occasional unlit wall sconce and the faded remains of stained and dirty wallpaper.

"Do you know," whispered Sophia, "there used to be an enormous art collection here. Aunt Agatha told me it was the pride of the county. Now, look," she said as she waved at a particularly telling square stain on the wall. "It has all been removed."

Anthony nodded grimly, already guessing what had occurred. "Come, let us begin this ridiculous search."

He turned her down one hallway, but was stopped when she paused to address him. "Are you angry that we are here, Anthony? Can't you see that something dastardly is going on here?"

"Of course I can see that," he snapped. "Young Lord Blakesly has probably imprisoned his father, sold all the man's art for his expensive London lifestyles and is likely gleefully running through the rest of his inheritance."

She nodded, as if they were agreed in their suspicions. "Then why do you object?"

"I cannot see the sense of bringing females upon a rescue mission."

"We are not all frail flowers," Sophia returned sternly. "Even Lydia shows uncommon sense at times. Besides," she reluctantly admitted, "Reginald would never truly endanger us. Lord Blakesly is likely on the third floor where he has gone with Aunt Agatha. They have the dangerous task. All we have to do is—" Suddenly, she cut off her words, a fiery blush heating her face.

He studied her, his suspicions growing by the second, but she would not say anything. Even as he watched her, Sophia appeared to grab hold of herself, perhaps even steeling herself to some task.

"Sophia?" he asked softly, a note of warning in his voice.

"Come, Major," she said briskly. "We must search these rooms." She started off with obvious determination, leaving him no choice but to follow.

They met no servants as they moved. They simply wandered down the second-floor hall, opening one door after another. Each room was a bedroom with covers over what few furnishings were inside. There was dust everywhere and, occasionally, the unmistakable signs of rodents.

Anthony would have thought it a complete waste of time if not for Sophia's odd actions. At first, it was she who opened the doors with a force that belied her shaky hands. It was as though she steeled herself to thrust open each door. But as each room was revealed, she hesitated, then pulled back, suddenly unsure.

"No one here," she would say quite unnecessarily. Then she would hastily pull the door shut and move on.

After some five rooms, she could not manage it any longer and allowed him to perform the necessary task of opening doors while she hovered awkwardly behind him. The whole situation was bizarre, to say the least. He might have been amused, taking time to admire the way she filled out her gown, if not for her clear agitation.

"Sophia—"

"One last door on this side," she said, her voice unnaturally high.

"Of course," he responded, mentally bowing to the inevitable. He had no doubt that everything would become clear if he could but wait patiently for it. But patience was hard to come by. Why would she pick now, of all times, when they were in search of a reputed madman, to act out some bizarre scheme? It was foolhardy. And yet, part of him relished it. Part of him was beginning to smile every time she started, becoming more skittish by the second.

It was not gentlemanly of him to be so amused. But that was part of what he adored about her. She constantly surprised him. For a man who had thought he would never see anything new in life, Sophia was a joy he could never fully appreciate.

And yet she was not his.

With a groan, he turned to face the last door. "Shall I open it?" he asked. "Or would you care to?"

"No. No, thank you. You go ahead." Then she shifted behind him, poised as if to either push him in or run for her life. He could not tell which.

It did not matter. He was prepared for either eventuality. He leaned forward and turned the doorknob, though his attention was focused more on the woman behind him. To his complete surprise, the door did not open.

Frowning, he twisted the doorknob with more force, only to have his initial thought confirmed. "It is locked."

Behind him, he felt Sophia start with surprise. "Locked? Are you sure?"

"Hello?" interrupted a soft, muffled voice from the other side of the door. "Is someone there?"

Anthony looked at Sophia, wondering if she could have heard what he had.

"Please, can you hear me?" it continued.

"Yes," answered Sophia as she bent down to look through the keyhole. Her entire body went rigid with shock. "Oh, no," she gasped, pulling back to let Anthony see as well.

Peering inside, he saw a petite brunette coming to the door. He caught a glimpse of a beautiful elfin face spoiled by an ugly bruise across her cheek. Then she was leaning into the door, speaking urgently.

"I am a prisoner here," said the woman. "You must help me escape."

Anthony thought to say a number of things. The soldier within him had dozens of questions for the woman, not the least of which was, why was she incarcerated in the first place? He had met madmen who appeared perfectly normal. Though he doubted it was true, he could not dismiss the possibility that this woman was imprisoned for entirely appropriate reasons.

Sophia, apparently, had no such qualms. She pushed him aside as before, kneeling again at the keyhole.

"The door is locked," Sophia called through the door. "Where is the key?"

"Mr. Sween has it."

An entirely different thought entered Anthony's mind. Could the search for Lord Blakesly be a ruse? Could it be that Kyle actually searched for this woman? That would explain a great deal. After all, the man could not openly admit that he was looking for a woman he had no relation to whatsoever; he would have to invent some other story.

Whatever the truth, it was clear this lady had a good deal of the answers. So, with sudden resolve, he slipped a slim wire out of his pocket. "Let us see what we can do without a key."

"Major!" Sophia exclaimed as he gently set her aside and began working on the lock. "I had not thought this part of the standard military education."

He merely shrugged as he concentrated on his task.

"You would be surprised at what one learns in the army."

"Do not open that door!" boomed a voice from behind them.

Anthony spun around, hiding the wire while cursing himself for letting his thoughts become distracted. He had been thinking so much of Sophia, he had let his guard slip. Now they were caught by Mr. Sween, and the man suddenly seemed to have grown a foot. Gone was his obsequious smile. He seemed taller, firmer, and a great deal more dangerous, especially since he was flanked by two large footmen.

Anthony tensed, confident of his abilities to handle the two, plus the annoying Mr. Sween. Unfortunately, the last thing he wanted to do was fight three men in front of Sophia before knowing exactly what was going on. He first had to understand the precise nature of the situation. But before he could begin speaking, Sophia rounded on the butler.

"Whatever can you mean in locking up this poor woman?"

"She is Lord Blakesly's niece, and she is subject to the same fits as his lordship. I will ask you again to leave her alone. She is quite dangerous."

"No, I am not!" cried the woman from within.

"Nonsense," sputtered Sophia as Anthony gripped her arm, trying to quiet her through his touch alone. "I demand an explanation at once!"

Clearly, she was not willing to be quieted. He tried a more direct approach with her, making sure his voice carried a note of warning that he hoped she would understand. "Perhaps he is right, Sophia," Anthony suggested smoothly. "She did seem a bit distraught to me."

Sophia spun toward him. "What?"

"I think we had best leave the young lady to Mr. Sween's care," he continued calmly. "Really, Sophia, you cannot let madwomen run around. They may seem lucid, but in my experience, they can turn violent without a moment's notice."

"But—"

He pressed his fingers to her lips, stopping her words even as he began to move her away from the locked doorway. "Come along, Sophia," he said, as if she had not spoken. "Your tender emotions have quite overwhelmed you. Trust me in this. I am sure Mr. Sween would not have locked that door without a good reason. We must rely on his judgment." He turned to the man, doing his best to appear sincere. "You are caring properly for the woman, are you not?"

"Of course, Major. The younger Lord Blakesly cares deeply for Melissa. We are doing our absolute best to keep her from harming herself or others."

Beside him, he felt Sophia stiffen. "Melissa!" she cried, already turning toward the door, but Anthony tightened his grip, preventing her movement.

"You see, Sophia," Anthony began before she could say more. "There is nothing to worry about. And now we must return to the gardens. Getting lost as we did, I fear we have left the others for too long."

"Major—"

"I believe the stairs are this way."

"Anthony—" There was a note of desperation in Sophia's voice.

"Trust me, my dear. Please."

At last, miracle of miracles, he felt her relax. Turning, he saw that though clearly upset, she was willing to accept his leadership for now. With a pleased nod, he pulled her down the hallway, heading toward the opposite wing. She went willingly, and Anthony experienced a moment of euphoria at the sensation.

He glanced behind him to see if they were being followed, but Sween had apparently lost interest in them.

The man unlocked the woman's door; then he and his footmen disappeared inside.

"Anthony," Sophia began, her voice soft.

"Wait a moment until we are outside, please," he returned, a plan already forming in his mind. He did not intend to abandon the poor woman in the room, but he could not act until he was sure Sophia was out of danger. He began to consider his options. "We must find Percy," he finally said. "You should be safe with him."

He felt her begin to stiffen, and he sighed. He should have known her compliance would be short-lived. They got as far as the stairs before she dug in her heels.

"Sophia." The word was a low warning, but she was having none of it. Before he could do more than draw breath, she lowered her shoulder and shoved him into a door right behind them. He stumbled backward, catching himself painfully on the wood as the door shuddered beneath his weight.

He heard her curse. A most unladylike word that had him smiling despite their awkward circumstances. "What are you doing?" he demanded.

"Oh, just get in the room!"

"What?"

She twisted out of his grip, then quickly reached behind him and turned the doorknob. "In!" she snapped, giving his chest a quick shove for good measure.

Anthony blinked, shocked to his toes by this new, demanding side of Sophia. It was a moment later when he realized he actually liked it. In moderation. "Whatever you wish," he said mockingly as he ducked inside the nondescript bedchamber. "You had only to ask."

Sophia followed a moment later, looking harried and perhaps a bit devious. It was that last part that bothered him. It was exactly how she had appeared before she went off to rescue those damned fighting cocks.

Suddenly, he decided waiting for her to explain all

their reasons for coming here was no longer going to work. The situation had changed, and it was time he knew everything. Lord Kyle and Sophia had different reasons for coming on this trip, and Anthony was tired of being kept in the dark. Folding his arms across his chest, he regarded her with a firm expression.

"Enough foolishness, Sophia. It is time you told me what is going on."

She hesitated, clearly startled by his commanding tone. "Foolishness?" she practically squeaked. "We need to—"

He did not give her time to finish. "Tell me, Sophia. Now. And then, I promise you, I shall deal with the young lady." *After I am assured of your safety*, he added silently to himself.

Chapter Fifteen

Anthony's patience was fast wearing thin, and still Sophia seemed to hesitate, shifting uncomfortably as she finally stumbled into her answer. "Uh, as to why you are here, that is somewhat complex," she admitted. She delayed things even further as she carefully shut the door behind them.

"Sophia," he warned, but she rushed into her speech, preventing him from saying more.

"It's really quite simple. You see, Reginald had this idea. Actually, it may have been Aunt Agatha's idea, but I am not entirely sure." She abruptly quieted and flushed a deep scarlet.

Anthony's misgivings became a great deal more alarming. Whatever was going on here had obviously sent Sophia into a tizzy of awkwardness, and they were fast running out of time. He had no idea how long it would be before the dangerous Mr. Sween started searching for them. "I have no interest in what Lord Kyle wants," he snapped. "And why do you do every mad thing he suggests, anyway?"

"I do not blindly follow his dictates. You should know that, as I have never followed yours!" Sophia returned, equally hot. "I would think that would be obvious by now."

Anthony ground his teeth, knowing the truth of her words. "Yes, I have long since realized you are your own woman. In truth, I would never change that."

"I am not a peahen," she continued, oblivious to what he had just said. "Nor do I think . . ." She stopped, frowning as she at last comprehended his words. She looked up, surprise and delight coloring her features. "Truly? You understand that I will not be ordered about?"

"God, yes," he practically growled. "Now, perhaps, would you please tell me what madness Lord Kyle has involved you in?"

But she did not answer. Instead, her pert mouth curved into an impish smile. "Are you perhaps somewhat jealous of Lord Kyle?"

Anthony felt the last of his frayed temper rip free. "I am nothing of the sort!" he bellowed, only to have Sophia clasp her hands before her in delight.

"You are! Oh, wonderful. Then there is hope. But I cannot seduce you at the moment, Major, as much as I might like it, for I have another thought in mind—"

"Sophia!" Anthony took a menacing step forward, and then her words hit him, wiping all other thoughts from his mind. "What did you say?"

She dropped her hands on her hips. "I am trying to explain, Major, just as you asked. I feel we must provide an escape—"

He shook his head. "No! What did you say before that?"

"Hmm? Oh, about the seduction? Well, that was the original plan, you know." Then she waved her hand in a dismissive gesture. "But, never mind that now. I absolutely feel we must help that poor girl escape this horrible place."

She began pacing the room, clearly deep in thought, obviously hoping for his help. Unfortunately, Anthony could not seem to think at all. All his blood was pounding through his body, and none of it was going to his brain. When Sophia chanced to pass directly in front of him, he suddenly caught her, spinning her around to face him directly. He took care not to grip her too tightly, but he refused to release her until he had a straight answer.

"What do you mean, seduction?" His words were deliberate. Slow. But no less forceful.

As usual, such tactics had no effect on her. She merely pushed his hands away with an irritated gesture. "Oh, do not be so single-minded! I am talking about engineering an escape. It is obvious that that girl is being mistreated. Did you see her bruise?"

Anthony felt his hands spasm on Sophia's arm. Clearly, she would not be distracted. He would have to focus on problems other than his own. "I saw the bruise," he said softly.

"We cannot allow that to continue!" Sophia broke free, resuming her pacing. "We must find a way to get her out of this horrible place. But how?"

Anthony took a deep breath, trying to remain calm for both of them. Unfortunately, it was extremely difficult given that the word *seduction* continued to clamor in his brain. Nevertheless, he persevered. The first task was to quiet Sophia's fears for the incarcerated Melissa. "I quite agree that she must be rescued. In fact, if I am not mistaken, your Lord Kyle is intent on accomplishing that very thing. That is, no doubt, the very reason we are here today."

"Oh, no," she countered, clearly a bit exasperated. "Do try to keep up with me, Major. You see, Reginald thought to come here so I could seduce you. It had nothing to do with an escape."

Anthony nearly moaned out loud. There was that word again, but it made no sense. Before he could pick one of the hundreds of questions pushing to be voiced, the door flew open and Lord Kyle sauntered in.

"My, my, what do we have here?" he drawled.

Sophia spun around, throwing her hands up in disgust. "Oh, not now, Reg. We have more important things to worry about. And shut that door!"

Lord Kyle lifted his quizzing glass and frowned. "Really, Sophia, I am quite disappointed. I had thought you would have accomplished the deed by now. I was hoping to catch—"

Folding her arms across her chest, she scowled at the man. "I will not seduce Anthony, or at least not now, so you may put that thought right out of your mind. I have another plan altogether."

Lord Kyle lifted an eyebrow. "Another plan?"

Anthony groaned and settled on the bed. His leg ached, and apparently insanity was infectious. He was holding on to his reason by the tiniest thread, and now Lord Kyle was adding more confusion to the mix. Fortunately, Anthony had long since learned it was best to merely ride along with the nonsense, doing what he could to mitigate the damages. Especially when Sophia was involved.

"Major, whatever is the woman talking about?" demanded Lord Kyle.

"She intends to engineer an escape for the young lady prisoner," he commented, his tone as exhausted as he felt. "Be so good as to explain that you are already doing that."

"What young lady?" exclaimed Lord Kyle, his expression suddenly intent. "What prison?"

Sophia shook her head. "Anthony has it all confused.

He says that you intended to come here and effect a rescue in the first place."

Reginald let his quizzing glass fall from his hand and his voice dropped to a lower tone. "I do intend to remove Lord Blakesly directly. I have already discovered him. He was chained up in the most abominable way upstairs."

"Oh, my," Sophia moaned. "Now we must engineer two escapes!"

"It has already been done—" cut in Kyle.

"As I told you, Sophia," inserted Anthony.

"—but I knew nothing about a woman."

Sophia leapt forward. "We cannot leave her here! She is being hurt."

Lord Kyle reached out, grasping Sophia and pulling her to face him directly. "Describe to me this woman in detail and her circumstances," he said, his expression fierce.

"It is the most awful situation—"

"Where is she?"

"I absolutely will not allow you to ignore her."

"Sophia!"

Anthony tried not to listen as the two began bickering like magpies, but he could not block them out. In the end, he decided it was best for him to take control.

Pushing off the bed, he strode over to them. "Sophia! I understand your concern, but you cannot expect to simply open the door as you would a cage. There is something else at work here. It is dangerous!" He would not let her be hurt.

"What is that to the point?" she asked, her expression as stern as that of a mother protecting her children. "I would not treat a dog as that woman is being treated."

"Sophia," returned Lord Kyle, his expression nearly distraught with frustration. "If you do not tell me where this woman is, I swear I shall strangle you right now."

Ignoring him, she planted her fists on her hips and glared at both men; then she focused on Anthony. "Last month, I went to free those roosters unaided, and the event was ill-conceived, ill-timed, and it landed us both in gaol. This time, I am asking for your assistance so that such a disaster will not occur again."

Anthony paused, his emotions colliding in a tumult. On the one hand, the knowledge that she was at last turning to him for help was a great joy to him in ways he could not even express. But she was asking him to willfully endanger her.

"Can you not simply rely on me?" he asked softly.

"I trust you implicitly," she responded. "Which is why I have asked for your help. But if you do not wish to be of assistance, I shall be forced to work on my own."

"Good God," gasped Lord Kyle, clearly appalled. "You cannot do that! These men are well paid to keep things exactly as they are."

Sophia spared not even a glance for her friend. Her entire being was focused on Anthony. "You must help me," she entreated.

What could he do? The woman he loved had just pleaded with him to assist her. He could not refuse. With a sigh, he turned to Lord Kyle. "How did you obtain Lord Blakesly's release?"

"I cannot bribe Mr. Sween. Blakesly's son is paying him too handsomely to even consider it."

Anthony nodded. "I imagine the elder Lord Blakesly tried before with no success."

"Yes." The one word was grim and held a wealth of undercurrents. Anthony did not wish to guess what the elderly gentleman had been through. "Of course," added Lord Kyle with a grin, "Sween's assistants were somewhat less loyal. I bribed them."

Anthony returned the smile. "Good. How did you intend to set the escape in motion?"

Lord Kyle shrugged. "I had intended to create a commotion by discovering you in the midst of a seduction, then spirit him away."

Anthony raised an eyebrow as his gaze sought out Sophia's scarlet face. "This was all part of some mad scheme?" he asked, suddenly hurt. "You would endanger yourself and your reputation for this?"

"No!" she answered hotly. "The one has absolutely nothing to do with the other—"

Before she could explain, the door burst open and Lady Agatha barreled through. "What is going on in here?" she cried out. Then her eyes widened as she focused on the tableau before her. "Really, Sophia," she gasped. "Both gentlemen? I do not believe that was the plan."

At which point Sophia threw up her hands in disgust. "Oh, not now, Aunt Agatha. I have finally got them doing exactly as I wish. You cannot mean to interrupt us now."

"But—" stammered the poor lady.

Lord Kyle turned politely to the elderly lady. "We are attempting to rescue Lord—"

"A prisoner," interrupted Sophia.

"Good," said the dear lady with a smile. "I was hoping we would do something here. It is so dismal, I cannot think Blakesly enjoys it."

"Not Blakesly," returned Sophia curtly. "The woman!"

Anthony finally managed to clear his mind enough to set his goals. His first priority was to keep Sophia safe. Second, to assist in the rescue. And lastly, to have a long discussion with Sophia about exactly what she had been planning to do here.

First was the issue of her safety. Since he could not remove Sophia from the environment, he simply had to stay by her side. As for the rescue attempt, he turned to Lord Kyle. "Is the elder Lord Blakesly set to escape?"

Kyle nodded. "All we need is a distraction, then we can get him to our coach."

Anthony began cataloging possibilities. "The ruckus must be large enough to distract Sween and his staff for a very long time. Did you have any *other* ideas?"

Lady Agatha stepped forward. "A distraction, you say? I have just the idea." Then she turned to her niece. "Sophia, have you ever seen Lydia's mother in the midst of hysterics? She is most excellent at it."

Sophia's eyes widened. "Er, no, I haven't." Then she shook her head. "But what help can that be? Lydia's mother is not here."

Lady Agatha grinned. "What the mother can do, I am sure the daughter can, too. I shall set her to it immediately."

Anthony nodded, thinking that might just accomplish what they needed. He turned to Kyle. "Can you go with her and ensure their safety?"

Kyle hesitated. "But the woman—"

"Sophia and I will handle that."

Lord Kyle appeared to waver, but Sophia stepped forward. "Anthony can pick locks. Trust him, Reg. He shall set everything to rights."

It took Kyle a moment, but eventually he relented. "Very well," he said. Then, with a nod to them all, he extended his arm to Lady Agatha. "Shall we?"

The older woman dimpled at his courtly manner, but when she spoke, it was on a regretful sigh. "I still think a seduction would have been better. But I should have expected Sophia to be contrary. She was ever so, you know. Why, even as a child . . ."

They left, with Lady Agatha still chatting away. In truth, Anthony had an urge to follow them. He would quite prefer hearing about Sophia's childish antics to this dangerous mission with his beloved, but at least he would have her standing nearby, easily protectable and once again alone with him. He now could focus on his third goal—a pointed discussion about Sophia's intentions.

He turned to face her, his determination quite clear. "Soph-umph!" The word was cut off as she literally fell into his arms. Indeed, it was all he could do to keep standing as he found himself holding the most tempting and delectable woman.

"Thank you, Anthony. I am sure this will work excellently," she said, her voice infused with enthusiasm—and something else. Gratitude?

He smiled down at her, his head lowering automatically toward her lips. She was stretching upward to him, her expression open and eager. But he stopped himself.

Now was not the time. Nothing could progress between them until he understood what had happened. This morning he had left the Rathburn household with the certain understanding that she wished nothing to do with him. That she had suggested her mother, in fact, assist him in finding a different bride.

But now? He shook his head. Now she spoke of seduction and threw herself into his arms. He did not know which was fact and which was fiction. And hard as it was—indeed, it was perhaps the hardest thing he had ever done—he forced himself to set her aside. He gently stood her back on her feet and watched as the joy dimmed in her eyes. Then, he folded his arms to keep his hands off of her and straightened his spine.

"Sophia, I must have my explanation. Now."

She looked away, her demeanor downcast. "Of course," she said softly. "I understand." Then she paused, obviously gathering her courage. "It began this morning, really, when you visited me. I suddenly realized—"

At that very moment, the air was torn by a piercing scream. Anthony recognized the voice immediately, as well as the tone. It was the sound of a woman having severe hysterics, and it could only be coming from Miss Smyth.

The timing, as usual, was perfectly wretched. They had

to go rescue Melissa now, and there would be no more confessions from Sophia.

He looked to her and saw that rather than exhibiting consternation, she appeared relieved and all too ready to abandon what they had just begun. In fact, she was already moving to the door, but he could not allow her to leave him just yet.

He reached out, grasping her arm and pulling her close to him. So close that he felt her heart beating wildly in her chest. Then he whispered into her ear, "This is not done yet, Sophia."

She lifted her gaze, meeting his uncompromising stare. After a moment she gave him a sweet, mischievous smile. "Of course not," she returned. "I still have to accomplish your seduction." Then, while the blood once again drained from his brain, she rushed out the door.

Sophia paused outside the door, searching the hallway and the stairs as best she could. Thankfully, the second floor appeared empty except for herself and Anthony. Glancing down the stairs, she caught sight of Lydia in the midst of loud hysterics. She was gasping and screaming and falling over near the base of the staircase.

Aunt Agatha was right; Lydia did indeed have a talent for hysterics. And what she couldn't accomplish, Percy completed, as he too appeared completely distraught by his fiancée's difficulties. The mayhem was quite impressive.

In fact, two burly footmen stood nearby as confused witnesses. They seemed literally dumbfounded, though whether they were simply stunned by the noise or hampered by Reginald, she couldn't tell.

Reginald, apparently, had chosen the task of distracting the many servants who kept appearing. First there were the two footmen, then a couple of maids, and finally the cook, all who had come out to assist or gawk, she couldn't tell which. Whatever their inclination, Reg kept them busy as he alternately bellowed orders, then gestured wildly, then stood in the way. She heard him order people to move furniture, then bring smelling salts, then brandy. He loudly criticized the cook's food for inspiring this display. Naturally, the cook took insult to such a thing, and soon was hotly defending himself.

With the servants effectively embroiled, all that remained was Mr. Sween, who now came barreling forward, his face red, his voice amazingly powerful. That was when Aunt Agatha stepped in. First, she fluttered forward, somehow managing to "accidentally" knock the large man to the floor. Then she hampered him, constantly sending him back to his knees all under the guise of fussing over Lydia and Percy, who were now threatening all sorts of action, legal and illegal.

Truly, it was quite amazing.

A sound above her made Sophia look upstairs to the third-floor landing. It was difficult to see, but from her angle, she could just make out an elderly man being wrapped in a large rug by two extremely large men. She might have been alarmed—indeed, she was on the verge of rushing upstairs—but the man, presumably Lord Blakesly, spotted her and grinned. Then he could do no more as he became completely encased in fabric and was summarily thrown over one of the men's shoulders. In less than a moment, the other footman opened a doorway to what was likely the back stairwell and both disappeared through the door with their burden.

Sophia smiled, impressed by Reg's handiwork. Servants were forever taking rugs outside to beat them. The two men were not likely to be stopped. And that meant the elder Lord Blakesly had been rescued.

Excellent! That only left Melissa.

She turned, looking about for Anthony only to discover that he was already at the lady's door, working at the lock. Horrified that she had allowed herself to be distracted, Sophia rushed to his side, noting that he worked the wire with amazingly deft movements. He did not even look up as she joined him.

"You should go down to be with the others," he said, his voice low and urgent.

"Absolutely not."

She heard his sigh, but he made no more comment. Unfortunately, he apparently made no progress either. The door remained locked.

"Hurry," she whispered.

"It has been a long time since I did this," he muttered.

Sophia looked over her shoulder. The hallway was still empty, but she was sure the mayhem from below was beginning to lessen. In fact, she thought with a frown, she was sure of it. It was not that the sounds had ceased; she could still hear Lydia and Percy with absolute clarity. It was simply that the noise was muted somehow, as if they had gone outside.

She paused. If Mr. Sween and his servants were outside, that gave more freedom to herself and Anthony to engineer Melissa's escape. Unfortunately, it also meant that Mr. Sween was one step closer to getting control over things. After all, the man definitely wanted all of them outside. How long before he sent servants back to look for herself and the major?

"I do not think we have a lot of time," she whispered to Anthony.

He did not respond, too intent on his task. Then, suddenly, she heard the snick of the lock, and Anthony was grinning at her as he abruptly pushed open the door. Sophia did not wait. She rushed forward, heedless of Anthony's urgent warning.

But there was nothing to fear. The room was exceedingly sparse, empty except for the woman, a broken wardrobe, and a sagging cot. She had thought to grab Melissa and escape. Unfortunately, she now saw that the woman was chained to her cot.

"Oh, Major," Sophia cried. "You shall have to work on another lock." Turning, she was gratified to see the major already kneeling in front of the chains, his hands deft as they inserted his wire into the lock.

Satisfied that Anthony would soon accomplish his task, Sophia turned to the woman, seeing both the tears that streaked her face and the sudden blossoming of hope in the lady's eyes.

"We are engineering your escape," Sophia said softly. "We will take you from here."

The woman nodded, her gaze lifting anxiously to her closed bedroom door.

"Don't worry," continued Sophia. "Mr. Sween is being detained." Then she leaned forward, capturing the woman's attention. "What are you doing here?"

"I am not insane. Truly, I am not!"

"Of course you are not," Sophia responded automatically. "That is why we are rescuing you. But why are you locked up?"

"I am Melissa, Lord Blakesly's niece. I found out what was happening here, and I was furious. I told Simon I would go straight to the House of Lords. That he would be punished!"

"For locking up his father?"

Melissa nodded. "It has been awful. Simon locked me up here, too. He said it made little difference to him if Mr. Sween imprisoned one or two insane patients." She looked down at her hands, and once again, Sophia saw tears slip down her face. "No one came looking for me. No one."

Sophia enfolded the girl's dainty hands in her own. "We were told you eloped with some Scotsman."

"It's not true!"

"Of course not," Sophia soothed. Then a sound penetrated her thoughts. Heavy footfalls were coming directly toward them. Worse, she could not hear Percy or Lydia anymore. "Hurry, Anthony. I hear someone coming."

"I know," came his terse response.

Sophia bit her lip, wondering what to do. Thankfully, at that very moment the lock clicked and Melissa's chains slipped away. Anthony rose to his feet, helping the lady to stand.

"We must hurry," was all he said.

But there was no time. The footsteps were too close now, running down the hall to this room. Sophia and Anthony exchanged a tense glance, then the major shifted forward to just inside the door.

She knew what he planned. He meant to fight whoever came through that door. He intended to come to physical blows despite his injured leg and the fact that he might be severely outnumbered once the fighting began. Sophia did not know whether to be thankful for his bravery or to hit him over the head for being so reckless.

Then it was too late as a man suddenly appeared in the doorway.

Anthony pulled back his fist, his swing already in motion just as Sophia cried out.

"Wait! It is Reginald!"

Anthony shifted, pulling his punch until it landed with an impressive thud in the wall. Reginald did no more than flinch. His gaze was trained on the woman, his motion barely arrested as he barreled into the room. Sophia, on the other hand, was horrified by the look of pain on the major's face.

"Anthony!" she cried, as she rushed to his side.

"I am fine," he ground out through clenched teeth as he cradled his hand.

"But your hand—"

"I am fine!"

He would not let her see it, so she could only stare at

him while the oddest comment slipped from her lips. "I am most impressed, Anthony. You have a mighty right cross."

He glanced up, apparently startled by her admiration. "I *had* a mighty right cross," he grumbled. "I believe the wall won that particular round." Then he looked in her eyes and shared a strained smile. For a split second, all the awkwardness, all the anger and frustration slipped away. They were merely two people who cared for one another.

"Melissa!"

"You are alive."

Both Anthony and Sophia turned at the voices behind them. The sight that greeted them was both astounding and heartwarming. Reginald and Melissa gazed at each other as though they barely dared hope it was real. Their eyes were huge as they drank in each other's features, moving toward one another slowly until their hands at last clasped.

"You are hurt!" Reginald said.

"You came for me," she whispered, her dark brown eyes liquid with unshed tears. The adoration was clear in her tone, and Sophia felt a surge of joy at the sound. Truly, Reginald had found his love at last.

Then the major was interrupting, his voice gruff as Sophia moved toward the door. "Reunions later. It is time we were out of here."

Lord Kyle seemed to come back to the present with a start as he gathered Melissa close to his side. "Percy and the others have Lord Blakesly in the carriage. I told them to leave. We must be sure of Blakesly's escape."

"Leave?" exclaimed Sophia. "But then how—"

"The woods," interrupted Anthony. "We can walk through the woods. It is not far to the village."

"Exactly," confirmed Kyle. "But we haven't much time. I left Sween with a bit of a domestic crisis on his hands.

But it won't be long before he finds these two missing and comes searching for us."

Indeed, Sophia noticed that the house was ominously silent. Whatever chaos remained was being quickly fixed. There was no more time.

Reginald turned to Melissa. "Can you make it?"

Melissa smiled back at him, her voice gaining strength with each word. "I can walk to the ends of the Earth, if you help me."

"We should split up," said Anthony firmly. "More tracks will confuse Sween; he won't know which to follow and he'll be terrified we'll reach town before him. You go west. Go as fast as you can." He glanced anxiously at the frail woman in Reginald's arms, and Sophia shared his concern. Truly, despite her brave words, Melissa did not look very well. They would make slow progress.

"We'll make it," Reg stated firmly.

"Very well," Anthony continued. "Sophia and I shall draw them east, then circle round. We shall meet you in the village. Let me go look to see if it's safe."

Lord Kyle nodded, gratitude shining in his eyes. "Thank you."

Anthony did not seem to notice. He was busy searching the hallway, his body obviously tense and anxious. Behind him, the other three stood with equal fear, awaiting his signal.

Chapter Sixteen

"Now."

It was the signal, and Sophia tensed to run. Returning with a quickness that belied any injury, Anthony grabbed her hand and neatly swept her down the hallway. She had only a split-second to glance behind her and see that the others followed. Unfortunately, it was clear Melissa could not move very quickly. Sophia was about to say something when she watched Reg lean over and lift her into his arms.

The woman began to object, but Reg just shook his head. "You are not heavy," he said in clipped tones; then his whole attention was fixed on moving forward. Just as they reached the staircase, a maid stepped out into the hallway. She was a large woman with thick arms, and she gasped when she saw them. Sophia half-expected her to draw back into the staircase in fear.

Unfortunately, she did not. Instead, she bellowed in a

voice that carried clearly through the house: "Right 'ere, Mr. Sween!"

Sophia heard Anthony's rough curse, and she heartily seconded the thought. Especially as she looked down the staircase and saw Mr. Sween come tearing out of the front parlor, a pistol in hand. He spotted them immediately. Worse, he saw Melissa as well, and his face contorted with fury.

Sophia lost track of events and everything became a blur. All four of her group of escapees picked up speed, dashing down the stairs and out the door. Reginald and Melissa ducked quickly into the western trees, while to the east, Anthony waited. He bellowed in fury, then seemed to purposely run into a bush, breaking several branches as he moved. Sophia remained directly behind him, her hand held in his iron grip. He kicked up some gravel as Mr. Sween appeared from the house, then shouted a curse as two footmen followed.

It worked. Mr. Sween and his cronies cursed back in loud roars, not even looking west as they tore after Anthony and herself.

Suddenly, it was as if her feet had wings. Together, she and Anthony practically flew past the formal gardens and into the surrounding woods, quickly ducking in and around the trees. Despite the cramp in her side and her improper shoes, they did not stop for what seemed a dozen miles. Then, it was only to slow down to a steady walk. Anthony helped her along.

It was some time later before she found the breath to speak. It was even later before she dared voice her fear.

"Anthony, do you know where we are?" She was completely lost. The seemingly endless wood seemed all the same to her. For all she knew, they could be going in circles.

Thankfully, Anthony nodded and pointed. "The village is about two miles that way."

She looked nervously behind her. "Do you think they will follow us?"

Anthony shifted awkwardly as he glanced behind him. "I think we lost them. But we should keep going just in case."

"I assure you," she said dryly, "I have no intention of stopping until I am safely inside my aunt's house. Then, I firmly intend to have strong hysterics."

He smiled at her, and she felt some of her fear slip away at the sight. "You won't be able to match Miss Smyth's performance."

"You may eat those words," she said dryly. It was only now that some of the reality of what they had just done began to hit her. "Mr. Sween had a pistol."

Beside her, Anthony nodded grimly, but his grip was gentle as he helped her over a fallen log. "He is gone now."

She nodded, but her thoughts returned to their narrow escape. "What about Reginald and Melissa?" she asked. "Do you think they are all right?"

Anthony's face was expressionless as he spoke, but his tone held a wealth of something she did not understand. "Lord Kyle is a resourceful man—much more than I gave him credit for. I am sure he will keep his lady safe."

Sophia smiled wistfully as she remembered the rapt expression on Reginald's face. She had never seen him look so passionate, even when discussing clothing. Yes, Reg would keep Melissa safe.

"They make a nice couple," she said softly.

"Then, you do not mind?" His surprise was poorly masked.

"Mind?" she asked. "Mind what?"

"That he is in love with her." Anthony spoke stiffly, as if he was trying to shield her, and Sophia could not help but smile at his concern.

"I am ecstatic that they have found one another. Reginald needs someone to love."

Anthony opened his mouth to respond, but at that moment, he stepped in a gopher hole and his foot turned beneath him. He stumbled, barely catching himself before cracking his head on a tree.

Sophia was beside him in a instant. "Oh, my," she moaned softly, "your leg. You should have traveled in the carriage with the others." She offered him her hand, but he shrugged it off, his expression stony.

"I am certainly capable of a walk in the country."

"Don't be silly; this is more than a walk, Anthony. We have just run for miles, and there are yet two more ahead of us." When would men use the brains God gave them? Couldn't he see how much he was asking of himself?

Rather than reassure her about his health, he simply turned his eyes away. "Never fear," he said, his voice gruff, "I will be able to keep pace with you."

"I did not ask you if you could keep pace with me!" she snapped. "I wished to know if your leg pains you." She had not intended to speak so curtly, but she was beginning to feel the strain of the last few hours.

Anthony squared his shoulders, but he did not comment. She could see she had hurt his pride, and suddenly her patience with him wore out.

"Major Anthony Wyclyff! From all you've ever told me, you would not have made a wounded man under your command go on a forced march, so why should you be so cruel to yourself? Good Lord," she cried to the skies, "save me from men and their pride." Then she turned to face him directly. "It is a hurt leg, Anthony. Nothing more. You are more of a man than I have ever met, but even you have limitations. And if you reinjure yourself, do not think I will sit by your bedside crying and praying that you survive. I do not intend to go through that again!"

With that she stomped off, her head held high as she

tried to keep tears from spilling down her cheeks.

She felt the major's gaze on her as she walked, but she did not care. She could not care, or she might wonder just what she had revealed with her impetuous statement. She was only just realizing how difficult those days had been for her. Even sick, Anthony had been a powerful draw for her. She had wondered each day as she walked into the hospital if he would be lucid or delirious, prayed nightly that he would hold on for one more day, one more visit when she could sit beside his bed and hold his hand and pray some more.

She must have loved him even then. Their visits together at the beginning, before the fever took hold, were clearly stamped in her mind as the most memorable, most wonderful of all her days in London. He had made her smile and laugh and wish she were a nurse just so she could remain by his side a little longer.

And then his fever had climbed, and in a month, they'd told her he died.

"Well, well, look what I found," purred Mr. Sween from directly beside her.

Sophia was caught completely by surprise. One second she was moving away from the major, desperately trying to control her emotions, then a second later, she was trapped against Mr. Sween, his arm around her throat, his pistol pressed to her temple. She barely had time to gasp before the hideous man tightened his hold, constricting her throat so that it took all her energy just to breathe.

Choking, she looked at Anthony, seeking reassurance, strength, anything that would calm the panic clamoring within her, but he had turned away. His stance, normally so straight and correct, sagged as he leaned against a tree trunk.

And if the effect of their fight weren't terrible enough, on the opposite side of the tree, a huge bear of a man—

Sween's henchman—eased forward, a heavy club poised in his thick hand. Clearly he was heading for Anthony, creeping along right where Anthony could not see him. And the brute would be upon him in seconds.

Sophia would have cried out. She did struggle, desperately clawing at the arm around her throat, doing her best to draw enough breath to scream in warning, but she couldn't. All she managed was a high wheeze—and the certain knowledge that her struggles were only making things worse. Mr. Sween tightened his hold enough to make dark spots appear in her vision, and she was becoming distinctly light-headed.

In the end, the powerful Sween won out. She ceased fighting, choosing to remain conscious rather than be suffocated because of her struggling. All the while, the other brute crept closer and closer to Anthony, his huge club poised to deliver a killing blow.

Tears burned in her eyes. Was she doomed to always watch helplessly while Anthony died?

Then the beastly man was beside Anthony, bringing down his club with enough force to shatter a skull. Except Anthony wasn't there. Swifter than she thought possible, he had slipped around the tree, coming up behind his assailant. And while the brute was off balance from his swing, Anthony delivered powerful blows to the man's torso.

At first, they didn't appear to have any effect. With an angry roar, the man straightened, brandishing his club once again, but before he could strike, Anthony landed two more blows, this time to the brute's face. A third sunk deep into the man's belly, and with a startled grunt, the ogre fell.

Anthony straightened, a self-satisfied smirk on his face. "It appears, Mr. Sween, your henchman isn't as well trained as you thought." His expression darkened. "Now, kindly release Lady Sophia and run as far from England as you can. I assure you, your employer will be doing the same very, very soon."

For a moment, Sophia thought they had won. Mr. Sween appeared stunned, worried enough that his hold on her throat had slackened, allowing her breath once more. But within moments of Anthony's statement, her captor suddenly redoubled his restraint, dragging her against him and pressing his pistol even harder against her forehead.

"Oh, I don't think all is lost yet," the man sneered. "I, after all, have Lady Sophia at my mercy. Now, you shall tell me exactly where Melissa is or I shall be forced to do unimaginable harm to this delicate creature."

Sophia tensed, unsure what Anthony's reaction would be to such a threat. She imagined all sorts of terrible things, all of them ending with a bullet in her head. Anthony was fast, but even he could not bridge the distance to Mr. Sween before the hateful man pulled the trigger.

She closed her eyes, envisioning the worst, but then she heard the strangest sound—laughter. Her eyes flew open, only to see what her mind flatly refused to believe. Anthony was laughing—a full, derisive, belly-holding laugh.

Mr. Sween, it appeared, was as startled as she, his grip once again loosening on her, allowing her to take a few normal breaths. All the while, Anthony was holding his sides, laughing for all he was worth.

"Good God, Mr. Sween," Anthony chortled. "You are a fool. What do you suppose the lady and I were quarreling about?" When the villain had no answer, Anthony continued, his tone mocking. "She thought I cared for her." Again came the derisive laughter. "I ask you, Mr. Sween, what use have I for an aged, penniless spinster? Go ahead." He waved a mocking hand at them. "Use her. Kill her. Do whatever you will. I doubt anyone save her aunt will even notice." Then he straightened, a strange look on his face. "Except, of course, that whatever you do to her is yet one more nail in your coffin when you and Lord Blakesly are held up before a magistrate. For you only have that one pistol, and I shall kill you the moment you fire it."

Sophia stared at Anthony, her blood running cold. At last it had happened. The man she loved was loudly disavowing any interest in her, abandoning her to her fate as she always knew he would. She stood stock still, waiting for the chilling ice to take hold of her soul, freezing out the pain of his betrayal along with every other emotion she could possibly feel.

She waited, and yet it did not come. Because she did not for one moment believe Anthony meant what he said. He would never betray her, she realized, and never abandon her. She knew it as deeply as she knew that she loved him, and together, they would certainly find a way out of this mess. This was simply a ruse.

Indeed, she now understood it was her turn to add to this little scene. Stiffening in mock outrage, she lunged, not at Mr. Sween as he no doubt expected, but at Anthony, screeching as if she were a betrayed lover. She didn't really know what she was saying, except that she called Anthony every foul name imaginable.

As soon as Mr. Sween recognized that he was restraining her from attacking Anthony, his hold slackened even further. And in that moment of confusion, Sophia turned. Twisting as best she could, she clenched her fist and swung, burying it deep into Mr. Sween's belly, just as she had seen Anthony do to the other brute.

His foul breath exploded out of him, and in that moment, Sophia dropped, well aware that the man's pistol was still aimed directly at her head. Fortunately, Anthony had seized the opportunity as well, rushing forward the moment she began her attack. As Sophia fell to the ground, Anthony grabbed her attacker's gun hand, twisting it in his powerful grip.

The gun went off, but the ball flew upwards, harmlessly crackling into the trees. Then Anthony fell on Sween, raining blows on him faster than Sophia could see. The hideous Sween could not muster a defense and soon lay unconscious, stretched out beside his fallen henchman.

A bare second later, Anthony was beside Sophia, pulling her into his arms, alternately clutching her and holding her away, scanning her for injuries. "Are you all right? Oh, Sophia, if he has hurt you—"

"I am fine," she cried, "but you . . . Are *you* hurt?"

"I have not a scratch on me." He pulled her into another fierce embrace. "Sweet heaven, when I saw him grab you—"

"I thought that man was going to club you—"

"I wanted to rip him apart—"

"I tried to scream, to warn you—"

"I didn't mean those things I said. You didn't believe them—"

"Not for a second, Anthony. Not even for a second."

Then they were kissing, their mouths fused together as they expressed all the things that could not be said. The fear, the terror of the last few moments, drained away to be replaced by a fierce hunger, a need to touch and be touched.

She would have happily spent the rest of her life there, enmeshed in his arms in the middle of the woods, but Anthony had better sense. Breaking away, he closed his eyes, his breathing labored as he spoke.

"We cannot stay here. That shot will have attracted others." She looked down at the villains stretched out at their feet, then she watched in dazed awe as Anthony threw her an apologetic look. "I adore this gown, sweeting, but I am afraid I have need of the fabric." Then, before she could respond, he dropped to one knee, swiftly tearing strips of her skirt and using them to bind the unconscious men. "It will not hold long, but it will certainly be adequate for us to make our escape."

He finished his task, then quickly grasped her hand. Together, they dashed off into the woods, heading for safety.

The next morning, when he appeared, Baron Riggs seemed a good deal more congenial to Sophia than the last time they'd met. His manners were impeccable as he set to business, taking notes as she gave him her version of events.

Almost everyone who'd taken part in the past day's adventure was present, including Melissa and Lord Blakesly the elder. Everyone had time to give their own story, detailing the rescue with excited voices. But it was Melissa and her uncle's accounts that held them all riveted. The horrible privations endured at Mr. Sween's hand gave Sophia chills, making her all the more pleased by the part she had played in their rescue. Indeed, Lord Blakesly the younger had a great deal to answer for—especially now that Mr. Sween was in custody, telling his own version of events and blaming it all on the young peer.

The only one missing was Anthony, as he was the only one not residing with Aunt Agatha. Sophia tried not to fret. It was too early for morning callers, she told herself, and the major preferred to follow the niceties of society. But as the day wore on, Sophia's confidence began to flag. Surely, she told herself, after all they had endured, he would not disappear now.

Well after luncheon, the baron finally stood, putting away his notes. "This has been a most productive day," he boomed, smiling at the company at large. Then he began the necessities of taking his leave. It was not until he was bowing over her hand that Sophia noted his keen gaze on hers. Then, he spoke in an undertone. "The Major has already explained to me that your previous escapade was a ruse, deliberately established to distract young Blakesly. I trust there are no hard feelings."

"Of course not," Sophia responded, doing her best to cover her surprise.

"Excellent. I cannot tell you how happy I was to hear that the two of you were already married. It put me entirely off my port, thinking I had ruined a woman such as yourself." Then he frowned. "Though how your secret nuptials distracted Blakesly, I cannot begin to imagine. But, then, Major Wyclyff is a seasoned campaigner . . . knows a good deal more about these things than I do, I imagine."

"Thank you for understanding," Sophia responded, her smile growing brighter by the moment. She should have known Anthony would find a way to save her reputation. Despite the baron's purported discretion, she had no doubt that the news of her "secret" nuptials would be spread far and wide by now. Now if only Anthony would appear so that she could set about thanking him properly.

She had descended into another stewing silence when Reg startled her, bowing over her hand and taking his leave as well. "Must be off to get my own special license," he said as he turned his fond gaze to Melissa. "You don't mind hosting my fiancée and her uncle, do you?"

"Of course not," Sophia exclaimed as she bestowed a kiss on his cheek.

"Won't be long," he continued. "I'll be back in a trifle, and then we'll be married and they will both come live with me. Would invite you for Christmas, but I understand you may be in India." Then, before she could answer, he dropped his voice, giving her a scandalous wink as he spoke. "Still, I do wish I had been able to interrupt a seduction."

Then he was gone, and Sophia was left staring at her aunt's full parlor, wondering if indeed things were going to turn out as Reg expected. Despite all evidence to the contrary, Sophia knew that she had left things with Anthony in a highly unsettled state. They had been arguing when Mr. Sween captured her. Maybe he had thought back to that. Certainly he was nowhere to be seen this morning.

Still, if it meant waiting a day or a decade, she would remain steadfast to Anthony. He was her love, and she would wait for him, knowing he would some day return to her. It surprised her how easy it was to make that vow, now. She loved him. Naturally, she would wait for him.

If only he would appear so she could tell him.

By nightfall, her spirits had sunk very low. The rambunctious party had quieted, the distractions ended, and everyone had gone to bed, exhausted by the excitement. Everyone, that is, except Sophia. She sat at her window, staring out into the starlit sky, silently asking the moon what had happened to Anthony.

There was no sound to alert her. No whisper, even, that she was no longer alone. But she turned nevertheless and saw him standing, dusty, tired, and yet still gloriously handsome, in her door. "Thank goodness I can pick your front door lock," he said with a grin. "I wouldn't have wanted to wake the house."

She was up and in his arms as fast as her feet could carry her. He barely had time to shut her door before she flung herself at him, and then they were kissing, their touch as passionate, as gloriously all-consuming as ever.

"Sophia," he murmured against her lips.

She pulled back, needing the time to draw breath. He apparently did not. He began raining kisses upon her neck while she sighed in delight. "But where have you been?" she asked.

"London. Bribing yet another magistrate to say he married us three months ago in the hospital. Our Baron Riggs is not so easily cowed, you know. He wanted to see the papers straightaway. He said if he did not have proof I'd done right by you, he would clap me in irons right next to young Blakesly."

"Oh, Anthony, he didn't."

"He did, and rightly so, if I let a prize such as you escape my grasp." He returned to her lips, kissing her with a thoroughness that set her bare toes curling. When he had finished, he looked into her eyes. "Sophia, I have waited longer for you than any other woman. I have bribed two magistrates, become a butler, spent a night in gaol, even braved a madman's lair to win you. If you say you still fear marriage to me, I believe I shall kill you."

She smiled at his longsuffering expression. "That would be like fearing to draw breath. Anthony, I am only alive when I am with you." She snuggled deeper into his arms. "I never even knew what it was like to enjoy the company of a man until you made me laugh. That first time I appeared in the hospital—I do not even remember what you said—only that I laughed freely for the first time."

"I said that for an angel of mercy, you were too damned tall."

She chuckled, his words still able to affect her. "Yes, and you added that I made a bedridden man crick his neck too far."

He lifted her fingers, stretching them out one by one on his palm. "That is how I got you on my bed. You sat right down and held my hand."

"And once you touched me—"

"You touched me," he corrected.

She quirked an eyebrow at him. "Once *we* touched, there was nothing we could not speak of—"

"Or argue about," he said. He seemed somewhat amused by that.

"Nothing we could not share," she amended.

His smile faded as he spoke. "But then came the fever.

And it was painful for you to watch, painful to feel?" he asked.

She gripped his hand in memory, her sight blurred. "It was more than the fever. I had been groomed for a rich, titled husband."

His expression seemed to freeze. "And I am neither."

She released a bitter laugh. "But the others were nothing compared to you. It became torture just to be around any of them."

"So you gave away your dowry and came to live in Staffordshire with your aunt." It was not a question, but she answered it anyway.

"Yes." Her gaze dropped to the floor, but he lifted her chin, forcing her to look into his eyes.

"What was all that about you seducing me?" His voice sounded thick, almost husky, but his words were clear enough to make her cheeks flame.

"I . . ." She bit her lip. "It was Reginald's idea."

"Why?" he repeated, his tone leaving no room for escape.

She tried to squirm away, but as usual, he would not release her. "I had come to realize something."

His smile was slow in coming, but no less brilliant. Or smug. "And what did you realize?"

Sophia watched the easy spread of his grin and felt a little indignation pull at her. She straightened her shoulders and pulled backward, but he held her fast, his lips drawing close enough for him to whisper into her ear, "What did you realize?" His voice was almost triumphant.

"You think you know what it is?" she challenged.

"I do. I think it is what I realized in gaol. The morning after I first made you mine."

Sophia pulled back, raising an eyebrow, trying to make her expression haughty. "Major Wyclyff, you presume too much!"

He would have none of her indignation. Instead, he

grinned. "Kiss me and tell me you love me."

"I will not!"

"You will."

"Never!" She said the word—meant it even—but his eyes were seductive, his presence clouded her mind, and worse, his touch sent shivers of delight all through her body.

"*Do* you love me?"

She could not stop herself. "Of course!"

"Then say it!"

"I will not be commanded by you!"

His grin was almost blindingly bright. "Then perhaps we should say it together, my stubborn dear. *I love you.* I love you with all my heart, and I have loved you since you first held my hand in the hospital. I have loved you when you buried corsets and inoffensive furniture, and when you decided in your tenderhearted wisdom to release three wagons of dangerous fighting birds. I *love* you, Lady Sophia."

Her knees were melting with his every word, her heart bursting with joy. She had not believed she would ever hear those words, not from him. And yet, despite all the exultation singing through her veins, she said something entirely different.

"We were supposed to say it together."

He rose up from where he had been nuzzling her neck. "I know, but I could not wait for you. I have been wanting to tell you since I first kissed you."

She arched into his caress, her eyes shutting in delight. "Why did you wait?" she asked. "I vow it would have saved us a great deal of trouble."

He pulled away slightly, moving so his hands could have better access to her body. He stroked her sides in long movements. "I was not fully aware of my feelings until much later. I'd told myself all sorts of reasons for wanting you as my bride. By the time I realized, you had become too difficult to contemplate spending a lifetime with."

She stiffened, suddenly worried. "And now?"

He grinned and shifted his hands to brush across her breasts which made her knees shake with desire. "Now, it is too difficult to contemplate spending a lifetime apart." He lowered his head, and she raised her lips to meet his, eagerly sharing the emotions that flooded her senses. But all too soon he pulled back and his hands stilled and fell away. Soon he was not touching her at all, and his expression was grave. "Sophia," he asked as he dropped onto one knee. "Will you marry me?"

She took a deep breath. This was an important moment. She knew that when she said the words, she would commit herself to a lifetime spent by this man's side, traveling the world as part of his entourage. She would be his wife, giving up everything she thought she'd wanted. But she would be at Anthony's side, and they both knew now that she would never be so simple a thing as his ornament. After all they'd been through, she found the words were simple to say.

"I love you, Major Anthony Wyclyff. I have loved you from the moment you teased me into sitting on your bed and holding your hand. I loved you when you showed up at my breakfast table as my terribly insolent butler and when you lied to protect my honor after our night in gaol. I love you, and I cannot understand why I fought it so hard." She reached out, touching his face as she finally faced her deepest fear. "But what if I lose you?"

He grabbed her hand, pressing a kiss into her palm. "I can't predict the future, but I have no intention of returning to a battlefield, my love. There is no reason to expect I will live anything but a long and happy life."

She bit her lip. "I cannot watch you die. Not again."

"They say there is a potion for immortality in India. Perhaps we should go find it." His words were glib, but his expression was not. He drew her into a tender embrace. "We must love while we can, Sophia. There are no guarantees. But I love you, Sophia. And I believe that nothing, not even death, could keep me from your side."

She looked into his eyes, and for the first time ever, she found the courage to believe what he said. "I love you," she whispered. "I will marry you." Then she began to smile. "And I intend to seduce you at the earliest possible convenience."

He grinned, and she could see joy light his dark eyes. Then she was not looking at anything, but feeling a hundred different sensations. She had meant to seduce him, but she found she was the one being seduced. His hands were everywhere, stroking her body through her nightrail. She quickly became impatient with the barriers between them, and she began tugging at his clothing. Thankfully, he helped her, his movements as urgent as her own. Soon they were together, naked upon her bed.

She marveled at the feel of his glorious body. "This is wonderful," she whispered as she wriggled against him. She felt his smile as he kissed her face, lovingly teasing each one of her features before easing down the side of her neck.

The stroke of his tongue on her nipples, her belly, and the inside of her thighs surpassed anything she had ever experienced before. He did not need to exert pressure to spread her legs. She arched willingly into his embrace, aching for whatever he chose to do.

His nibbling bites traveled from the back of her knee, up the inside of her thigh, at last ending in the most intimate kiss she had ever known. Her body bucked and strained with a pleasure she had not thought possible.

She was totally exposed to him now, open as she had never known. Once, she would have fought such an experience with every ounce of her strength. Now, it all seemed natural and perfect. She felt her icy walls melt, and she was overwhelmed with heat and love. She was with Anthony, and she was safe. She was cherished and protected and loved. And, in return, she would give him her all.

His fingers were inside her now, stretching and stroking and doing things that had her writhing beneath him. She whimpered with the feel of it, the wonder.

"Anthony," she cried. "My love!"

She felt him look up, placing tender kisses at the base of her belly. "My love," he echoed, his voice deep and hungry. Then he pulled himself up, lifting her hips as he moved, placing himself at her entrance.

She did not wait for him. Wrapping her legs around him, she pulled him forward crying out in pleasure as he pierced her. Caught off guard, he fell forward, dropping onto her as he buried himself inside. She reveled in his weight.

"Sophia," he rasped.

"You are mine now, Major. I will not release you. Ever."

He grinned, though the expression was strained. As he began to move, she felt him shift and pulse inside her with each incredible stroke. "My love," he gasped. "You are mine."

"Yes. Oh, yes!"

Not slowing his rhythm, he pulled back and looked at her. She gazed back into his eyes and was caught there. With every thrust, she arched to meet him, feeling the brush of his chest against her breasts, the heavy weight of his hips, and the heated push of his body. But she never lost sight of his eyes.

This time, unlike the first, she knew what she wanted. She knew where they were going. And this time, as the coil wound tighter within her, as her breath came in short gasps and his hot breathy moans heated her face, she knew he sought the same thing.

Looking into each other's eyes, their bodies moving as one, together, they soared, and found joy.

Nearly dawn, Sophia thought as she stretched languidly in her bed. Turning to gaze at Anthony's serene face, she smiled in wondrous memory of their night together. Slowly, as she watched, his eyes opened, his gaze fuzzy with sleep, his body warm and tempting as he drew her closer against him.

She wriggled deeper into his arms, feeling his body come awake wherever they touched. "You have turned me into a wanton," she said happily.

"I have turned you into a woman who feels and laughs and loves."

She grinned. He never seemed to tire of hearing those words, just as she never tired of hearing him say them to her. She loved him, and he loved her. "You realize I cannot change back," she said. "I will never go back to being the Ice Queen again."

He shrugged, sending waves of sensation through her body. "I never liked that anyway."

"But, if I am not the Ice Queen, then I shall always be releasing caged animals and going to rescue mistreated young ladies."

He groaned, but rather than argue, he caught her hand and began kissing her fingers, one after the other, surprising her by the sheer eroticism of such a simple act. But she had to stop him. There were things they still had to discuss. She reluctantly drew her hand away.

"Anthony, you know there are a thousand impediments. I have no dowry."

"I do not want your dowry."

She shook her head, forcing him to listen by shifting slightly away from him. "I gave it all to Geoffrey. He is trying to rebuild the family estate."

"I do not care."

"He will."

Anthony sighed, apparently resigned to the discussion. "I will speak with Geoffrey when the time comes."

"But what about—"

He stopped her words with another kiss, and she found herself melting into his arms, her fears forgotten. He was willing to work through anything, everything. When he at last raised his head, she smiled up at him.

"We should be married very soon," she said dreamily. "There was no babe before, but there might be one now."

He paused, his expression uncertain. "Does that upset you?"

She grinned. "Of course not. I should simply adore having your child. And since you have turned me into a wanton . . ."

"We shall be married today." His words were a crow of delight.

"Geoffrey will insist on giving over my dowry," she said, her smile fading with the thought. "Anthony, he does not have it. The property was sold. The money spent."

"My dear," responded Anthony as he began to caress her intimately. "After what we have been through these last weeks, do you believe a lack of dowry might stop me? Besides," he added with a grin, "it appears I have won my wager with Lord Kyle."

Sophia pulled back far enough to peer into her love's eyes. "Wager?" she asked, suddenly suspicious. "What wager?"

He didn't answer, choosing instead to try and distract her with a deep kiss. It worked. For now. She was far too happy to worry about any male nonsense—with either Lord Kyle or her brother.

She knew her idyll would not last for long. There was still their true wedding to accomplish, not to mention preparations for their journey to India. And her brother would probably make a fuss about trying to provide her with a dowry. But all that paled beside her love for Anthony. Especially as he reached down to stroke the fire that blazed between them. In that heat, she found their love had burned the last of her fears away.

And don't miss

Miss Woodley's Experiment

Coming in April 2002!

Chapter One

"Lud, you foolish boy! You cannot expect us to believe that you have been languishing in the Yorkshire wilds, can you?"

Geoffrey Rathburn, earl of Tallis, winced at the lady's strident tones and dodged her fan as it playfully rapped him on the arm. He had barely entered his mother's ball ten minutes earlier when the lady and her daughter literally cornered him between the staircase and a huge towering column.

"Truly," he said, his bored drawl showing distinct signs of wear, "I am afraid I must disappoint you, but I was—"

"Faith thays you were thpying for the Home Office," said the woman's pasty-faced daughter who, unfortunately, had not mastered the art of a fashionable false lisp without spitting. "How romantic," she crooned as she fluttered her eyelashes at him.

"Nonsense, Anora," snapped the girl's mother. "No doubt his lordship was enjoying masculine pursuits."

The girl pursed her thick lips, forcibly reminding him of the Yorkshire sheep he had seen two days before.

"Oh," said the girl with a sly wink. "Mother has explained all about men'th needth. I'm thure I understand. Explithitly."

Geoffrey had the grace not to choke, but it nearly cost him his tonsils as he suppressed his natural urge to gag. Finally, when he was able to draw breath, he managed to give the girl and her domineering mother a weak smile. "Then, I am sure you will understand that I must wish my mother a happy birthday." He bowed as politely as he could manage and began pushing his way through a veritable tide of matchmaking mamas and their ever-hopeful, ever-boring daughters.

If only he had known his mother planned to put him on the marriage block tonight, he would have worn a nose ring and a saddle instead of his fashionable evening wear.

To think that two days ago he had been missing London!

Struggling to maintain his sense of humor, Geoffrey maneuvered his way through the female throng until he caught up to his mother, who was gracefully holding court in one corner of the rented ballroom. She looked elegant as always, her silvery hair caught up with ivory combs that perfectly matched her cream-and-burgundy gown.

"Many happy returns, Mother," he said as he dropped a light kiss on her cheek.

"Geoffrey!" she exclaimed, twisting her diminutive frame to see him more fully. "You made it after all!"

He dropped into his best courtly bow. "In the flesh, Mother."

"Oh, darling, you sound glum. You are not going to spoil my birthday just because I decided on a slightly larger celebration than usual this year, are you? With that monstrous Corsican running wild on the Continent, I felt we all needed a little extra cheer."

"How very patriotic of you," he agreed.

She gave him a searching glance, then pouted prettily. "You are angry with me."

He sighed, knowing his mother was incorrigible when it came to restraining her expenses. She was a society butterfly through and through. It was part of her charm. So he smiled, reminding himself that they were finally getting their financial heads above water. If his mother celebrated in a slightly larger than appropriate style, it was only in anticipation of the successes to come.

After five years of dedicated labor, the Tallis fortune was beginning to recover.

He felt himself relax, his gaze traveling over the expensive hothouse flowers, the full orchestra, and the elaborate dinner buffet. "No, Mother, I am not angry," he said, surprised that he did, in fact, mean it. "Truth be told," he added with a cheeky grin, "I am in the mood to celebrate."

"Excellent," she said as she snared an elegant crystal flute from a nearby table. "Because I have wonderful news of my own." She wormed her arm through his and drew him aside, her eyes alight with secret information.

He tugged lightly on one of the curls that had escaped her elegant coiffure. "Let me guess. You have found the elixir of life and have grown twenty years younger." He leaned forward, whispering into her ear. "That is not a secret, my dear, because you do not look a day over thirty."

"Oh, my foolish boy," she said, blushing to the roots of her silver hair. "Drink up." She pressed the crystal flute into his hand, and he obediently sipped, savoring the best champagne—the only champagne—he had tasted in the last three years. "It is Sophia," whispered his mother. "She is to wed Major Wyclyff in four weeks!"

Geoffrey stopped in midsip, the champagne going sour in his mouth. He slowly lowered his glass. "What did you say?"

"Isn't it wonderful? We shall announce it tonight." She was smiling, her face glowing with delight. "In truth, they have already wed . . . in secret, but the formal event is to take place in four weeks."

His sister was to wed? To be formally wed? In four weeks?

"I swear I had begun to lose hope," she continued. "I am practically beside myself with delight."

Geoffrey was happy for his sister as well. After five Seasons, Sophia deserved to find love and marriage. It was just that everyone, including Sophia herself, had come to regard her as a sweet *maiden* woman. She had told him that she would never marry. She insisted he use her dowry to purchase new sheep stock.

By God, she had insisted!

Now she was to marry in four weeks' time. Where would he find her dower money?

"Drink some more, Geoffrey. You look pale."

He barely heard her. "Can they not wait at least until next year?" If he had a few months, perhaps he could scrape together some of her portion. "They need not wed immediately," he repeated, speaking as much to himself as to his mother. "I can manage something in a few months."

Gradually, his mother's prolonged silence penetrated his mind, numbing it with added fear.

"Mother?"

"They cannot wait, Geoffrey. Sophia is . . ." She glanced quickly around to make sure they were alone, then dropped her voice to the barest of whispers. "She is in an interesting condition."

Geoffrey gaped at his mother. Pregnant? Sophia, the woman once dubbed the Ice Queen, was pregnant? His blood started to boil in brotherly anger. By God, he would show—

"They are in love, Geoffrey."

"But—"

His mother's voice suddenly turned sharp. "Geoffrey Lawrence Thomas Rathbun, I have approved this match. If you do anything to hurt your sister or Major Wyclyff, I swear I shall never forgive you!"

Geoffrey turned to his mother, his eyes wide in shock at her tone. She had not called him by his full name in twenty years. Slowly, his indignation began to ebb. "You want this marriage?"

"Absolutely."

"And Sophia?"

"Is in alt."

Geoffrey saw the finality of it in her eyes. His sister would wed. In a month. "Then, I suppose all that remains is for me to provide her dowry," he said bleakly.

He drained his champagne, his eyes burning from the unfairness of it all. Four weeks. How would he find Sophia's marriage portion in so short a time?

"We do not have it, do we?" His mother's voice was low, almost fatalistic.

They both knew she referred to Sophia's dowry. As much as she pretended to know nothing more than the latest *on-dit*, his mother was not stupid or willfully blind. She was well aware of their financial circumstances; she just had never been able to spend accordingly.

"No," he answered in equally low tones. "We do not have it."

"Well . . ." She averted her eyes, leaning over to grab another glass of champagne, which she pressed into his hands. "I believe Major Wyclyff will still marry her without—"

"*No!*" His explosion drew the attention of more than one curious guest, and he quickly moderated his tone.

"What kind of man would take his sister's marriage portion?"

"She insisted!"

"I should not have done it!"

"But you did, and rightly so. Sophia does not blame you in the least."

"Confound it, Mother . . ." He ran a hand through his hair. "It is *her* money."

"Speak with Wyclyff. I am certain he will understand."

"Absolutely not! The man needs the money almost as much as we do." His hand clenched spasmodically around his glass. "It is Sophia's money. She should have it." He just did not know where he would find it, short of selling off everything he had just worked so hard to achieve. Getting that money, in four weeks' time no less, would put them back to where they were five years earlier, when nothing would have saved them but an heiress.

Oh, God. He glanced around the room with renewed understanding. He saw the glittering jewels, the rich fabrics, the money represented in each and every young girl in the room.

"Good God, Mother, is that why you have filled the room with heiresses?"

She sighed, confirming his worst suspicions. "I knew you would go prickly," she said. "Men are so fastidious when it comes to their honor."

Geoffrey bit back his retort, knowing acid remarks would not help the situation. Instead, his gaze followed her gloved hand as she gestured at all the flowers of polite society. "They are all here, awaiting your attention."

"And they would all fall prostrate before me at the altar, no doubt," he said, frustration making his words too sharp. Why had he worked his back to near breaking these last years if not to avoid the Marriage Mart? He felt like one of his own sheep at a county fair.

"Come along, dearest," said his mother as she drew him

toward the edge of the ballroom. "There is one young woman I especially wish you to meet."

Geoffrey allowed himself to be pulled, but his steps became heavier and slower with each passing moment. It had been bad enough five years ago when he had tried his hand at winning an heiress. He had nearly succeeded, the delectable Amanda Wyndham hand-in-hand with him at the altar. Except that Amanda turned out to be someone else, a girl desperately in love with Stephen Conley, the fifth Earl of Mavenford. Bowing to fate and his own second thoughts, Geoffrey had quietly stepped aside, annulling his own hasty nuptials so she could marry her true love.

It had not all been bad. The parting gift from Mavenford had given Geoffrey the breathing room to rebuild his family's finances. But, now, five years of heartbreaking labor later, when Geoffrey had finally wrested them clear of debt, he suddenly had to find his sister a dowry commensurate with the Tallis name.

Which meant Geoffrey once again needed to wed an heiress.

For the first time in years, Geoffrey felt a great fury build within him. He was angry at the greedy mamas who pushed their nursery-pure daughters at him in hopes of winning his title. He was angry at his father for throwing his children's inheritance away at the gaming table. But most of all, he was furious with himself.

By all accounts he was an intelligent man, a financial genius willing to spend long days shearing sheep and long nights studying how best to maximize his yields. Yet for all his labor, he had still failed.

It was a bitter taste in his mouth.

Geoffrey dug in his heels, stopping directly in front of a side doorway. "No."

His mother paused, turning to him in surprise. "What?"

"I said, no."

"No what, dear?"

"No more champagne, no more dancing, no more insipid girls."

"But—"

"I am tired, Mother. And not in the best frame of mind to tease smiles out of frightened young heiresses."

"But—"

"No."

Geoffrey allowed his mother to study him with her intense green eyes, letting her read the fatigue on his face and the worry that had etched fine lines into his features. He was at his limit. She needed to understand that.

"Very well, Geoffrey," she finally said, her smile fading. "Perhaps you could go upstairs and enjoy a brandy in peace? The music room is decidedly pleasant this time of evening."

Geoffrey smiled, gratitude welling up inside him for the temporary reprieve from the Marriage Mart. Dropping a quick kiss on her cheek, he ducked into the side hallway and bolted up the stairs.

He needed time to think. To plan.

God, four weeks!

He reached the room and poured himself a brandy, not even bothering to light a candle. Taking a deep breath of the surrounding darkness, he loosened his cravat and wondered what he would do. He knew the answer. He was intimately acquainted with every aspect of the Tallis fortune—or, rather, lack thereof. Though he searched for an escape, mentally reviewing every sheep, every acre of the family land, he knew there was no hope. There was no way he could provide Sophia's dowry and still pay the mortgage.

He had to find a rich bride.

But he could not bring himself to accept it. Not yet. The very thought was like a noose tightening around his neck.

He had only just poured himself a second glass of the restorative elixir when he glanced at the open window.

Was that a leg?

And a hand braced on the sill?

A girl was climbing in the window. Bloody hell, they were mounting the greenery to get at him!

He was torn between the equally desperate urge to laugh hysterically and to flee screaming in terror. Was there no end to the female mind's determination to get him wed?

Like a man drawn to probe his own sore tooth, Geoffrey's gaze slowly returned to the intrepid woman. The leg was actually quite lovely, curved nicely and shining with pearly whiteness in the moonlight.

In the distance below, he could hear the murmuring of his mother's guests, no doubt milling through the ballroom searching for him. There was nowhere for him to run, he realized with a distinct sense of fatalism. He might as well enjoy the show.

Dropping peacefully onto the settee, he gave himself up to total enjoyment of the lady's wriggling as she tried to squirm in sideways through the narrow window. He caught a glimpse of golden blond curls escaping an elegant chignon, heard the gentle rustle of white silk, and then all was eclipsed by the sight of the shimmering skirt pulled taut against a nicely rounded bottom.

In truth, it happened quite quickly, but Geoffrey knew those few seconds would be forever etched upon his memory. The mysterious woman had given him just enough of a view to enflame his senses, and then, with a final whisper of white silk and a couple of tiny hops, she was inside, everything covered and in its proper place, her back toward him.

"Oh, do pull the stick out of your hair," he drawled. "It quite spoils the effect."

The girl gasped and spun around to face him, her eyes wide with shock.

Was it possible? Had she truly not expected anyone in the room? Geoffrey shook off the thought. Why else would a girl climb the greenery if not to find him?

"I congratulate you on your ingenuity," he commented, his sense of humor softening the bitterness in his voice. "Consider my curiosity well and truly piqued."

The girl frowned at him, her brow furrowing in thought. "Thank you," she commented, though her words seemed a bit distracted. "I am counted quite clever."

"I could not agree more. So clever, in fact, that I cannot wait to know more." He leaned forward and, with a quick flick of his wrists, lit a nearby candle.

"No!"

But it was too late to stop him. The candlewick caught and they were both bathed in the soft glow of its light.

She was a pretty thing, older than he'd first guessed. In the flickering light, her eyes appeared rich blue pools fringed by impossibly long lashes. Her lips were the dark red buds of a woman who had . . . just been kissed?

Yes, he thought, as he felt his body tighten in response. She *had* kissed someone. And, she was definitely older than he first guessed, perhaps as much as twenty-one. His gaze dropped, following the graceful curves of her fashionable dress, noting the small, pert breasts and an enticingly slender waist. The rest was hidden beneath her skirt, but his mind had no difficulty replaying his delightful memory of her creamy white thigh and slender leg. It was not until he noticed her slim foot, tapping in annoyance, that he returned to the present.

"My apologies for staring, fair vision, but it is not often I get to look on a woman brave enough to attempt such a climb."

"Then you clearly do not have any sisters," she said congenially.

He nearly choked on the thought of his sister, the cool Sophia, forgetting herself so much as to climb a ladder, much less a tree. "On the contrary, my sister is the epitome of serene consequence." He grinned. "I much prefer the leaf-strewn variety." He gestured to the rose-and-orange-colored leaves still clinging to her hair.

She gasped, her hands quickly flying to her coiffure as she tried to find the offending objects. Keeping his wicked grin in place, Geoffrey uncurled from the settee and moved closer. "Please, allow me."

He was quite careful not to disturb her coiffure as he withdrew the fall colors from her hair, but he could not help noticing the silky texture of her golden tresses. Then, suddenly giving in to a wicked impulse, he deftly pulled out two of the pins anchoring her chignon.

"Oh, dear," he said with false chagrin as her curls tumbled free. "How clumsy of me." Then he sighed with delight as he touched the riotous glory of her hair.

Unfortunately, he was not allowed to linger, for she quickly backed away from him, her mouth pursed in disgust. "Oh, bother. It is forever doing that."

Geoffrey had to choke back his laugh, unaccountably pleased when she had little success repinning her hair. Stepping away lest he be tempted to pluck out the remaining pins, he gathered up his brandy. "Come, fair vision, share a drink with me."

"And I have lost my fan!" she cried, oblivious to his offer. She began scanning the floor for the missing item. When it did not present itself, she ran to the window to lean out, peering into the darkness. Geoffrey knew he must say something quickly or she would be climbing back out to find it.

He stepped forward, taking her slender hand as he drew her away from the opening, which, he now noticed, was disconcertingly high off the ground, and the tree a rather precarious distance from the window.

"Please, allow me to introduce myself. I am Geoffrey Rathburn, son of your hostess."

"The earl?" The words were apparently startled out of her, and she leaned forward slightly, as if to get a better look at him.

"One and the same." He released her to bow in his best courtly manner, his smile widening as she stumbled into an awkward curtsy.

"Good evening, my lord," she stammered, her eyes drifting back to the window.

He could not mistake the meaning. She intended to search for her fan despite the depth of the plummet if she slipped. He quickly poured her a glass of brandy. "Please, I suddenly find myself unaccountably lonely. Will you not share a glass with me?"

She hesitated a long moment, and he held his breath waiting for her response. It was truly wicked of him to keep her here. He ought to encourage her into the ballroom, via the doorway, but he had yet to solve the puzzle of her unorthodox entrance. After all, she might be a beautiful thief come to rob his mother's guests. It was his duty to learn more about her.

"Come," he coaxed. "What harm can there be in a simple glass?" He raised his eyebrows, quietly challenging her adventurous spirit.

She did not seem to notice. "I think I should go back out into the tree."

He felt his mouth go slack. "Just to find your fan?"

"My fan?" She frowned; then suddenly her expression cleared. "Of course not, silly. To think."

"You think in trees?"

"Usually." Her eyes once again wandered to the towering oak. "Only I thought that in the moonlight, my white dress would be rather conspicuous, and even Aunt Win would not approve of my climbing trees at a ball.

So when I saw the open window, I decided to try to think in here."

"Hence your rather precipitous entrance," he said dryly, oddly piqued that she had not been searching for him.

"I had no idea the room was occupied. I will go back to the tree." As if that resolved the matter, she stepped to the window and lifted her skirt in preparation for climbing the sill.

"No!"

She paused, her eyes wide with surprise, and he racked his brain for a suitable reason to keep her with him.

"I, uh, cannot let you go out. You might fall—"

"I never fall."

"But you might."

"Do not concern yourself, my lord. I admit I did fall once. My father said I bounced quite nicely, and although I did break my arm, it healed in a few weeks. In fact, the confinement forced me to catch up on my studies. So, all in all, it was a positive experience."

When he had no response to that, she nodded politely to him and jumped neatly to the windowsill.

"No! Uh, just think of my mother."

She frowned. "The countess?"

"Why, yes," he continued, finally thinking of something suitable. "It is her birthday today, you know. And although you might bounce quite nicely, it would give her the vapors just to think of it."

Her frown deepened. "Why would your mother have the vapors if *I* fell?"

He shrugged, a smile pulling at his lips. "I have no idea, but I assure you, she would. Therefore, as her son, I must insist you refrain from climbing the trees. At least during the remainder of the ball."

She sighed heavily as she nimbly dropped back to the floor. "Oh, very well. But then, where am I going to think in peace?"

"Why not right here? I assure you, I can be quiet."

She eyed him narrowly. "Promise?"

He nodded, his lips pressed tightly together to hold back his smile. Then he pressed the brandy into her hand. She took it but did not deign to drink. Instead, she settled neatly into a nearby chaise as he returned to his place on the settee.

Unfortunately, despite his promise, he found it exceedingly difficult to sit in silence with the odd creature. She stared down at the floor, idly tugging at her hair as she apparently fought with her thoughts. Then, every once in a while, she released a sigh so heavy, it seemed to press her deeper into her chair.

He could not stand more than ten minutes of it. "Perhaps you would do better if you thought aloud," he offered.

Her body jerked slightly as she glanced up at him. "You promised to be quiet," she accused.

"I did not realize you would be so very loud."

She tilted her head, clearly confused.

"You are sighing. Quite loudly. I am surprised they have not heard it downstairs." He was teasing her, although he kept his expression somber, and suddenly she smiled, her entire face lifting with an inner delight.

"Do not try to gammon me, my lord."

"I would not think of it."

Then she sighed again, and her long lashes closed over her eyes, making dark half moons on her cheeks. "It is nothing, really. My aunt would tell me it is undoubtedly all my fault."

Geoffrey touched her hand, pushing her brandy toward her mouth. "Take a drink, angel; then you can tell me what happened."

She opened her eyes, obediently sipping from the snifter. Then she spoke, her voice trembling with self-recrimination. "It *is* my fault, my lord. I am cursed with the most insatiable curiosity. Or perhaps," she added on a softer note, "it is the weakest of wills. It has gotten me into more troubles than I can count."

Geoffrey narrowed his gaze, noting for the first time that the girl's hands trembled slightly as she held her brandy and that her throaty whisper was not a seductive affectation but a sign of true distress.

He silently cursed himself for his stupidity, suddenly remembering the rosy blush of her just-kissed lips. The girl certainly had not been running him to ground; she had been escaping something—or, rather, someone. Someone had just accosted her, and at his mother's ball no less.

Anger burned within him, and he silently swore to avenge this odd creature before him. He barely gave thought to such uncharacteristically gothic behavior on his part. It was simply necessary. But first he had to ascertain the facts, and as delicately as possible.

"I am counted quite discreet," he offered softly as he reached forward, capturing her small hand in his. He had not intended to touch her. He merely wanted to discover the name of the boorish gentleman. But somehow he found himself possessing her small hand, caressing its velvety softness. "Tell me from beginning to end what happened."

She gazed at their entwined hands, slowly tilting her head, as if considering the sensation. Then she abruptly stood, pulling her hands away as she began to pace. "Do you know Alvina Morrow? She is to wed Baron Heise next month."

Geoffrey blinked, wondering if she was trying to distract him with an *on-dit* or whether it was important. "I have only recently returned to London and have not had the pleasure."

She shrugged slightly, her gown shifting in the soft light, giving Geoffrey a distinctly unchivalrous thought.

"It makes no matter. She is a dear friend of mine. She had an offer from an earl but turned him down for the German baron."

Geoffrey remained silent, his attention focused on the shifting planes of her face. He had not realized a person's features could be so totally expressive.

"We were having a comfortable coze just yesterday," she continued. "And I asked her about her choice. Her mother had been mad for the higher title, you understand."

She glanced up at him, and he nodded, silently encouraging her to go on.

"She said she loved the baron. Actually, she said it quite a bit more eloquently than that with a great deal of heartfelt sighs and doe-eyed looks, but that was the essence of it."

"Then I congratulate her on her good fortune."

She glanced over at him, clearly catching the cynicism in his voice. "You do not believe she was in love."

"As I do not know either party involved, I am unqualified to judge."

She shrugged, and again his gaze wandered to the shifting fabric of her gown. "I did not believe her either. I asked her how she knew she was in love, and . . ." Her voice faded, and she frowned down at her brandy. "She said he made her tingle when they kissed." Even in the soft candlelight, he could see the blush staining her cheeks as she continued speaking.

"Naturally, I thought it was all nonsense, but I did check my father's library, especially the Greek love poems." She looked up, pinning him with her dark gaze. "Did you know that literature offers hundreds of references to various physical responses?"

He gaped at her, not quite sure how to respond. "I, uh, believe I am familiar with some of the references."

She nodded, as if pleased with his intellectual abilities.

Then she spoke again, her words punctuated by the swish of her skirts as she paced to the window and back. "I have never been kissed, you understand. Harry's and my family have had this understanding since we were born. Our properties connect, and so I wondered if . . . if—"

Geoffrey finished her thought, his tone excruciatingly dry. "If you would tingle when he kissed you?"

She shrugged, her gaze back on her brandy. "I was curious."

He sighed and tried to keep his voice bland despite the anger still burning within him. "Angel, did he hurt you? Do I need to summon a doctor?"

"Oh, no!" she exclaimed. Then she bit her lip, and he was sure she struggled to restrain a grin. "Unless it is for Harry, er, Lord Berton, that is. I am afraid I hit him rather soundly. I . . . I may even have broken his nose." She paused to gulp some of her brandy. "It is quite ironic, really, as he is the one who taught me to punch in the first place. We did grow up together, you know."

Geoffrey did not know what to say. Here he was delicately trying to ease her past the trauma of an overamorous beau, only to discover the girl handled the situation quite neatly on her own. And with fisticuffs, no less. "Please, tell me what happened," he urged, suddenly more relaxed.

Her hand strayed to her lip, touching it lightly. "We were taking a turn about the garden, and then I asked him to kiss me." She frowned as she continued. "Do you know, he never gave me a moment to explain my interest when . . ." She blinked and looked directly at Geoffrey, her eyes growing wide. "When he kissed me!"

Geoffrey felt his eyebrows raise in surprise, fairness compelling him to defend the unknown Lord Berton, ham-handed though the boy must be. "You had requested as much."

"Well, of course I asked him to kiss me. But not with such . . . such . . ."

"Enthusiasm?"

"Wetness!"

Geoffrey was grateful he had set down his own brandy, otherwise he surely would have spilt it.

"It was like pressing my lips to a wet fish," she said. "Then, when he put his hands . . ." She raised her own hands and waved them about the area of her bodice. "Well, that is when I hit him." She glanced at him with an impish grin. "Knocked him flat, I fear."

"I feel certain he deserved it," he commented, startled by the grim satisfaction he derived from the image.

She shook her head, her eyes filling with genuine distress. "Oh, no. I did truly ask for him to kiss me. It is not Harry's fault the experience was so . . ." She wrinkled her tiny nose. "So repellent. Truly, my lord, if this is a foretaste of marriage, I am afraid I shall not be able to bear it." She poured herself some more brandy before delicately sipping. "It was not at all pleasant." Then she looked back at the tree, its leaves fluttering silently in the moonlight. "You see now why I went in search of a tree."

Geoffrey smiled, amused by her phrasing even though he did, indeed, see the crux of the problem. It was not that the woman had been heinously attacked, although clearly the overeager Lord Berton had much to learn about the gentler sex. It was that the poor girl contemplated a lifetime of carnal relations with a boy who could not even make a first kiss pleasant.

Geoffrey mulled over the situation, a wicked thought stirring his loins. The girl was beautiful. And curious. He could do no less than teach her that Harry was definitely not representative of his gender. In fact, was not that what riding instructors taught—to get directly back on the horse that threw one?

Lifting his brandy, he kept his voice lazy, with just the

slightest hint of challenge in it. She would not know that, inside, his blood pounded in his ears in anticipation.

"I would not worry about marriage overmuch," he drawled. "It was just one kiss, you know, and a bad one at that. There are other men who are less, um, wet in their attentions. One might even expect you will find someone to make you tingle."

He smiled at her, a long, lazy smile born of too much brandy and a beautiful girl who turned to him for advice on kissing. She responded in kind, her sweet lips lifting in a delicate curve, her eyes alight with curiosity as she considered his words.

Suddenly, she nodded. "You are quite right, you know. It was only one kiss. Certainly not enough evidence to warrant a lifetime of chastity."

"Heavens, no."

She tilted her head, her gaze wandering over him in a way that made his skin heat with a sensuous hunger. "I suppose there must be others who could handle the situation with more skill."

"Scores." His voice was rough with desire.

"It is not as if Harry and I are engaged. There was merely an understanding. In fact, my aunt financed this entire Season just so I might have the opportunity to meet other eligible gentlemen."

He watched her take another sip of brandy, her perfect lips pressing against the edge of her glass, parting to allow the entrance of the dark liquid. "I, myself, am counted quite an eligible gentleman," he commented, his gaze still on her moistened lips. "And quite good at kissing."

Her eyes sparkled with the candlelight. "Indeed, my lord?"

"Absolutely."

"And do your ladies tingle when you kiss them?"

He set down his glass, only vaguely aware of the inappropriateness of this conversation, more deeply aware of the rosy glow of her skin in the candlelight, the gentle lift and lowering of her breasts as she breathed, and the slight parting of her sweet, red lips.

He wanted her.

"I have never thought to ask," he replied as evenly as possible. "Perhaps we could try an experiment."

"Why," she suddenly exclaimed, "that was exactly my thinking. Exactly what led me to Harry—"

"Forget Harry," he said abruptly. "Focus on gathering more information."

She set down her glass with a determined click. "An excellent suggestion. Stand up, my lord."

He blinked. "I beg your pardon?"

"Stand up. Harry kissed me standing up. I feel that in the interest of fairness, we should duplicate the situation as closely as possible."

Geoffrey frowned at the half-full brandy glass in his hand, wondering why he felt completely foxed. "I beg your pardon?"

"You do wish to know if your ladies tingle, do you not?"

Geoffrey looked back at her, his mind feeling slow and dull. Suddenly, he had an odd surge of sympathy for the unknown Harry. "Uh, yes," he began. "I suppose I do."

"Well, I promise to share all my information with you."

He grinned, delighted that she had taken up his suggestion with such alacrity. Except that honor required him to mention the pitfalls of her plan. "You do realize this is most improper."

"Nonsense, my lord. This is science."

He nodded, pleased with her explanation. This *was* science, he told his conscience. He had his duty to perform in the name of investigative research. He pushed himself upright. "You wish me to stand?"

"Yes. Right about there." She pointed to a spot directly beside her left shoulder, and he dutifully stepped forward, his body tightening with anticipation.

"Do not forget to touch my bodice," she reminded him.

"I shall endeavor to remember."

She peered at him, apparently confused by his dry tone. "Unless you would rather not. I would not wish to impose. You are being most helpful."

His grin widened. "I shall attempt to force myself. In the interest of scientific discovery."

She returned his smile with a pleased one of her own. "Excellent, my lord. I was sure you were a game one." She lifted her head. "You may begin."

He looked down at her upturned face and had the oddest sensation of falling, sinking deep into the swirling sparkle of her dark blue eyes.

"My lord?"

"My name is Geoffrey."

"Geoffrey." His name was like honey on her lips, dizzyingly warm as it heated the air between them.

She lifted her chin a bit more, raising her lips to his, but he did not take them. Not yet. Instead, he traced the curve of her face with the tip of his index finger, noting the exquisite lift of her cheek and the soft brush of her eyelashes. She was clearly startled, her mouth parting in surprise that he had not simply claimed her lips.

"Harry did not do that." Her voice was thick, and he grinned at the indication of his effect on her.

"My apologies." But he did not stop. He let his hand trail lower across her brow, skating across the tip of her nose until he outlined the gentle flare of her lips. He felt her breath, warm and seductive as it caressed his fingers. Pressing downward, he let his thumb trail inward, soothing the flesh abused by the impatient Harry.

He felt her breath catch and her body melt against him. His restraint gave way. His resolve not to frighten her crumbled beneath the silken heat of her body, pressed as it was against him. He claimed her lips abruptly, almost savagely. Her lips tasted of the brandy they had sipped, dark and rich and full of promise. She tasted sweet, her innocence fresh, her response open and easy.

He deepened the embrace, pulling her harder against him, opening her to his plunder. He took it all, tasting, exploring, touching her totally with just this one kiss. She responded eagerly, learning his movements and adjusting to them, meeting them, then adding her own unique flair.

It was a kiss to enflame passion, and he nearly lost himself to it. Only the muted sounds of the orchestra beginning another set kept him from disgrace. With a supreme effort of will, he broke away, stunned by the pain the movement caused, shocked by the raggedness of his own breath.

His only comfort was that if he was discomposed, she was even more so. Her eyes were dazed, turned dark and wide with passion, and her lips were a haunting red, urging him back to their forbidden depths.

"Angel," he rasped. "I think we had best return you to your heavenly realm."

She blinked, clearly coming back to herself with an effort. "What?"

He smiled, pure masculine pride salvaging what the kiss's unexpected intensity had stripped away. "I asked if that was a satisfactory experience." He was teasing her. Her answer was written clearly across her face and body.

She appeared to rally her scattered thoughts, straightening her shoulders and smoothing down her skirts. "I believe you are right, my lord. I will definitely have to conduct more research before committing to a lifetime of chastity." Then, suddenly, she frowned at him. "Especially since you forgot to touch my bodice."

He gaped at her, then suddenly the ridiculousness of the situation overcame him in a wave of hilarity. Lord, but the woman was a complete hand. Standing before him now, she was as cool and composed as the most proper matron in his mother's ballroom. Only he knew what fire lay just beneath her calm exterior. Whatever man was lucky enough to marry her would enjoy a lifetime of ecstasy in his marriage bed. Assuming, of course, the man was not too stupid to discover it.

He reached out a hand and smoothed a curl away from her eyes. "You almost tempt me, my dear. But now, I think I should call your . . . aunt?"

She nodded, though disappointment clouded the dark crystal of her eyes. "Mrs. Winnifred Hibbert. She will be with the dowagers."

"And what is your name?"

"Oh!" She colored slightly in embarrassment. "I am Caroline Woodley. My father is Baron Alfred Woodley."

He bowed in his best courtly manner. "Then I am most pleased to meet you, Miss Woodley. Now I shall fetch your aunt."

It was not until much later, after the orchestra played the last dance, after the candles were extinguished and the ballroom doors closed that Geoffrey relived the exquisite moments of their kiss. In the darkness of his bedchamber as he gazed out on the delicate rose of a new dawn, he recalled her words.

I will definitely have to conduct more research.

More research? Into kissing? The girl could not be serious.

Could she?